Losing the Plot

Paul Wheeler has written extensively for film, television and the stage, and is the author of several novels including *And the Bullets Were Made of Lead* and *Bodyline*. He was educated at Exeter College, Oxford and the University of Chicago, and before becoming a full-time writer he worked at the Foreign & Commonwealth Office. Paul Wheeler is married with two grown-up children and lives in Kensington.

Losing the Plot

PAUL WHEELER

PHŒNIX

A PHOENIX PAPERBACK

First published in Great Britain by Victor Gollancz in 1998
This paperback edition published in 1999 by Phoenix,
an imprint of Orion Books Ltd,
Orion House, 5 Upper St Martin's Lane,
London WC2H 9EA

A CIP catalogue record for this book
is available from the British Library.

ISBN: 0 75380 850 1

Printed and bound in Great Britain by
The Guernsey Press Co. Ltd, Guernsey, C.I.

I would like to thank my agents, Michael Sissons and Anthony Jones, whose expertise made my career as a writer possible. And I would like to thank my wife Alex and my children, Lara and Sacha, whose extravagance made it necessary.

Once the Land-Rover left the tarmac and turned on to a dirt track, a fine red dust started to blow in through the windows. Breathing hoovered it into their nostrils, making them cough, so the driver wound up his side and the man in the passenger seat followed suit. He turned to a third man seated behind, who seemed unaffected.

'Sorry 'bout this, Bruce,' he said. 'But me 'n' Seb are new to Africa. We ain't gone bush enough to get used to it.'

The man in the rear didn't reply and they drove on in silence for a while, the suspension inadequately countering the pitted surface, tossing them about like balls in a lottery bubble.

'What part of Oz you from, Bruce?' the driver asked.

'Melbourne. And the name's Bob.'

The other man in front laughed and spoke in a Leeds brogue: 'Hode yer sweat, lad. All you lot are called Bruce back home. It's nowt personal.'

His cheerfulness wasn't matched by the Australian, who kept glancing at his watch. The sun was settling on the horizon; it would be dark in fifteen minutes.

'Helloooo, possums!' trilled the Cockney, winking at his mate. 'Know who that is, Bruce?'

Their passenger sighed. 'Barry Humphries. Look, how much further?'

'Not far.'

One started to warble 'Waltzing Matilda' and the other

joined in. There was no twilight in Ethiopia. When the sun set, it was like the house lights dimming in a theatre.

'What made you go in for famine relief, Bruce?' the Londoner asked.

It was stifling with the windows closed, and their faces glistened.

'It seemed like a good idea,' he replied, dislike clipping his diction.

'Well, someone's got to do it,' Yorkie said. 'I mean t'bloody niggers aren't gonna help 'emselves, right? Not when there's blokes like you to wipe their arses.'

The Australian felt a profound surge of fear sweep through his stomach. They had driven for over an hour hardly exchanging a word. Why were they suddenly trying to provoke him?

'Bin up north lately, cobber?' the Yorkshireman called over his shoulder. 'North of England, I mean.'

'No.'

'There's parts of Leeds, 'ole areas, I bet if you was to take a picture, you couldn't 'tell it from fuckin' High Street, Bombay.'

'Hey, listen, I don't appreciate this kind of conversation, so why don't we just get where we're going and leave the rest out?'

'Ooooh!' sang Sarf Lunnon. 'Touchee. What's up, Bruce, you into poking nignogs or what?'

'Why are we going this way?' the Australian asked, watching the dark African plain bump past.

'This is where the journos said.'

'We usually meet in town.'

Sarf gave his profile and shrugged. 'Don't ask us, old son. All we do is fetch 'n' carry, don't we, Seb?'

'Thassit.'

The engine began to hiccup. The Cockney tapped the dials with a knuckle.

'Whassup?' asked Yorkie. They lost speed and went forward in fits and starts.

'Beats me,' the driver muttered, braking. He pulled the bonnet release and got out. His friend peered round at the silent landscape.

'You get lions round here?'

'Anyone know anyfing 'bout motors?' Sarf called, holding up the bonnet.

'Christ, Harry, you said you was a mechanic.'

'I lied. Here, Bruce, I bet you know what to do. Come and take a butcher's.'

The Australian froze. Why had he trusted them? Because they'd given the password agreed with the newspaper guys, that's why. He climbed out, feeling his knees weaken.

'Listen,' he said. 'Don't do this. Please.'

The Yorkshireman had stayed in his seat but now he stepped down, coming up behind the Australian, one arm held stiffly by his side.

'Don't do what?' Sarf asked, pointing to the engine. 'All I want is you to figger out what's wrong.'

The shot created a mass rise of birds clear across the landscape.

They dragged the body fifty feet off the track and left it in a gulley. The Londoner glanced up at the wheeling vultures.

'No need to bury 'im. Be nuffing there tomorrer 'cept his shoelaces.'

They returned to the Land-Rover.

'Hate Aussies,' Yorkie muttered. 'We had a few in the

Bradford League. They'd stand in t'slips and talk while you was batting. Say things to put you off. Sledgin', they called it. Totally out of order that, in my book.'

The vehicle performed a wide U-turn and disappeared into the darkness.

DATE: MAY 13

FAX TO: ALAN TATE

FROM: MORT DELANNOY, MOVIELINE INTERNATIONAL,

          LOS ANGELES

Unspeakable Behavior

Good morning, Alan,

Thank you for your rapid delivery of the rewrites. We appreciate the speed, which must have meant giving up your weekend. In return we are giving our reactions right away.

1)   There is still far too much explanation as to how Brandt is killed. We feel the audience will turn off at the word 'existential' Hillary uses when they cut the body down from the beam. We know you were only following our previous point, that it is more visual to have him found hanging in the garage rather than carbon monoxided inside the car but you don't need to elaborate. Cut pages 14 and 15 and reduce the scene to a brief description of a body that has been suspended for five days. Any pathologist will tell you what happens. Don't go apeshit with the details but specific enough to make it read authentic.

2)   We looked again at the rhythm of the second act and prefer the original. Sorry, Alan, we are pains in the ass, I know, but that's the movie business. So please return to Susie getting laid after the third murder but before the fourth. So we go kill fuck kill and not fuck kill kill. It's a matter of pace. Two killings one after the other can get tedious, so interspersing with sex gives the audience time to relax before the bloodfest of murder four. Besides, Susie's motivation has always been to feel horny after finding a corpse, so we're not going out of character.

3)   We had a lot of feedback in the office regarding

11

the similarity of names Hillary and Mallory. Hillary over here is more a female name, you know Clinton, so when people read it they think the hero's a woman. Please call Hillary Mallory and find another name for the cop. We like Bernstein, playing against the cliché that there aren't any Jewish policemen. (Maybe there are in England but we have to think how the story will play in Abilene.)

4)   You still have too many British words in the dialogue. We don't talk about 'hands in the till.' No one knows what a till is. Say 'cookie jar.' We appreciate Hillary (now Mallory) is a Brit but put somewhere early on he spent time in the US. Maybe his girlfriend keeps telling him he's got an American accent. Could be a funny running joke?

5)   The script is still too long, Alan. Don't go over 110 pages max. There's a lot of speech you can cut in the third act. Look at some of the classics again and see how it's done. *True Lies* hardly had any dialogue in the last hour, mainly because Arnie can't speak English, but it didn't need it. Just slash and burn is what the script needs from page 80 to the end.

6)   Our research turned up the fact US audiences don't want to hear any reference to cancer. Can you find another reason why Susie has a mastectomy? We think it's a great idea to have her minus a tit and will get us approval for realism, but try and suggest she lost it through some kind of accident. One of our partners says she knows a case of breast amputation after a skiing fall.

   Listen, Alan, we all think you're doing a great job and we're pretty sure these changes aren't going to take much work. We're almost there, old buddy. People who have heard about the script are showing great interest. The feeling is we're onto something good here.

Talk to you soon. Give my love to dear old London.

MORT

'This is starting to sound like the scene in *The Sun Also Rises*.'

'What scene?'

'One character asks, "How did you go bankrupt?" And the other replies, "Two ways. Gradually, then suddenly."'

'I never saw that film.'

'Nor did I, but I read the original material.'

The trouble with writing scripts for a living is that you start talking in side-of-mouth phrases, the ones that get the big laughs from an audience. I know a writer who blamed his divorce on his compulsion to answer anything his wife said with a Groucho Marxism. "Guess what, John, a lorry driver whistled at me today." "Probably thought it was another lorry." That sort of thing. He just couldn't bite his tongue. Even when she was halfway out the door and swimming in tears.

'I've left my number on your desk, if you ever want to talk.'

'I'm glad you left *something* . . .'

When actors crack jokes on the screen, they follow a scenario that's been carefully rehearsed and refined. On the runway of life, you never know what's taking off next. Not that calling Hemingway's book the original material squeezed a smile out of Richard. Solicitors, like public executioners, have a different take on life's funnier moments.

'They gave you three months to vacate, Alan. You never once rang Maxie and asked for longer. There's not much I can do without a pretty good reason to plead hardship.'

Why do people meet to discuss their most private matters

in crowded restaurants? Here we were, picking over the bones of my deceased marriage in between shoving alien matter through a hole in the head and being asked every five minutes by an eager-to-please manager if we were enjoying the meal. Worse, a couple at the next table, who'd finished a bottle of white before they even ordered, were screeching with laughter. Their fun was strangely superimposing itself on our discussion: they went into paroxysms after Richard made his last remark. It was as if, by some glitch, a laughter track had been supered over *Hedda Gabler*.

'I know,' I said.

'I mean, is there some reason why you haven't moved out?'

'Not unless you count not having anywhere to go. Doesn't that classify as hardship?'

'If you can prove you can't afford to rent—'

'I can't. The Inland Revenue are on their final demand. It's written in blood and has a noose as a logo.'

There I go again. As if I were writing a scene of a man facing ruin in a Chevy Chase movie. Not even the people next door laughed at that one. Richard just played with the stem of his glass and swallowed a belch.

'They might want to know whose BMW was in the drive.'

'It's leased.'

'How much a month?'

Now they cackled. I sneaked a look to see if they were listening, but the woman said: 'That was always the big debate. Do you swallow or spit?' I noticed his foot was resting on the tip of her shoe. While Richard went on about writing to Maxie to beg a few more weeks before she and the kids moved back in, I wondered about the situation next door. She wore no wedding ring; he looked a few years older.

14

This was not a cheap restaurant and he had ordered for her: foie gras, Dover sole, and a Montrachet the waiter had treated with respect. Boss softening up ambitious junior executive. Her face was flushed. Whether from the wine or the lubricious conversation wasn't clear. I didn't give much odds on the office seeing them back that afternoon. I should have been envious. Genital liposuction hadn't played a role in my life for a while. But waiting for her to explode into another guffaw, wincing at the Sarah Ferguson dialect, I remembered the words of a well-travelled uncle when I was a youth. He put me off Englishwomen for life when he said to go down on them needed the breath control of a pearl diver.

'—anything in the pipeline?' Richard was asking.

'Not much,' I replied. Writers call eavesdropping research. They are able to chat fluently with someone while their ears pick up conversations across the room. It takes a bit of practice, like patting your head and rubbing your stomach at the same time, but it comes in handy when your companion is either a leaden bore or, in this case, telling you things you don't want to hear.

'What are you doing at the moment?'

I explained about the Hollywood job, how they kept delaying payment on the revisions by asking for further changes. How I'd told my agent to threaten them with the Writers' Guild if they didn't come across with the money. He tried to look as if he had the first idea what I was talking about. I suppose if he started banging on about the legal intricacies of quitclaim compensation, I would have reacted the same way. Anyway, it certainly wasn't in my interest to lie and say I was over-employed.

'After you pay your tax, is there anything left?'

'Is there ever?'

I'd known Richard the best part of thirty years. We had met at Oxford. I'd often bragged about how my solicitor was also a close friend, how we used to play cricket at weekends. People were envious. They said their lawyers were crows who regarded them as roadkill. 'You mean sometimes he doesn't even send you a bill?'

There's a snag to this. You like to look good in front of your friends. If he had been a stranger, I'd have had no problem saying I was finding it harder to get work. We deride Americans for hiring shrinks, boasting that Europeans get personal advice free from old mates who know us better than we know ourselves. However, discover you have developed an urge to bugger horses and I know who I'd rather confide in, and it wouldn't be my friends.

'Do you want me to write to Maxie?' I could see the pain in his face. He had known her almost as long as I had. Maybe that was the problem. A stranger might have been stricter with her demands. But I had insisted he handled things.

'No,' I said. 'I'll move.' I did a Montgomery Clift into my wine, bravely concealing the vulnerability of my soul.

'Hi, enjoying your meal?'

I thought more about the 'gradually/suddenly' thing on the train home. Make that the train to the Home Counties house I was about to lose. After Maxie left, life had been like the first months of the Second World War; nothing much happened. We agreed that for the sake of the children we wouldn't be shitty to each other, even though they seemed oblivious of our existence except when they needed money. It would all be civilized, avoiding the trainwrecks that friends had made of their marriages. So for a time there was this phony peace. I moved in with Jackie, promising never to bring the kids round. Actually, Jackie had insisted on that more than my wife. At twenty-four, her maternal instincts were still waiting to blossom. Maxie and I would meet now and then, amicably wondering where we'd gone wrong. Neither of us probed deeper than admitting to a mutual boredom. When I was younger, my friends would go on about how lucky I was to work at home. No British Rail hell, no office politics, get up when you like and so on. I, on the other hand, envied their pub lunches, the gossip and camaraderie around the photocopier. Most phone calls I got were for Maxie, and she was usually out at art college. I'd be so desperate for human contact, I would pass an hour discussing the relative merits of Sainsbury over Waitrose and make notes about upcoming jumble sales.

Then things changed. Her lawyer said she had to wash or get off the bidet and that's when matters escalated. His letters made me out to be Vlad the Impaler. Richard told me to pass them on to him and what followed was a legal El Alamein. Lawyers love it: they also love each other, so there was nothing personal in their manoeuvring. Richard sometimes called to read out their latest bombardment. If I'd received it, I'd have opened a vein there and then, but he merely said they were trying it on. He should care; his marriage made the Longfords seem like *Who's Afraid of Virginia Woolf.*

Six months of exaggerated politesse were followed by an escalating campaign of forays and counter-attacks. Unfortunately, the fact that I had initiated the break-up by banging a researcher I had hired, meant that in this Alamein I played Rommel. My ammunition ran out and my supply lines were severed. Maxie, disliking the suburban isolation, regrouped at her mother's with the children, and when Jackie met someone her own age, I moved back home. For a while everything carried on as usual. I had a suspicion Maxie felt sorry for me in a *schadenfreude* way.

The 'suddenly' part started when the money was finally settled. Within a week, I went from writing the occasional cheque when my conscience stirred, to arranging a haemorrhage of Direct Debits.

Then a court order arrived to vacate the family seat.

I now know what the man meant in the Hemingway novel. I suppose all life is gradually/suddenly; childbirth, sex, death.

The thing was, I liked our house. We had bought it on a mortgage with the money from my first successful film, *Assignment Berlin*. There followed a dozen jobs with handsome fees which paid off the loan within five years. None of the scripts was ever made, but that didn't matter. In my business you can go a long way on one well-received production. There are writers in Hollywood making a half million a year whose last picture featured Gabby Hayes as the romantic lead.

We had even installed a combination lock on our entrance. I'm talking about the gate at the end of a fifty-yard drive. Canadian pine and Cambodian monkey trees, apple orchards and rose gardens littered five acres of lawn. I loved it, despite the neighbours who were dredged from the depths of the City; men who found refuge from Jews, blacks and women in the local golf club.

I told myself I had an estate. And I got it by writing.

Writing stories. You've no idea how much that means to someone from a two-up, two-down semi in a small Midlands town, where to expect more from life than to work in an office and support Notts Forest was regarded as presumptuous. Men who were at home all day showed neighbours not that they had cracked the secret of life, but that they were on the dole.

For a while after we moved in, I'd wander round the place, leaning on the trees and pretending I was H. G. Wells. I even took up pipe-smoking to get deeper into character. I can't think of one single moment I wasn't completely happy there. Until now. The gradually/suddenly scenario had a deeper resonance. Work was harder to come by. At fifty-three, most writers are conscious of younger people treading on their heels. Producing scripts is a young person's job. It's, well, it's like sex. (Funny how, since Jackie departed, I seem to compare everything to humping.) You need stamina, passion and energy to get to the end. And after a short pause, you're expected to do it all over again.

For some time, I had found myself exhausted after doing it even once. Writing, I mean. When I was younger and starting out, I had a reputation for being quick. Producers joked that if they asked me when I could deliver the screenplay, I'd look at my watch. I'd work all night and see the dawn rise over the top of the Underwood. Television companies would say, 'We need it by Tuesday, get that quick writer, whatsisname, Lyle.' If my name had been Lyle, they'd have called me Tate. I could handle three assignments at once. The money poured in. We spent weeks abroad during the school holidays. I played the role of a globe-trotting Byron, staying in ever larger hotels, filling shelves with albums of family photos taken in Venice, Rome, Moscow, China.

During these extended absences, I failed to notice that television drama was changing. Instead of ruggedly handsome heroes creating mayhem in crowded streets to nail the villain, later to be congratulated by a grateful Scotland Yard, action series became more authentic. Police procedure was scrupulously documented. A force once portrayed as trustworthy lads under the Blue Lamp began framing people, faking evidence. Hospital dramas wallowed in fountains of blood. The ratings proved this was what the public wanted and everyone became experts. People learned how to defend themselves in court, how to handle arrest, and occasionally the papers told of a man performing an operation with no training beyond watching surgical soaps. This rush to realism played havoc with writers of my generation. It meant you now had to leave the house, hang around the practitioners, learn the lingo. Spend a week in a car with two racist, homophobic, misogynist coppers. Stake out the local casualty ward and wade through the Saturday night gore.

Ambitious young scriptwriters leaped aboard with glee. Older hacks preferred to watch it on television and use that as our research. We became fleas feeding on larger fleas.

The result was fewer commissions. What happens in my business is your agent puts you up for a job and the producer will ask to see a sample of your work. So I pull out a sepia-tinted seventies script or a fuzzy video and send it over. A thirty-year-old kid developing a series with a name like *Armed Response Police Squad* would read a piece where middle-class criminals smile as the tweed-suited detective invites them to surrender and ask, "Tell me, Chief Inspector, how did you know it was me?" "When you ordered Barolo to go with the *boeuf en croûte*, sir. Not the choice of a true connoisseur." The result was silence. Or worse, I'd hear they turned me down on the grounds that I was too expensive.

If I had scripted my life, I would have found a way to tie up the ends, round off the vicissitudes of what Margaret Thatcher once called a funny old world. Driving from the station, I'd pause outside the gates to reflect for a moment. My lips would twist into a wry but accepting smile. Like Dustin in *Kramer vs Kramer*, when Meryl says he can have the kid after all the divorce court fury. Then I'd punch in the combo, the gates would swing inwards and I would drive through as the camera rose and the final credits music swelled to tell us there was life after adversity. A truer, more worthy life. *Arbeit Macht Frei*, as Himmler put it.

But taking off from the unrehearsed runway of life had presented an unwelcome irony. When failed cabinet ministers resign, they quote the reason as wanting to spend more time with their families. My decline coincided precisely with the moment when I had lost mine. Dustin had his son to watch TV with, while I was headed for the last scene in *Damage*: Jeremy Irons ending up in a flyblown Arab village looking at videos of the family he has lost.

Strange how potent cheap movies are.

DATE: MAY 18

FAX TO: ALAN TATE

FROM: ELAINE MORGENSTERN, MOVIELINE

          INTERNATIONAL, LOS ANGELES

Dear Alan Tate,

I am responding for Mort Delannoy who is out of town but who read your rewrites on *Unspeakable Behavior*.

We must be upfront and say we were all deeply disappointed in the changes, many of which weren't called for in his May 13 fax to you. We accept that the story is set in the UK and that all the main characters are Britishers but we were hoping for a major US distribution deal. Potential for this is severely limited by making so much of the dialogue incomprehensible to middle America.

However, dialogue can always be fixed. What is of deeper concern is your refusal to address the clear reservations on the draft that Mort expressed.

1) We checked out with our expert on the state of a corpse left hanging in a garage and his findings are greatly different from yours. Maybe British pathologists employ less scientific language but to simply say in the narrative: 'Brandt looks like a pheasant that has been left to hang too long and would need a special kind of cook to disguise the fact' is too obscure. And what is this about hanging pheasants? Over here we shoot them with shotguns.

2) We note that you have now situated the sexual intercourse sequence involving Susie between murders three and four but what happened to the trucker? Who suggested she masturbates to a keep fit video? As written the scene makes a mockery of the serious import vital to the integrity of the concept.

3) You renamed Hillary Mallory but now we see the

policeman is called Tiffany. Tiffany is even more a female name than Hillary, which is why we wanted it changed to Mallory. Apart from anything else, Tiffany is a trading company name let alone probably owned by whoever made *Breakfast At Tiffany's* in the sixties. We still would like him to be Jewish. Mort suggested Bernstein, and that's what we would like to see from now on.

4)   About the British flavor to the dialogue see above and go with Mort's idea that Mallory spent time in the States when he was a student.

5)   Your previous script that Mort told you was too long was 120 pages. Your rewrites have cut it down to 56. This wouldn't even make an hour on TV. Please replace 50 pages. Your covering note referred to *True Lies* and Schwarzenegger's ability to replace words with action and we know you were only trying to follow Mort's advice. But reduced this much, you make Mallory sound like something out of *One Million Years BC*. No bankable actor would look at a script that reduces his part to a series of grunts.

6)   We thought long and hard about the mastectomy thing and have reluctantly decided to abandon the concept. We had an actress in mind when we conceived the notion who had undergone a breast removal but she is uninsurable owing to a felony conviction involving illegal substances. Susie has five sexual encounters in the script and it's going to be hard to make them convincing without nudity. So please delete all references to mammary amputation.

We received a call from your agent who expressed concern that you were being asked to do more revisions than are called for in your contract. Our legal department points to the phrase 'and such revisions shall be completed by the writer with his/her best efforts.' We do not regard your last work as falling

into that category and will say so to the Writers'
Guild should you or he feel it necessary to consult
them.

   We look forward to hearing from you,

                           Elaine Morgenstern
Since time is of the essence please e-mail your work
in future. Our address is: screen @emline.bev.com

Quite a lot of time is spent in script conferences debating whether a certain action is 'out of character'. Drama is controlled by a set of hard and fast rules. Who laid them down, I've no idea. Aeschylus probably. Coming up with the notion of theatre, giving actors words to say on a stage and inviting others to listen, he must have thought, hang on a minute, we can't just have a bunch of people talking like they do in normal life. You can hear that every day in the marketplace. Theatre is life with the boring bits missed out. (Well, there's always room for a Pinter.) We need to work out a structure. A beginning, middle and end, so the audience can leave wishing life were like that. Or in the case of Greek theatre, thanking the Gods life *isn't* like that. Mothers not safe from their own sons . . .

Since life *is* mostly boring bits, it follows that drama can never be true to it. Every day the papers report us acting wildly out of character. Loyal, compassionate, cheerful members of the community suddenly chop up their children, or vanish to reappear living with a fisherman in the Gambia. Put that on the screen and no one would believe a word.

Take me, for instance. I spend twenty years in monogamous devotion, then find myself unaccountably mounting a virtual teenager in a production office late one night while going through her research for my screenplay. Freud might say it was in keeping with my infantile neuroses, but when I thought about it later, it seemed as daft as kicking a nun.

Today, I woke up with thoughts I never imagined I would entertain in a million years.

They were triggered by what happened last night. The bell had rung from the gate.

'Hello.'

'Is that Mr Tate?'

'Yes.'

'Mr Alan Tate?'

'If this is double glazing—'

'Carter and Burns Collection Agency.'

'No thanks.'

'Sir, we have an order to repossess a BMW, registration number—'

'I've had no warning about any repossession.'

'This is it.'

'I meant on the phone.'

'Our clients say you've ignored repeated demands for payments and you're four months in arrears.'

'That's ridiculous.'

'Sir, we have to take the car.'

'It's inconvenient right now.'

You can't see the gate from where I was standing and it was getting dark. They could have been Home Counties thieves. We read about them in the local *Argus*. 'Be on the alert. Crooks are posing as charity collectors . . .'

'Open the gate, Mr Tate.'

I heard the speaker snigger, presumably at the rhyme.

'How do I know you're who you say you are?'

25

'Ring our office. My name is Harris and my colleague is Jonas.'

He gave a number. I left it a few minutes to make them think I was checking, but I knew they were kosher. However, before I pressed the gate release I saw them coming up the drive. How did they do that? Climb over? What was the point? They couldn't take the bloody car away with the gates shut.

When I went outside I saw they were open. By now Harris and Jonas were already unlocking the BMW with a master key.

'Look here, what gives you the right to invade private property?' I barked, sounding like any of my neighbours.

'This,' the man in the car said, holding out a paper. His expression put me in the wealthy git category. It was a standard form listing the particulars of the soon-to-be-deprived victim typed in erratically. My name appeared, not on the top line, but below in the address box, the address in the box below that and so on. I wondered if this constituted a loophole in a court of law, like a misplaced comma in a will.

'You can't get much job satisfaction, doing this for a living,' was all I could find to say. The man looking in the boot slammed it down, glancing at the house and the grounds. He got tons of satisfaction. Another self-important toff bites the dust.

'Was it Lloyd's?' he asked.

'Lloyd's?'

'One of the names, were you?'

'No.'

'It'd break your heart, some of the things we see when we have to collect the Roller. The old lady pissed out of her mind, husband with a shotgun under his chin. Kids chucked out of Eton. It's horrible.'

'Then why do you do it?'

'Someone has to. And it's a job,' the one turning on the engine shouted above the noise. 'You know, the thing that pays the bills.'

I was handed a pen.

'What you do then, squire, if you don't mind me asking?'

'I write.'

'Write what?'

'Telly, films.'

'Go on!'

'That's it.'

'Anything I might have seen?'

'You watch much?'

'Nah. *Blind Date* now and then. Football.'

'I've never written for either of those.'

He looked at my signature.

'Is your autograph worth anything?'

'Only to your client,' I said. Neat. Could use that one day.

He stuffed the paper in his pocket.

'You can always reclaim the car once you pay the arrears,' he said as he got in beside his mate. I watched them shoot off scattering gravel, and screech to a halt beside their van which was parked between the gates to prevent them closing. One nipped across and backed it out to let the BMW through. Then they were gone with a sardonic toot on my ex-horn. What I wanted to know was how did they find out the combination code? Only one other person knew it. Maxie.

The police have a way, I once saw on television, of breaking down a suspect by passing on a devastating piece of news before leaving him alone in a cell for twenty-four hours.

"Oh, by the way, Kevin, your mum told us she washed blood off your coat." Then they watch the poison seep in as he sits by himself, no cigarettes, no magazines, nothing to do but think how his mother wrecked his alibi.

The rest of the evening I brooded on what had just occurred. Client calls in the repo men. There's a snag: the gates are locked. What if the bloke refuses to let them in? Hang about, he's got a wife who leases another of our motors. Different address for the last six months. Uh-huh. Like that, is it? You're allowed to effect entry after being refused. "Hello, Maxine Tate? Are you married to a Mr Alan Tate? . . . Oh, I see, I'm sorry. The fact is, we have to take back his car and we were wondering if you knew the combination of the gates? Whoa, slow down, not so fast . . ."

Why? She'd got everything she wanted. The house, a whacking great maintenance award, private health insurance, school fees, my balls. Even then, she couldn't resist giving the knife a last twist. How do I get to the railway station? Apart from a kid's bike in the garage or a two-mile hike, I was paralysed.

The scenario began to sound familiar. *Sunset Boulevard*. Screenwriter William Holden needs money to keep his car. His agent abandons him. Then he meets wealthy ex-star Norma Desmond. Where are the Normas when you need them?

So we come back to the next morning when I woke up a changed person. No more Mr Nice Guy.

The house was in both our names. The problem was, during the months of guilt and remorse, I told Richard to let Maxie have what she wanted. I remember him muttering about the dual ownership, as if embarrassed to bring harsh materialism into the problems of two dear friends. I'd said

28

forget that. Some sentimental streak persuaded me that offering it to her would make her reply, "No, darling, I know how much it means to you. I'll get a flat." It was completely out of character for her not to act this way. Just like finking on the gate number. Even Meryl had second thoughts about depriving Dustin of their son in *Kramer*. She'd shown a compassion that made us leave the cinema liking her for the sacrifice, her refusal to exact the entire pound of flesh.

'Richard, morning, it's Alan. Listen, this dual ownership of the house. Any way I could rethink what we decided?'

'What *you* decided.'

'Yes. I was wondering . . . I seem to have been overly generous in the settlement. I mean, no one's going to accuse me of depriving my family. I just thought maybe we should put the house up for sale and split the proceeds. Maxie'd get at least four hundred, maybe five, which'd buy her a big enough place to see the kids through till they leave home.'

'Mmm.'

I admire professionalism. The way lawyers, accountants, agents, drop into noncommittal grunts just at the moment you want their wholehearted approval.

'Can we set it up?'

'You should talk to Maxie.'

'I can't. We're not in that area of possibility.'

'Knowing her all these years, I'm sure she'll co-operate.'

I've known her every bit as long as you, mate, and I can tell you now, it's a waste of time, was what I thought.

'Do I have to?'

'Well, yes, actually.' He sounded more like her lawyer than mine.

'Why?'

'Because you signed the agreement awarding it to her.'

29

'And that's it?'

'You could try saying you weren't of sound mind, but you'll need a psychiatric report.'

'What? I go down and wank in front of Buckingham fucking Palace?'

'That might do it.'

'Richard—'

'Alan, listen.' I detected a sharper tone. 'It's over. Legally, all the loose ends are tied. As my namesake once remarked: "You can't put the toothpaste back in the tube."'

It's true. Not just about the toothpaste – his name really is Richard Nixon. He caught terrible flak during Watergate.

I was sufficiently self-analytical to realize I was moving into the next stage of despair: paranoia. My oldest friends were turning against me. Who knows, perhaps during our friendship I had inadvertently insulted Richard. At Oxford maybe. Could I have unknowingly screwed someone he was keen on? Has he just been biding his time to get even? I ran him out once when he was on 93. Surely not . . . ? Suppose he secretly nurtured a passion for Maxie. Too shy to mention anything but fantasized each time he woke up that it was my wife next to him instead of Christine. When she arrived from the States, he had circumvented work permits and fin-agled her a job in a solicitor's firm, where she was billed as an expert in American law, a talent not noticeably apparent in her career as greeter in a Chicago cocktail bar where we'd first met. She told me she was taking a break from managing the Stockyards, but all I noticed were the breasts. Years later, she still often reprised the story to emphasize Richard's kind-ness. How he'd been so clever to find her work. Could I have been so blind . . . ?

There was a film – Bette Davis? Joan Fontaine? – where

30

a secret love simmers for twenty years and is consummated only when the woman's husband dies and the thwarted lover comes home after years helping lepers in Africa. No, it was *Passionate Friends*. Ann Todd, Claude Rains, Trevor Howard. Todd was married to the director David Lean at the time. Still, what did he know about love that didn't end up with people dying in the snow or talking about spaghetti in Venice, or getting something in their eye on a railway station? Lean was terrible with love stories. Good at Dickens and big canvas war sagas, but when it came to romance he was way below Michael Winner. Maybe it wasn't *Passionate Friends* . . .

In the same way you can't concentrate on the opera because you're plagued with thoughts about your car being towed away outside – you were late, you dumped it in the first space you saw, was it a double yellow line? – so the notion of a conspiracy to have me end up in cardboard city made it impossible to think of anything else all day. The more I picked over the debris, the more certain I became of having been unbelievably blind all these years to a Maxie/ Richard liaison. When an automatic pilot whispered, 'A hell of an idea for a film,' I was outraged. 'For God's sake, can't you see *anything* outside of screenplays?' I yelled into the bathroom mirror.

It isn't true to say I never did research.

I knew a journalist who, back in the seventies, had been one of an elite corps of investigators for a Sunday broadsheet. There was no problem he couldn't solve, no subject he hadn't at some time touched on in pursuit of a weekly crusade. If I required a character to know about the incidence of dyslexia among the Masai, Roger at some point would have talked to someone who kept track of these things.

Times moved on and he was long retired from newspapers.

Recently he had found some cushy quango in Oxford and I rang him at home, where he spent more time than I did, and explained I was working on a story that required a private eye to verify a leak of privileged information. A country house theft. The crooks had somehow gained access to the combination lock fastening the gates, enabling them to bring in a pantechnicon and strip the place.

'Easy,' he said, laughing at my naivety. 'They get it from the people who installed the system.'

'What?'

'You'd be amazed how vulnerable clerks are to a bung.'

I tried not to sound too surprised.

'I'd thought of that, but I need something more dramatic. I don't want the audience getting the answer before my detective.'

'Inside job. The owners are deep in hock. They need the insurance.'

'Weeell, maybe but—'

'Wife has a lover, hates the husband. It's his stuff, inherited. She married for the money and social whichwhat, finds it unbearable in the sticks, meets Flash Harry the way women do, and before you know, she's slipped him the number and he brings in the lads. She's getting revenge for hubby forcing her into anal sex. Or how about—'

'Roger, let me think about it,' I butted in. Boy, quangos don't sound what you'd call time-consuming. He would have still been going at midnight. "Aliens. Superior intelligence works out the numbers . . ."

I hung up and wondered about telepathy. He seemed to latch on to the revengeful wife so quickly. Was there an edge to my voice that betrayed my suspicions?

The phone rang. I hoped it would be Maxie saying she

32

was having second thoughts about reclaiming the house.

'Hello?'

'What do you know about horses?'

It was Tim Roberts, my agent.

'Only that you can make glue out of their hooves.'

'Keep that to yourself. *Animal Doctor* are doing a fifth series and they're looking for writers.'

'Animal doctor? You mean a vet.'

'It's called *Animal Doctor* because the BBC have already got a series called *The Vet*.'

'How many are they doing?'

'The usual, thirteen, ten, whatever. Why?'

'I'll only come on board if I can do three minimum.'

There was a pause. Or was it a sigh?

'They won't guarantee how many.'

'Tim, what do I get? Seven, eight grand an episode. And for that I have to deal with teenage script editors. I'd rather flog my arse in Piccadilly Circus.'

'OK. I'll tell them you aren't interested.'

'Hang on. *They* came to *you* asking for me?'

'The producer's taken on a researcher called Jackie Wainwright.'

'Christ, she's pimping for me?'

Tim wasn't a man to delve. He knew about her and me but wasn't interested in over-the-fence gossip.

'He said he admired your work.'

'*Animal Doctor*?'

I knew the name. It had been running for years. The British public never get tired of watching their favourite actors give enemas to pigs. Good solid ratings, but they were running out of ideas, Tim explained.

'They want a fresh mind on the job.'

'Who do I have to fuck?'

He gave me a number. I left it until late afternoon to call so as not to seem desperate and fixed a meeting. At one time, you went either to the BBC Centre in Shepherd's Bush, or a handful of commercial companies at expensive West End addresses. All that had changed. The independent producers, the indies, had arrived. All you needed to be one was a back room and a phone. And a name that sounded cute: Inebriated Newt Enterprises, something like that. And they're all over the place. Instructions how to go there can get complicated: 'Take the tube to Kentish Town, walk down the High Street as far as a pub called the Rat and Parrot, turn down the narrow alley beside it till you get to the canal, cross the bridge and you'll see a white building to your right . . .'

Eight thousand per. Ten per cent off for Tim, leaving seven two. It would see me started in a flat, maybe get the car back. Persuade them to commission a couple more; twenty thousand would do nicely.

When I was young and starting out, things were different in many ways. Receptionists at television offices were terrific looking. (I'm talking commercial companies here: the BBC's all bore the impoverished civil servant stamp you see working desks at the Job Centre.) Like air stewardesses in the days when only the elite flew and rich husbands were there to be snagged in first class. As soon as everyone could afford air travel, the staff became ageing skivvies.

Unmarried and seeking to nail everything that moved, I came on strong to these front women. I was a writer. I met famous people, I made lots of money and had a Chelsea address. Good enough to get one's kit off for. Nowadays, like airline customers, there are far too many of us. Now they just fling a security tag across and tell you to sign in

34

and sit until someone comes down. They could all lose around thirty pounds too. I'm not saying this because in my fifties I'm no longer their fantasy figure, nor even because they no longer react to my name: "Not the Alan Tate who wrote the 1979 BAFTA award-winning *Choke on My Vomit*?" I am just recording the truth as I see it.

Jackie came out of the lift and saw me in the foyer trying to look absorbed in *Screen International*, while a TV set nearby showed Ivana Trump being interviewed on a morning show. The sound was down, and Ivana's smile gave nothing away as to the philosophical depth of the probing.

'Hi. You're looking good,' she said, presenting a cheek before leading me to the lift. 'How are things?'

'Fine.' Why does everyone say that, I wondered. 'You?'

'Terrible,' she answered, cancelling my observation. 'I think I'm pregnant.'

Luckily, no one else got in as we rose to the fourth floor. I tried to fix on a way to reply without revealing my inner turmoil.

'You *think*?'

'I've never been three weeks late before. Not ever.'

'What about whosit, Drongo?'

'Terry? He buggered off. Said I talked about you all the time.'

Flattering, but it wasn't what I wanted to hear. I wanted to hear: "I don't need his help, even if he is the father." But she didn't say anything. The doors opened and I was led through a maze of desks and PCs to a line of glass-walled offices. I tried to remember the last time we'd had it off.

Shows that run for years quickly lose the people who first develop them. They move on to weave their magic elsewhere and are replaced by older hacks. Tired, lacklustre, seen-it-all jobsworths who only dream of retiring to write poetry, but know they'll never be able to afford it. The good news is they're probably familiar with your work. The bad news is they don't give a shit, since they know the public would watch the series even if it were written by gerbils. 'Alan Tate,' a balding fellow said when Jackie opened the door. He waved to a chair, revealing a large sweatmark in his armpit. '*Trade Wind*, Beeb, nineteen seventy something.'

'Coffee, tea, Coke?' Jackie asked.

'Perrier?' I countered, and she said she'd see if they ran to it.

Leaving me without the name of the man I was hoping to squeeze for twenty thousand.

'That's right,' I said. 'We had some fun on that.'

'Fun?' He lifted an eyebrow. 'What's that?'

I gave him a grade two laugh. Laughter tracks on sitcoms are graded. Grade six is the best, reserved for when someone either says "shag", mentions the name of the Prime Minister, or turns to the camera with a pained glare and says, "Bloody hell!"

'I know,' I agreed. 'The days you could think of a series idea coming to work and get a green light by lunchtime.'

He presented a raised thumb. This was going well. Here were two old pros who didn't have to do the bullshit.

On the walls were photographs of the show's main characters, all of them in wellies and standing fore and aft of a large farmyard beast. Well lit and make-up in place, they looked like models showing off Versace anoraks. Someone had even washed the cows. Their hooves *gleamed*.

He watched me scan the pictures.

'Great show,' I said.

Jackie came back with a Diet Coke and no glass.

36

'Sorry, that's all there was.' She knew I hated Diet anything. Remove the caffeine and all you have is the taste of rusty metal. And the can had been nearer an oven than a fridge.

'That's fine,' I said as she fluttered her fingers and went out. I hooked the ring pull and warm fizz shot out over the floor.

'Shit, sorry.' She'd shaken it up!

'This carpet's had more than Coke spilled on it,' Baldy said. I wondered what he meant. Egos? Blood? Semen?

'As I was saying, it's a terrific series,' I schmoozed on. 'Kept its original feel. That's why you're still getting over twelve million viewers.'

'Thanks.'

Christ, what *was* his name? He'd story-edited *Trade Wind*, a show about an old clipper ship, known more for its soaring background music than its drama. Like *Chariots of Fire*; a great tune buffing up a ho-hum tale.

'So what have you been doing?' he went on breezily. Why was he delaying the start of the meeting? An alarm bell rang in that part of the brain where experience stores up bad memories. They'd changed their minds about hiring me. They'd found out I hadn't seen a single episode.

I gave the modest response: 'A lot of unmade Hollywood scripts, some horrendous experiences with the French . . .' trying not to stir the natural reaction from television producers that once a writer scores on the big screen, they become condescending to the small.

'Bit of a comedown, vet stories,' he grinned.

'Not a bit. It's what they call real life, a concept Los Angeles regards as avant-garde.'

A lull followed. I stood to take a closer look at the photos.

Except for one actor, none of the faces registered. It was pre-watershed, transmitted during the 7 to 9 p.m. desert infested with British sitcoms and game shows. Only room temperature IQs turned on a set in these hours. But I carried on smiling and prodded the pictures. 'It's always the measure of a good series that the actors stick with it.'

'It's more a measure of how their agents can nail us to the wall once we get the required ratings,' he replied.

I related the story of a red-hot American legal series that was in its fourth run. An American writer who had worked on it told me that every so often one of the stars would approach the producers and ask for more money and their part to be given greater depth. The producer said he had been thinking exactly the same way and here was a script that he intended to shoot at the end of the current batch.

The actor would race home, believing she or he was on the way to A-list movie status and then read the script. It ended with their character committing suicide. Apparently all the principal stars had a similar scenario in the safe. It killed all complaints stone dead.

'Not a bad idea,' he said, followed by another lengthy pause.

'So,' I said. 'Vets.'

The door opened and he stood up, almost at attention. Turning, I saw a smart woman in a quiet but meaningful Krizia suit. She was around forty and projected a composed, solemn manner I had seen only in Los Angeles, where women have to behave like this to be taken seriously.

'Ah, let me introduce Marti Van Allen,' the producer said, showing his sweatmarks. 'Alan Tate.'

'How do you do,' she replied and gripped my hand with one that had been dipped in liquid oxygen.

'Marti, er, is our new supervising exec from Glamor Cable TV.'

'Ah.'

'Glamor has taken on co-financing of *Animal Doctor*,' Marti explained. 'American audiences loved the James Herriot series which proved there is an active appeal for veterinary-orientated stories.'

'But you don't make any of your own,' I said as we sat. She waited while Baldy scratched his armpit and her nose twitched ever so slightly.

'No. Research revealed that coast-to-coast attraction of veterinary medicine depends on the co-relationship with an English accent. I don't know if you are familiar with the United States, but our rural communities are spread over a vastly differing climatic and cultural area.'

'I know, I've been through most of them,' I said. She might have mentioned my credits on at least five American movies. She looked the kind to prepare herself before a meeting.

'Then you will appreciate that what is of interest to an Iowa farmer is not necessarily the same as that which appeals to someone with a spread in Texas or, indeed, Mississippi. Placed abroad, in Europe, all these regions may watch with equanimity.'

She spoke as if she were reading an autocue. I was wondering how she would respond in a shower.

'Yes.'

'Ted tells me you and he once worked together.'

Ted! Ted MacFarlane. That was Sweaty's name.

'Ted and I knocked conkers together,' I grinned. Her face clouded. 'What I mean, in my colloquially English way, is we have known each other a long time.'

'Ted, of course, is in charge of the series. However, Vermilion kindly consented to allow me to sit in on preproduction meetings.' She flashed a smile as Siberian as her handshake.

'The more the merrier.' I smiled. Inwardly I was doing anything but feel merry. Ted and I would have made a deal based on old times' sake. 'Listen, Alan, we don't need to fuck around with treatments. Go away and think of something, I'll put the commission through sight unseen . . .' But Marti sounded like a different bag of horsefeed.

'I assume you are familiar with the series,' she said.

'Hard not to be when it's been on for so long.'

'Do you watch regularly?'

'I missed a couple of seasons when I was in Los Angeles,' I explained. Is this where I drop Pacino's name? I once did a script for his people but he chose another project. 'But I never miss them when I'm home.'

'Obviously when something has been running for so long, it gets harder to find a fresh take on veterinary surgery,' Marti went on, going down her memorized cue cards. 'Have you had any time to think about stories?'

'Well,' I began. I hadn't thought of the bloody series at all in the four days between my call and the appointment. Only coming in on the bus had I wondered if they had ever done one about horse mutilation, a curious phenomenon that breaks out occasionally in the shires, for which nobody is ever caught. 'Yes, I have.'

My voice was pitched to make it sound as if the topic had been fomenting in my mind for years. 'I'm intrigued about this business of attacking horses.' Ted looked at Marti, who didn't take her eyes from a spot somewhere to the left of my chair.

'What business of attacking horses?'

I told her how young girls, going to ride their pony, would find someone had removed its nostrils, or shoved a spike up the vagina. Ted began to shuffle papers, but Marti never moved. She looked like she was thinking the idea had legs, so I pressed on. 'Or a stable lad discovers someone's been playing noughts and crosses on his nags with a Stanley knife. Vets obviously must go ballistic about stuff like that. I can see Pinkerton giving a terrific performance saving the animals' lives while at the same time helping the police catch the maniacs. It would explore the darker side of animal doctoring. A friend of mine owns horses down in the sticks, in the country, and he often says how scared he is—'

'Who?' Marti said, returning her eyes to mine.

'A friend, Maurice Jackson—'

'No, I mean who can you see giving a terrific performance?'

'Pinkerton. The vet. The main character. Him.' I pointed at the photo of the star on the wall.

'Pickering', Ted mumbled.

'Pickering,' I repeated. 'Sorry.'

Marti spoke for a minute about the unsuitability of a tale about animal sadists in a pre-watershed programme, especially if it involved young women finding their pet raped with a post. She looked at her watch, held out her hand briefly and left.

'Maybe we could do it without showing the grisly bits,' I offered, wanting only to be out of that office. Ted replied they actually had a storyline roughly on the same lines, only not so graphic. I asked how many episodes were still free and he made a pretence of looking down a paper and said there were only a couple. I stood, tried to ease the mood by saying things were simpler in the *Trade Wind* days – 'No American involvement' – which allowed him to feel he wasn't the one who had slammed the door in my face.

'Wait till she wants the fucking dogs to bark in an Iowan accent,' I grunted as I went out. He smiled wearily.

I hoped to reach the lifts without running into Jackie, but she was waiting. She had put me in a meeting with a fizzy Coke, plus the thought that I was the father of her child. Not the best foot to start off on, even excluding Cruella de Vil. I recalled the police trick of giving a suspect an anxious day in solitary, thinking about a fatal mistake. As a matter of fact, *Jackie* knew about that one. We had watched the scene together. It was in *Prime Suspect* or *Cracker*. The little sod! Has me brought in, then wrecks my concentration by saying she thinks she's pregnant. And she won, hands down.

Pinkerton! Telling them I was a fan, yet I didn't know the name of the main character. "Oh Mr Tolstoy, I just *adored* your Eileen Karenina . . ." Maybe she, Maxie and Richard had got together. Maybe every move I make for the rest of my life is going to be orchestrated by my enemies so that I wind up cadging change in an underpass.

'How did it go?'

'I think I may have bombed.'

'Oh, God! *How?* Ted was really keen to have you.'

'Marti Feldman took another view.'

'Who? Oh, *her*.'

Jackie loathed all women. Her mother, my wife, Joan of Arc. She never had a good word to say about any of them. Positively damning about Jesus's mum. She saw all females as competition. During our briefish fling, she would assume that the only reason I took a bus was because I was having an affair with the conductress.

42

'I know a bit about selling out to Hollywood,' I said. 'But I never expected to meet it in television.'

'She's a dyke,' Jackie explained, pressing the lift button. 'Shit, love, I'm sorry. I did my best.'

'My fault.' I hadn't had sex in weeks and the smell of her hair tightened my loins. 'Thanks for trying.'

'If anything else comes up, I'll give you a bell.'

I wondered about exploiting the double entendre of anything coming up, but decided this wasn't the moment.

'Give me one anyway.'

The doors closed and I left her looking sad, swamping me with remorse. This paranoia must stop. Of course she hadn't sabotaged my chances. Solitary workers are prone to unlikely fears. There had been a time when I was certain I was going to be mugged. I'd been reading too much *Daily Mail* and every time I walked around London, I'd be forever looking over my shoulder, clocking who was behind, turning down streets to check if they followed. Now it was betrayal. Poor kid. She knew I was strapped, with the divorce and everything. She was only trying to help. You're an embittered shit, I thought. You'll end up making nuisance calls or stalking.

I was a hundred yards from Vermilion when I wondered why she didn't refer to her late periods after I came out of the meeting.

DATE: JUNE 4

FAX TO: ALAN TATE

FROM: BERNARD CARLUCCI, LEGAL DEPARTMENT,

          MOVIELINE INTERNATIONAL, LOS ANGELES

Unspeakable Behavior

Dear Alan Tate,

Elaine Morgenstern has presented your latest revisions on this project to Movieline's legal department for assessment.

It is apparent that you have consistently failed to take note of the many detailed instructions given to you either by Mort Delannoy or by Elaine Morgenstern in their various faxes between April and end May. To whit:

1) Asked to replace fifty pages of script deleted between revisions three and four you merely restored those you had removed, ignoring the reservations made earlier about superfluous dialogue, thus taking the project back to a previous draft instead of forward.

2) This legal department does not take lightly the libelous references you make having renamed the police officer Bernstein. No employee of Movieline International at any time suggested you should refer to him as the illegitimate child of the famous songwriter Leonard Bernstein and Jacqueline Onassis. It can only be concluded that you are deliberately trying to damage the property by these inflammatory tactics.

3) Elaine Morgenstern clearly and unequivocally asked you in her May 18 fax to delete all references to mastectomy in relation to the Susie character. She did not, repeat not, require you to do anything more than that. Making Susie a quadriplegic amputee and

44

having the trucker leave her suspended on a coat rack after their sexual encounter was in extremely poor taste and makes it impossible for this company to retain your services. We hereby dispense with them, citing irreconcilable differences. We shall be writing to your agent with a copy to the Writers' Guild explaining our reasons to exercise cut-off as of this date.

Bernard Carlucci

The rental agency described the flat as West Chelsea. The ad said SW6, which meant Fulham to me, once the breeding ground of the now extinct Yuppie. It felt like going back to the beginning, the camp bed in a friend's Balham kitchen 'just until I get fixed up'.

Postal districts are important in London. SW3, SW7 mean young and successful. Meet someone at a party and say you live there, and it's kit off right away. Tell them you live in W8 and they'll pull a face and ask if you have a son. SW15, you're young but married with children, and as for higher double digits, you might as well come from Birmingham.

The flat was across the road from Stamford Bridge. Luckily it was summer, and except for a Murdoch-inspired soccer competition, there weren't meant to be any Chelsea home games during the hopefully short time I would be there. The two rooms, kitchen and bath were on the first floor of a small turn-of-the-century house and I was assured the neighbours were quiet. All I needed was a round-the-clock reggae fan. An unexpected cheque for five thousand helped me leave the house keys in the garage for Maxie and return to the city. A new cable company was buying up old series to transmit through Europe and I had written some episodes for one about a bunch of lovable Cockney sparrows. How they would go down in Albania wasn't my problem.

Of all my contemporaries at Oxford, I was the last to marry and the last to divorce, so I knew what it was like to return to the single life. Except for Richard and Christine, they had all hit the buffers, some more than once, and transferred from a spacious house to the silence of a poky flat. Their life followed a uniform pattern. First off, they wallowed euphorically in no longer having to lie about where they were last night. When I called in, the place stank of aftershave and the only thing in the fridge was a bottle of cheap champagne 'for later'. They were off to the meat markets and eager to let the evening take its course. After a few weeks of this, the mood changed. For a start, none of my friends had ever used condoms beyond the age of nineteen. We were the pre-AIDS generation, where the worst you could get was the clap, and that was sorted out by a genial jab in the buttocks at the local VD centre. And really, there were very few of these mishaps. The women were pilled-up, told their sex lives could now be as lively as men's, and for a while there seemed no reason for anyone to marry.

From the mid-eighties on, however, habits changed. AIDS became a fact of life, or death, although most hetero males felt immune, saying it was only a gay disease. They still do. Women, though, saw it from a different angle. They often had sex with bisexuals. Some were even married to them. So the daisy-chain syndrome was talked about in the ladies' lavs, the upshot being that while you were struggling to get an erection, they reached out and took a Branson from the bedside table. By the time you'd figured out how to roll it on, there was nothing to roll it on to, and for the rest of the night you spoke about the castration of marriage and she looked at her watch.

My friends then moved to the next stage, which basically rested on me pimping for them among Maxie's divorced friends. Or, as we grew older, their daughters. Somewhere you could park it without having to go through a top-to-tail medical. Naturally, this didn't go down too well with Maxie, although it was true to say that many of her dumpee acquaintances would have dropped them for Saddam Hussein.

So I knew what my new life entailed. The first night I lay in bed and heard an al fresco dinner party next door go on until one thirty. It was summer and the English moved their Marks and Spencer's chicken biryani into the garden. I heard the women's laughter grow more raucous as the wine slipped down and the jokes turned bluer. The whole world was going to get laid tonight and the only fingers on my cock were my own. I tried to shut out the gaiety of others by making a list of the pluses of my new situation. I need answer to no one, select whomsoever to spend the night with, watch any TV channel I liked; smoke, drink and fart in bed. I could plan a weekend without having to consider anyone else, never go to another musical, stay in clubs until the sun came up. Live the life of the post-war poets, fetch up in alien rooms with unknown companions; suck the juice from life instead of waving as it passed me by.

They were the pluses of my new life. As for the minuses, well – they were roughly the same.

Fulham is fine for anyone who hasn't spent the past ten years behind high provincial walls. Where you never saw a young black in a wool cap with a Tennant's Xtra Strength in his hand coming towards you after dark. All the old phobias about being mugged came rushing back. Should I cross the

47

road? That would be racist. Act like he's white, in a pin-striped suit and carrying a tissue-wrapped bottle of Côtes du Rhone. *But he's not!* Keep on this side, but walk near the kerb so you can dash into the street if he makes a lunge. Better to be killed by a car than stabbed in the neck. The immense relief when he passes without a glance. Quickly, turn round as if you're searching for a house number to make sure he hasn't doubled back; no fine, he's gone. Shit, here come three more.

Fulham is no problem if you're still youngish enough to handle the pull and shove of city life. But, as the duchess perceived, anyone who travels on public transport after the age of thirty is a failure. And those first few days passing Chelsea football ground, avoiding any but the best lit streets, I never felt more aware that the rest of my days would be a steady descent into hell.

'Jackie, hi, it's me.'

'Can I call you back?'

She doesn't recognize my voice.

'It's Alan.'

'Call you back.'

'Listen, I've moved, I'm—'

'I'll get the number from 1471.' Click.

It's only eight o'clock. In the morning. She must have been in the shower. No, she answered on the second ring. She was in bed. With someone. So? But when I was with her, she'd answer and chat for ages, with me lying there completely forgotten. Having spent the best part of a week hesitating to call, I felt angry that, after I'd summoned the moral courage, she hung up. To be exact, she was the only woman under fifty I knew who might, as a favour, assist my sexual requirements. A fortnight wanking to the sound of

48

couples splashily screwing in bath tubs – the weather remained sizzling, with open windows everywhere – had narrowed my original parameters.

As for pursuing my craft, I concluded that if I were on the way out, I would go in Malcolm Lowry style. Submitting storylines for *Jackanory* until something better turned up was too demeaning. Oblivion was what I sought. As my solicitor's namesake remarked as they were about to evict him from the White House, unless you have been in the deepest valleys, you will never appreciate the highest peaks. Or was it the other way round?

A hefty part of this scenario was self-pity. Even Jackie wouldn't speak to me. Why I would want to speak to *her* wasn't a question I dwelled on. She wasn't a particularly good fuck. Before I took up adultery, I'd assumed all the women decorating the newspapers, TV and King's Road were sexual contortionists. God knows, they start learning early enough. But Jackie just used to lie back and wait for the orgasm. And wait. A few perfunctory kisses and she expected me to pole vault into her. Asked to help things along a bit, and having her hand forcibly clamped on my genitals, she would sigh and give them a couple of tweaks as if she were fiddling with Playdoh. I suppose twenty-year-old men don't need foreplay; I can't remember. At fifty, you need a hard-core video playing on the headboard just to get into position.

Like most people of my age, I had learned most of what I knew from the movies. How to pick up girls, what to say, how to talk them into sex, how to run when they got pregnant. These rites of passage were cinematically explored during the permissive years of my early manhood. Albert Finney, trapped by Shirley Ann Field in *Saturday Night and Sunday*

49

Morning, chucking a stone in the final reel and threatening it won't be the last. They were the morality tales of the post-war era, laying down the rules of what was honourable and what wasn't. For a while, the bad guys always lost and virtue triumphed. Doris Day tamed Rock Hudson and had his baby over the end credits. Later on, studios followed the mood of the times and made heroes of the crooks. Audiences cheered Gordon Gecko in *Wall Street* and derided Forrest Gump for being so good. The guy was an imbecile, what else do you expect?

The pictures warned you to be on guard if a strange woman started talking to you. If they looked like Sharon Stone, they were after your wallet or the keys to the vault. Shelley Long types were safe enough, but they would end up smothering you in unwanted attention. Or, as in *Play Misty for Me*, try to turn you into shish kebab.

The one who spoke to me in the Groucho Club was somewhere between. I saw her come in via the mirror behind the bar. Late thirties, neatly dressed, composed. I liked how she didn't look round at the crowd. (There's a standard rule at the Grouch. If you scan the faces, you're looking for a job: if you don't, you're the one with the juice.) She moved through easily without having to shove. Some people are able to make even PR thugs give way with a look, and she was one of them.

She took the stool next to mine and in a Mittel-European accent ordered a Budvar. Nice. I had pegged her for Perrier and lime. Her dark hair was androgynously cropped, but her movements were liquid feminine. I might have recently felt like Jack Lemmon in *The Apartment* but this wasn't the raddled old whore he takes home, nothing like. Was she Czech, German, what?

'You probably think it is impolite to order a foreign drink,' she said. 'This is in no way a reflection on English beer.'

I reacted in a way you see only in cornball comedies. I looked around to see who she was speaking to. When she gave me her full face and lightly twitched her lips, I realized, oh gosh, it was me.

'I'm glad,' I said. 'I was about to have you thrown out.'

'Why? Do you know I am not a member?'

'I didn't mean that,' I back-pedalled. 'I was pretending to be outraged. You know, like "Disgusted, Cheltenham".'

'I have not yet been to Cheltenham.'

'It's in Gloucestershire,' I heard myself answer.

'Is it disgusting there?'

There is a slew of things you're told you should never try, like incest and folk-dancing, but using irony on foreigners is way top of the list.

I was about to plunge into a Who's-on-First nightmare when I noticed her lips had twitched further and were puckering into a smile.

'You do not mind I make a joke at your expense?' she asked.

'I forgive your Czech beer if you forgive my American Jack Daniel's,' was all I could come up with. She lifted her glass and clinked the rim on mine.

'Prost.'

At this point, the cinema kicked in. She'll invite me home. On the way, she'll say this alley is a short cut, where two men will jump me for my money. No, she's too well-dressed for that, and anyway there were far more flush-looking men in the place. What else? She wants an English husband so she can find work. She's got AIDS and wants to take as many as possible with her.

51

Running through my mental Rolodex of options created a pause.

'You do not mind that I speak to you?'

'Of course not.'

'I am not long in England and do not know if such behaviour is regarded with favour.'

'Where are you from?'

'I am from Hamburg born but now I live in Berlin.'

'In Germany, women go round talking to men in bars?'

'If they wish to, yes.'

'I should go there more often.' It came out like a leer, the kind of thing the man the club was named after might have said.

'You know Germany?'

'I once wrote a film called *Assignment Berlin*.'

'You are a writer? How wonderful!' She sounded genuinely impressed.

'Oh, not really. I just string words together,' I said, quoting Stoppard.

'You must not be modest. I am also in the film industry.'

It was hard to find anyone in this joint who wasn't, so this didn't come across as one of life's stranger coincidences.

'Really.'

'We have in Germany much production but few writers.'

'I suppose that's because—'

Because Hitler threw them out, since most were Jews, and they never went back, was what I was about to say.

'—because most of your directors tend to write their own films.'

'No, it is because the Nazis expelled them and since most were Jews, they never returned.'

What could I say to that? Is that a fact? Son of a gun!

'Yes.'

'This *Assignment Berlin*,' she went on. 'It was about the war?'

My track record for turning off employers was currently running at one hundred per cent, so I was reluctant to bring the Blitz into the conversation.

'Sort of.'

'I believe I saw this film on television. Was it about flying?'

'More about the brutality of mass destruction,' I hedged. 'What it does to ordinary men, you know, ordered to drop bombs on innocent civilians.' I was hoping she couldn't remember what she'd seen. The recurring theme of the picture was the way the bomber crew sang, "Hitler has only got one ball," as they watched the HE create pretty patterns below.

'You have written other films?'

In *Sunset Boulevard*, Nancy Olsen asks William Holden if she might have seen any of his screenplays. He said he had done one about Custer's last stand, but by the time it was made, the action took place on a patrol boat in the Pacific. Films are not written, see, they're rewritten.

'A few, nothing grand. No Oscars.'

Not that I hadn't worked out my acceptance speech.

"I would like to thank my agent Tim Roberts, whose expertise made my career as a writer possible. And I'd like to thank my family, my wife Maxie and children Lloyd and Sophie, whose extravagance made it necessary—"

'What are their names?'

'You don't really want to know.' The worst ordeal for a screenwriter is to see the film after his story has passed through a dozen hands. Talking about it comes a close second.

Her glass was empty and I pointed to it.

'No, I must go to dinner.'

Bang went my next move.

'May I give you my card?'

She reached into her shoulder bag and brought out a clip. I read: 'ANDREE BRUCKMEYER Operfilm Gmbh'.

'Alan Tate,' I said, holding out my hand. She held it a moment longer than was necessary and slid off the stool.

'May I telephone you?' she said.

'Yes.' I tried to sound calm, hoping she was not looking so much for a writer as for someone to run through what Valmont called the Latin phrases in *Les Liaisons Dangereuses*.

I realized I couldn't remember the Fulham number. It would have sounded daft to admit I didn't know where I lived, so I wrote down the one for the house. 'I'm not often there. Maybe I can call you.'

'If you wish. It has been very nice to speak to you.'

When Maxie rang a few days later, I had completely forgotten about Andree Bruckmeyer. She had played a supporting role in a late night fantasy where we had gone skinny-dipping in a lake amid a brooding German forest. She was wearing a horned helmet, the kind you see in Wagner. I had fallen asleep before we got to the sex and she soon drifted into my mind's attic . . .

'Some female with a foreign accent called,' Maxie said. Any women *I* knew were females in her lexicon, not to be confused with warm, generous and non-threatening ladies of her acquaintance. 'She said something about meeting you in a bar.'

'Andree Bruckmeyer. And it was the Groucho.'

'Let me tell you, she had quite a nerve.'

'Why, what did she say?'

'"Please I vish to Herr Tate speak." When I asked her name, she said: "Tell him I am ze woman he met ze ozzer night."'

'First of all, Maxie,' I said carefully, 'she doesn't talk like that, and second of all, why do you think she has a nerve?'

'How was she to know I wasn't your wife? You meet her only "ze ozzer night", give this number as where she can reach you, God knows why—'

'I'd forgotten this one.'

'—and unless you told her if a woman answers, it'll be my ex-wife, without explaining how come we still live together, she has a goddam cheek not to ask first, but just *order* me to fetch you.'

I was becoming dizzy. 'I'm sorry. Did she leave a message?'

'I gave her your number. Please try and remember it next time you go cruising.' The line went dead.

She still cares, I thought.

An hour later, Andree called and wondered whether I would like to come to Operfilm Gmbh offices in Mortimer Street. How was tomorrow? She sounded as if her interest was more professional than social. I rang Tim.

'Ever hear of a German film company called Operfilm?'

'No.'

'Andree Bruckmeyer?'

'No.'

'I met her a few nights ago and she wants me to go to a meeting.'

'Don't mention the war,' Tim said.

'Too late.'

'Then don't agree to support a single currency.'

'I just thought I'd check to see if I'm getting into some fly-by-night waste of time.'

When I was making tons of money, when stuff I wrote actually got made, Tim was much more conversational. Nowadays I imagined him, hearing who was on the line, asking the agency operator to butt in after thirty seconds with an important overseas call.

'Give it a go,' he said. 'What have you got to lose?'

'Well, nothing, but usually these things that come from outside the normal channels—'

'Look, I have to go, there's a call coming through I've been waiting for. Let me know how you get on.'

Thanks, Tim.

Before I hit the big time with *Assignment Berlin*, I pursued every sniff of a possible job like a bloodhound. If the dustman told me he had a producer on his rounds, I'd call him.

A television director I worked with took an option on a novel and asked me to adapt it 'for old times' sake'. And I did. Studio technicians told about Brazilian billionaires they knew who were dying to get into the movie business. 'They'll finance anything we send them, Alan. You write it and we'll split the profits.'

You write it for nothing, Alan, was the sub-text. All these projects ended in tears. Two-hundred-pounds-now-and-half-a-million-when-it's-made sort of thing. Any job offer not arriving through an agent is bound to be an exercise to get a script for peanuts, which can then be hawked around and hopefully sold on for serious money. We all get caught in the early days, when one word of flattery has you adapting the Bible for Bulgarians.

Depressingly, I was back following dodgy propositions. Something born from a ten-minute chat with a stranger. I was living in Fulham and pursuing hopeless offers. I was living in Fulham, pursuing hopeless offers and getting a bum's rush from my agent, my ex-wife, my solicitor and everyone who used to be classified as a friend.

When women are unhappy they eat themselves sick. Most men drink. When I'm staring ruin in the face, I take taxis. It's a morale thing.

'Mortimer Street, blimey,' the driver said as I climbed in outside Fulham Broadway underground station. 'West End this time a day, you'd be better off on the tube.' It took a minute before I was wishing I had taken his advice.

He adjusted the rear-view mirror so he could make eye contact while we nudged east.

'So what do you do, if you don't mind me asking?'

'I'm a writer.'

It just popped out. Maybe I had to tell someone to convince myself I was still what I had written in my passport. But I knew I had erred.

'What you write then?'

'Well—'

'Like Jeffrey Archer?'

'Not quite.'

'I suppose not, or you'd have your own chauffeur.'

'Right.'

I crossed my fingers and hoped someone would fall under his wheels so he'd change the subject.

'What then?'

'A bit of telly, stuff like that.'

Anything I might have seen? Do you watch much? Nah, the wife does, though. Ever see . . . ? It's wonderful to listen to people say they never watch television, but when you mention everything from *Breakfast News* to *Late Night Review*, they cough to the lot.

This one didn't go on like that. As he dodged up and

57

down side streets to penetrate the traffic, he started the other approach cabbies use when they have a captive writer in their grip.

'Have I got a story for you,' he said. God, no! Please ask if I ever met famous people, what were they really like, but not this.

'I once had Michael Caine in the back of my cab, and I told him and he thought I should definitely send it in. Even said he'd do it.'

Good old Mike, anything for a job.

'This is the gospel truth, I swear on my kid's life,' the driver said, locking me in his gaze through the mirror. We still had at least twenty minutes of the ride left, so I hunkered down in the listening-to-bores mode. Whatever you do, never take your eyes off theirs, or they'll keep reminding you to pay attention: "Did you hear what I just said?" "Yes, I heard—" "You looked like you didn't, so I'll say it again . . ."

The trick is to stare unblinkingly into their face and nod every five seconds. With a bit of practice, it comes automatically. Once you have the rhythm, you can drift off anywhere you like. Sex, shopping lists, what's on television, the letter from the bank. And when they finish, you go: "Amazing. You say it's a true story?" And everybody is happy.

'See, I'm Jewish,' the driver began, pulling up behind a long queue of buses. 'And I've been married twice. The first one didn't last long. She wasn't Jewish, and we had problems right from the start, my parents being orthodox and everything. I was a plasterer in them days and it didn't go down much with her people who thought the sun shone out of her, well, you know . . .'

While he droned on, I recalled the Groucho encounter.

58

Her handshake had definitely been a come-on. And she'd started the conversation. Her English was pretty good and with an office in London, the chances were she'd been here a while and knew you didn't go chatting up blokes in pubs as she said women did in Germany. All that stuff about 'I hope you don't think I'm insulting English beer'. You only have to be here five minutes and you find fifty different foreign beers on sale in every supermarket. No one goes into London pubs any more except football hooligans or, if the place is specialized, sado-masochists, Elvis lookalikes, gays and journalists. She was definitely looking for an adventure. She had only subsequently discovered I was a writer, so the professional contact was an afterthought.

'—don't know if you've ever been to South America, anyway, it don't matter since she came here when she was only ten years old to live with a German family who brought her up in Golders Green . . .'

I thought of Maxie, how she sounded pissed off. Throughout the divorce, she had been dignified, never dragged Jackie's name into the arguments. She'd acted as if it were a relief to accept the inevitable, that we had grown apart and the only solution was to call it a day. But there was an edge in her voice when she rang. 'Some female with a foreign accent called—'

'Met her at a football game, funnily enough. Spurs and Everton. Her foster father was football mad – here, do you know he took me to the '66 World Cup? He was gutted. Thought his lot would walk it. We had a laugh about it, Greta 'n' me. She saw the funny side. Actually she never liked them much, even though they spoiled her rotten. Anyway, as I was saying—'

I wish I could say I missed the kids more, but they were

both at an age when parents were marginal to their lives. Lloyd in his first year at Durham, Sophie doing A levels and virtually speechless at family gatherings, except when her friends telephoned. An hour of shrieks and gasps of amazement later, she'd hang up and go to her room for the rest of the night to play Leonard Cohen CDs. I had seen more of my children than most fathers, working at home, but in the end it doesn't make much difference. I could imagine them blaming too close a proximity with their father when their marriages failed or they went down for compulsive shoplifting. But we did have some laughs when they were younger.

'—changed when we married. Kept saying plastering wasn't a job she could tell her friends about, so why didn't I do summing else? That's how I came to cabs. She could speak German fluently and one time we went there. She liked showing me up in restaurants, not knowing what to order and that, and after a bit I realized it wasn't going to work, the marriage. She didn't want kids, either—'

When Tim got divorced, he came to stay with us, occasionally introducing us to a date. Lloyd was six and wanted to know why he was going out with a lady who wasn't his wife. Maxie explained that since Tim wasn't married any more, he could do anything he liked. 'He can't break the windows,' Lloyd replied, after thinking about it a while. The phrase stuck with us throughout our marriage. Whenever we heard somebody say, 'You can do what you like,' one of us reprised the wisdom of a six-year-old logician.

'—the letters kept arriving, once a month on average. Well, being in German, I had no idea what was in them. Greta said they were nothing, just local gossip about their town, Belem, it's in the north, near the Amazon—'

The taxi crawled round Marble Arch and I reckoned in

five minutes I would be out and away from this interminable story. What did he mean, have I got a story for you? What did he think I was, a soap opera hack? The everyday life of Jewish folk?

'—cut a long story short, when I remarried, we moved away from north London. Found a place near Epsom, since it's only half an hour from Heathrow and I could get a fare in from the airport then take one out at the end of my day—'

We edged through Marylebone. I used to live there when I first came to London, before Maxie. Shared with a friend from Oxford who had gone off to Australia. There's the flat, up there, first floor on the corner.

'—saw it in the papers. You must have seen it.'

'No,' I said on cue.

'A few years ago, when he was officially declared dead.'

'No, I didn't.' When who was declared dead?

'What number Mortimer Street you want, guv?'

'Er – one eighteen.'

'Amazing to see her name. Greta. It said she'd come to England in the fifties and never saw her father again. They didn't know where she was. I had a mind to ring up and tell them but I thought no, best leave it out. I mean, it wasn't her fault, was it?'

'No, of course not.' The cab stopped and he turned in his seat, his face flushed. He had hardly drawn breath for half an hour.

'Now is that a story or what?'

'Amazing,' I said, fumbling for my wallet. 'Absolutely incredible.'

'That's what Michael said. He said he could just see the film posters: "I Married Mengele's Daughter". He reckoned the title alone was worth a bomb.'

61

While he was sorting the change, I went numb. Mengele? The Auschwitz doctor? The Angel of Death? Had this man just told me the story of the *century*, and I hadn't listened?

I read once about a man at Los Angeles airport who told everyone coming into his newspaper shop about some chap called Schindler who had saved thousands of Jews from the gas chambers. No one paid any attention until Thomas Keneally heard it and wrote *Schindler's Ark*.

And I had just been offered a story about an orthodox Jewish plasterer who became Dr Mengele's son-in-law . . .

What could I do? Ask him to go over it one more time? Take him into the meeting?

'You should write it all down,' I said.

'I'm no writer,' he grinned. 'But you are. The bit about him meeting Eichmann in Rio is worth a film in itself, right? And the gold they smuggled out of Poland – and what about those letters he wrote her?'

Operfilm were on the second floor and occupied two interconnecting rooms. From the lift to the door which bore the name, the walls displayed German film posters. None of them meant anything to me except one featuring a tall blond woman in a nazi uniform holding a whip. I think I had seen it at the NFT during their homage to German expressionist porn.

The entrance door was open and I could see Andree on the phone speaking German rapidly. I may have mentioned I am a snob for foreign women and her voice gave me a flush of excitement. She might well have been discussing the merits of an Audi clutch over a Citroën for all I knew, but it sounded thrilling.

When she saw me, she ended the call and came out, smiling.

'Good morning.' I felt the firm fingers again. Her walls were splattered with studio photos of actors but I could recognize only a few: Curt Jurgens, David Bowie, Anthony Perkins. The rest looked out of Nordic casting.

'May I bring you coffee?'

It was twelve thirty. Usually meetings at this time segue into lunch.

'No thanks, I'm fine.' The less you drink the less you're likely to spill, was my new motto. She returned to her desk and steepled her fingers. We once had a Dürer print called 'Praying Hands' and they looked like that.

'I so much enjoyed meeting you the other night,' she said. 'I do not go much to the Groucho since I am not a member, as you know. However, the person with whom I was having dinner is.'

'I see.'

'Lucy Williams. You perhaps know this person?'

'Sorry.'

'She works in publishing. We are negotiating to buy one of her books called *Alien Ways*. Do you know of this novel?'

'Is it science fiction?'

'No, it is a story of a young American woman who comes to Europe and because of a car accident becomes blind and paralysed. She meets a man in the hospital with a face which in a fire has been burned away, but since she is blind, it does not matter. It is a love story.'

Only a German would seize on this as ideal romantic material, I thought, but 'Sounds interesting' is what I said.

'We wish Harold Pinter to write the screenplay.'

'Sounds right up his street.'

'Ah, you know where he lives?'

Was this another Teutonic attempt at a joke? I waited, but her lips stayed unpursed.

'No. It's a phrase. Whenever I speak to people whose first language isn't English, I am constantly reminded how ridiculously we speak sometimes.'

When I get nervous, my syntax goes to pieces. Forget you just passed up the story of a lifetime and concentrate. She put her hand in a drawer and took out three video cassettes.

'We found some of your films.' Lifting the first, she read: '*Three Against the Mob.*'

'There's inflation for you,' I grinned.

'Excuse me?'

'It was originally called *Two Against the Mob.*'

'Ah yes, two. Forgive me. I am a little unsure translating English numbers. This cassette is in German. They all are. Here is one which is . . .' she had to think, '*In Front of Early Morning*?'

'*Before the Dawn,*' I said. God in Heaven, they found that piece of shit.

'We greatly admired them all.'

'Thank you.' If they liked *Before the Dawn*, these people are pushovers.

She laid the cassettes to one side and produced a hardback.

'Do you know of this book?'

She showed the cover and I read: *A Run for your Money* by Gerhard Eisler.

'Doesn't ring a bell.'

'A bell?'

'No, I haven't read it.'

'It does not matter since we are not using it,' she said, placing it beside the cassettes. 'Only the story. The – the – *handlung*.'

64

'Plot.'

'Yes. The plot. Excuse me.'

'What's it about?'

'How it is possible to move large amounts of money over the world by touching one button.'

'Let me take a guess at the high concept.' Since I was dealing with cinema illiterates, I'd show them some glitz. 'Dirty money laundered in Luxembourg, used to buy arms for South American freedom fighters, brings down American President.'

'We are looking for a story where a man must find a billion dollars which has become missing in this manner. He must succeed, since we are hoping this role will be played by Harrison Ford.'

'Naturally. Harrison doesn't play losers.'

'I have spoken with my colleagues and we are in agreement that you are the person we wish to write the script. As I have said, we are an admirer of your work. You are an excellent writer.'

A playwright once told me that whenever someone comes to him with a movie proposition and precedes it by telling him he is a great artist, his first thought is, There's no money in this.

'Wait, hang on a minute, not so fast,' I blustered, taking care to sound good-natured. 'This story is about big business. I haven't worked in the genre for years.'

I hadn't worked in it ever.

'It is a film which will require a great amount of research. We have facilities in this area.'

'Look. Please don't misunderstand this, but why me? You and I meet in a bar. We have a few minutes' conversation. A couple of days later you find, God knows where, cassettes of my movies and are now offering me a job. How many other writers have you seen?'

She paused a moment to frame her words.

'Many. But none were suitable. They have not written five major films as you have done. Soon we must make a decision, or the development funds on this project will be withdrawn. I personally brought this idea to the company and I am most impatient to have a script. When we met, I decided I am able to work with you. This is most important. And then I saw your films. They are well constructed and I was excited by the stories. This is why you are the writer we wish to employ.'

Well, put like *that* . . . I waited. She fidgeted and I prepared myself for the worst. "Our situation, Herr Tate, is that we have only limited funds, so we propose that on completion of the film, you will receive—"

'May I know your answer?'

'I have quite a workload at present,' I said. 'There's a project with Warner's and I'm negotiating over a mini-series about Albert Schweitzer . . .'

'Perhaps when we discuss terms with your agent, we can agree a time when you can start.'

Discuss terms with your agent. They were kosher.

'I'm sure he'll work something out,' I said.

Half an hour later, I was on my way home with a feeling that a corner had been turned. I was back in work, dipping into the coffers of the German economic miracle. I figured Tim would ask for thirty thousand and I would be dealing with someone who showed distinct signs of wanting to mix business with pleasure. Who could I find to share this with?

DATE: 14 SEPTEMBER

FAX TO: ALAN TATE

FROM: TIM ROBERTS

Dear Alan,

Operfilm have agreed to a total fee of fifty (50) thousand pounds for a treatment, draft and two sets of revisions for their project working title: *Follow the Money*. Amounts will be paid:

     £5000 on signature
     £5000 for the treatment
     £10,000 commencement of draft
     £10,000 delivery of draft
     £10,000 commencement of revisions
     £10,000 delivery of final revisions

The fee to be set against a total price of £150,000 on commencement of principal photography.

I will send you a contract in due course but these are the relevant figures. Andree Bruckmeyer gave me lunch and expressed her keen desire to work with the author of *Assignment Berlin* so I gather you have found that legendary charm which you seemed recently to have mislaid.

She made it clear that before writing the treatment, she requires you to meet some of her bank contacts who will give you access to study their business procedures. Since lunch was at the Caprice and she had a driver waiting outside for three hours I would guardedly suggest Operfilm are pretty well fixed although, as she admitted, they have not made much of a dent in the US market to date. She is hoping *Follow the Money* will be their key into Hollywood. What she implied of course was that she is hoping *you* are their

key. So do a good job and as the Germans say, ' Upfucken
Sie nicht.'

Tim

P.S. The first ten thousand has just arrived.

Harold Wilson may have observed that a week was a long
time in politics, but when it comes to moving from suicidal
to euphoric, it was no time at all in the film world. *Fifty
thousand!* And ten in already. Tim's fax arrived seven days
after my meeting at Operfilm. Just as slow payers are treated
with suspicion, so are quick ones, and I rang him to quell
my nerves.

'What's the catch?'

'We haven't banked the cheque yet.'

'Did you like her?'

'Well, she was paying and she bought a bottle of '75
Musigny. If Carla goes under a bus, she'll be the first one I call.'

He told me Germany was currently drowning in development money and my chance encounter occurred the day
after Operfilm had been informed that unless they spent two
hundred thousand DM by the end of the month, they would
have to return it to the central fund.

'Actually, I mopped up the rest for a project one of our clients is preparing. There ought to be more Andrees out there.'

'So everyone is happy.'

'You still have to write the bloody thing.'

Andree called to say she was trying to arrange a meeting
with an executive at the Corporate Bank of Commerce and
Industry. The last few years, I'd lost interest in the financial
pages and hadn't heard of them. CBCI were thrown up
during the *grande bouffe* of the nineteen eighties. The first

thing they had done was take over a city building, rip out the Victorian walnut panelling and replace it with Carrara marble. Lear jets and Monaco assumed the roles previously played by Rovers and Brentford banqueting halls, and the telephone operators had French accents.

While I waited, I looked around for any port where I could shelter during the libidinous storm that blew up the moment I was back in the chips. The song may have pointed out that every man likes his lovey-doveying when the temperature is low, but for me the whiff of money gave me erections of flagpole proportions. I suppose it was the result of an impoverished youth, I don't know, but each time I land a big one, I have to keep my hands from straying in crowded places. I scan the top shelves of newsagents and imagine those dignified women television newsreaders going down on their partners. In short, I was in a constant state of horniness, my mind checked at the door while my lower half behaved like a stallion on heat. How else could I explain going round to Jackie's flat?

She hadn't returned my call after I caught her off guard that morning, nor did she respond to several later messages. What I did was draw a thousand pounds in twenties and drive past her building. Her car was outside, so I parked and stuffed the package under my jacket. When she answered the bell and heard my voice, she became hesitant.

'It's not really convenient right now—'

'Jackie, if you don't open up, I'm going to pin a note on the door describing the fox you have tattooed on your bum. I mean this. You can probably hear I'm using my serious voice.'

The lockbreaker buzzed, I shouldered inside and ran up the stairs.

'What's so important?' she asked, barely opening the door. For a second she stood blocking my way, but I pushed through, my hand under the bulge which made me look as if I had a pigeon chest.

'What you got there?'

I walked into the bedroom.

'Do you remember what you said when I landed the Hollywood job, *Unspeakable Behavior*?'

'What I *said*?'

'What you said you would like to do?'

'What was that?'

'You said you wanted more than anything else to lie on a bed of money and have me fuck your brains out.'

'I never did.'

'My memory is better than yours, Jackie. Trust me on this one.'

I pulled out the package, ripped open the end and shook. Actually, fifty currency notes don't go very far, not on a queen size, but it was the gesture that made me feel like a rich eccentric from the nineteen thirties. Stavisky, say. She ran a palm over the money, shuffling it like playing cards.

'Get 'em off,' I said, stepping out of my casuals.

'How much is there?'

'A thousand. I thought afterwards we might make a hole in it.'

When I dropped my trousers, I had a stand that was extending my boxers. She gave it a glance but returned to the cash.

'You get another job or what?'

'No, I won the lottery.'

She made no attempt to undress. I pulled down my shorts

70

and waited. The erection began to wilt, so I came up close and put my arms round her.

'You're randy,' she said. Perceptive, that was Jackie.

'For you,' I answered, bringing my hand up between her legs. The stand revived.

'You should have rung first.'

Jackie was never ever dry. Her labia were constantly humid. I never understood how she stopped them dripping down her legs.

'I don't like being taken for granted. No woman does.'

'Can we talk about this later?' I had this terrible feeling I was going to come prematurely and tried to concentrate on things I must not do. I must not screw up the assignment. I must not spend the money before I earned it. I must not let Maxie know I had a job worth fifty big ones.

She looked at her watch and yanked off her T-shirt.

'OK. But be quick.'

Ninety seconds should do it, I reckoned.

We rolled on to the bed and Jackie assumed the position of someone waiting to give blood. I thought it more romantic if she took off her skirt instead of just pulling it down along with her knickers.

'I shouldn't be doing this at all,' she said, lifting her bum to let the clothes pass. 'I thought I was pregnant the last time.'

I sprinkled some notes over her navel and climbed aboard.

'You know, I never said anything about doing it on money. You made that up.'

I fumbled for my cock and edged it inside her. She was so lubricated it fell out on the first thrust.

'Can you hold it?' I mumbled. 'Just till I get going.'

She sighed and slid her hand down. God, she was loose.

71

I couldn't feel the sides. Anyone this juiced up should have been panting with ecstasy, but I'd seen her more excited rolling on a pair of tights. I began to feel the first twinges of orgasm and tried to damp them down by wondering if Operfilm would pay me in DMs and send them to Liechtenstein. Could you open an account there with as little as fifty thousand? More tickling advances started to filter through. Of course, I would have to work out some system with Tim and his percentage, but it would certainly help to keep some cash out of the country – aaah!

'Can I get up now?' she asked, crossly.

Post-coital *tristesse* began at once. What the hell was I doing here? Am I so devoid of dignity that I actually pleaded with her to lie there while I virtually jerked off? What possessed me to take out a thousand quid and spread it over the bed? What crummy film did I see *that* in?

'Sorry it was a bit abrupt, but I haven't been exactly rampant lately,' I said. A twenty-pound note caught some discharge after Jackie disengaged herself and stuck to the end of my penis.

'Now I have to take another shower,' she muttered, and flounced into the bathroom. I lay for some moments wondering if men ever grew up, if there came a time when their brains controlled their bodies. If they were ever capable of regarding sex the way women do, as something rather special, not to be flung around like grass seed. We'll plant it anywhere for a thrill that lasts maybe ten seconds. Why didn't God put the penis where we can't get at it, so it would be the female who dictated when we shagged? Sticking it within easy reach, between our legs, was a serious design fault. The only people to profit by the arrangement were top shelf publishers. All pornography is based on the ease with which men can masturbate, plus the knowledge that they will never ever lose the habit.

A door closed somewhere. Then a voice called:

'Hello, honey. I'm home . . .'

The only variation on this hoary old comedy routine was that the voice belonged to a woman. I hardly had time to jump off the bed before Marti Van Allen walked in. She was carrying a laptop which she put down neatly before furrowing her brow first at me, then the money on the bed. Less then a minute had elapsed since I came and my cock was still semi-tumescent, making my attempt to pull on my underpants clumsy. Where were the snappy lines they have in farces when this sort of thing occurs? Why didn't some come to mind? I couldn't think of a thing. Well, except for:

'Oh, hi. Jackie's in the shower.'

I tried to dress with an insouciance I didn't feel. Would she recognize me as the man who pitched the X-rated storyline for a family vet show? Would recognition make anything easier? If she did, she didn't immediately show it, because she marched towards the bathroom and threw open the door.

Jackie was under the spray. 'Stay outside,' she called. 'Don't you come in here.' Marti pulled the shower curtain aside. 'Oh, it's you, love. You're early.'

'Who is that?' Marti demanded, flicking her head backwards.

'Him? Oh, just an old friend. Well, not a friend any more, actually.'

She was clearly scared. She turned off the spray and stepped out, reaching for a towel.

'No?' Marti's voice rose to a resonant top C. 'Then why is he waving his penis around the bedroom?'

'He, well, he dropped by and—'

73

'And why, may I ask, is there money spread all over the goddam bed?'

By now I had my clothes on, more or less. The underpants were back to front and I had wrongly buttoned my shirt, but there was enough covered to get out of there.

'The money?' Jackie was saying. 'Oh, that was just a joke—'

'For fuck's sake!' Marti yelled. 'Are you telling me you turn tricks while I'm out!'

'No, Marti, don't talk silly!'

'You fucking little tramp! I bet you never even used a condom. Where is it? *Show* me!'

Time to go. I stepped into my shoes and towards the door.

'Alan! *Tell* her!' Jackie screamed.

Congreve once remarked that hell hath no fury like a woman scorned, but he didn't say anything about men. If she had shown even the mildest interest five minutes ago, it would have ended differently. If I hadn't a mental picture of myself standing pathetically with my trousers round my ankles and of Jackie bristling with understandable contempt, then I might have helped. As it was, scorned to the eyebrows, I turned at the door and said, with one of those flourishes Burt Reynolds used to be good at: 'Same time next week, sweetie? Maybe you can persuade your friend to make up a threesome.' And left.

I liked the way I was able to get in the last word. It was neat. What comedy writers call 'a moment'. Usually tongue-tied in times of crisis, on this occasion I was proud of myself.

The fact that, while the lovers were tiffing in the bathroom, I had managed to snatch up less than a dozen of the twenties meant that I had paid dearly for the pleasure.

74

Andree had called while I was out doing my Cary Grant impersonations. Her message said I was to turn up at eleven tomorrow at the Corporate Bank of Commerce and Industry and ask at reception for Arnold Hall.

'He is a senior director and is willing to tell you anything you need to know.'

I like the City, with its atmosphere redolent of former glory. Despite the police controls following the IRA bombs and the newer glass monuments, many streets still retain a period feel, when men wore toppers and waistcoats and transacted business in handsomely decorated bankers' drafts. When the restaurants were foggy with cigar smoke and waiters were all over fifty. When Britain was the banking centre of the world, and if some upstart foreign state misbehaved, we confiscated their assets until they apologized. Today the pubs still smell as pubs should, of stale ale, and the customers lodge beer bellies on the lip of the tables.

CBCI stood out like – how did our dermatologistic heir apparent phrase it? – a carbuncle on the face of an old friend. Little was left of its Empire Gothic façade. The Eurovandals had even taken out the window frames to install triple glazing. The front resembled an old tart who thought she could still turn a few tricks if she piled on the make-up over a poorly executed facelift. What had once been a solid oak door entrance was now expanded into a marble and plate glass job you see on Rodeo Drive boutiques. A sign tolled the knell on the old days: 'This is a No Smoking Zone'.

I clattered towards the reception area. Fred Astaire would have made a classier approach. I sounded like a gauleiter going to see Hermann Goering.

The women behind the counter were reminiscent of the old television years. They looked like a Diana Ross backing group and greeted every visitor as if he were Mr Right.

'Ah, Meester Tate, Meester Hall is expecting you,' mine said, glancing at a screen. 'Eef you be so kind to sign the book, then proceed to ze fourth stage where you weell be met.'

I wondered how many receptionists in Zurich were handling the same work with "Hello, lovey, the old geezer's up the apple 'n' pears, mind how you go." In younger days I used to play the guitar. Well, three chords. After cricket, we'd convene in someone's house and a bunch of middle-class English yahoos would strain their tonsils to sound like Leadbelly: "May da Mi'night Speshul, shan a laht ona meee." I often mused on the odds of it happening that, at the same time, a group of toothless blacks were assembling in a Louisiana bayou around an upright piano, booming in public school tones: "And did those feet in ancient time/Walk upon England's mountains greeeen?/And was the holy Lamb of God/On England's pleasant pastures seeeen . . ."

Arnold's office was bigger than Mussolini's. Three-quarters of the floor was covered by two immense Isfahan carpets. I was treading on forty thousand pounds' worth of *schmutter* as I trekked to where two button-back red leather chairs faced a Chesterfield. A sort of three-piece suite for zillionaires. The windows looked out towards Canary Wharf standing alone in the East London swamps. Amazing to think that in a hundred years, when there would be a forest of these vertical sharpened pencils, historians would dig out old photographs and realize there was a time when there was just the one. Like seeing 1870s pictures of the Dakotas rising over Upper West Side meadows.

'Mr Hall will be with you directly,' the blond bespectacled

assistant murmured as if we were in church. 'May I get you something?'

'No, thanks,' I said, remembering the last time someone did.

She went out, turning to smile at the door. I wondered if she knew I was in the movie business. Although, judging her by the Donna Karan suit and surroundings, she'd probably regard going into films as a backward step.

Arnold Hall *was* only a moment, entering through another door. He looked around forty, but it was hard to tell. Suntans as dark as his made men look older. So did the conservative Gieves and Hawkes suit and the brogues. Here was a man who dressed to persuade people to take him more seriously than his age suggested. In contrast to power brokers in Hollywood, where sneakers and a back-to-front baseball cap are used to deflect attention from their fifty-plus years to a "Hey, guys, I'm in tune with the kids' market – how about a Diet Pepsi and a bowl of popcorn?"

We shook hands and sat facing each other. No small talk, straight in.

'Andree told me what you were looking for.'

A Rolex peeked out of his shirt cuff. So it's not all Carlton Club.

'I wish she'd tell me,' I said. His tan creased at the temples.

'Writers are the last to know anything,' he grinned. 'Did you hear of the Polish starlet who went to Hollywood—'

And slept with the writer, yes, I know that one.

'—and slept with the writer?'

I gave a convincing cackle. 'That's good.'

'I gathered she wants to make a film about computer fraud,' he went on, slipping a finger under the Rolex band.

77

'The idea is for someone to steal a billion and have the good guy find it.'

'Fiction, of course,' Hall chuckled.

'You mean in real life they get away with it?'

'It's been known. Not here, of course, not with CBCI. We pride ourselves on having the best FUs in the field.'

'FUs?'

'Forensic Units. They're accountants with attitude. Most insurance companies have small back rooms where smart young people have calculators in one hand and Glocks in the other. Ceaucescu, Duvalier, Tshombe stashed away entire *treasuries* . . . The FUs find out where and how they're laundered.'

'Sounds great for a series.'

'Be my guest.'

'I ought to say, I know nothing about big business. You're looking at someone whose only experience of managing money is to pay off one credit card with another.'

'That's all there is to it,' Hall replied with an expressive gesture. 'Every billion dollar thief begins by conning his bank manager into lending him a few extra bucks until the end of the month. Or he'll sneak a twenty out of petty cash with a phony voucher. Next thing, he's building a palace in South America with round-the-clock bodyguards.'

'But in the old days, if you wanted to steal money, you held up a bank. Nowadays you press a keyboard and that's it. Or have I watched too many movies?'

'No, you're right. Maxwell certainly didn't go round the pension companies with a sack marked SWAG. Have you ever been on a trading floor?'

'I saw *Wall Street*. And *Working Girl*.'

'It's not so hectic these days, but in the space of an hour

78

you'll probably watch a few hundred million bounce around cyberspace.'

I followed him to a screen on a table. It rippled with columns of changing numbers, making formal geometric patterns like a mobile Bridget Riley.

'Look out the window. See all that sturdy, rock-solid bricks and mortar? Makes you feel safe, doesn't it? Recessions come and go, wars, bombs, property developers, but the City remains impregnable. Like the Pyramids, Stonehenge. That's what we're told. And until recently, they were right. Now everything you see out there rests on this screen, these figures, these dots. You take your eye off them for a minute and, oh gosh, anyone seen Barings? It was here a minute ago.'

He certainly had the gift of the gab. I came in expecting some shifty-eyed spiv and found Ned Beatty in *Network*. Remember the scene when he mesmerizes Peter Finch? I was drawn to the screen, imagining each blip as another huge amount of cash shifting, untouched by human hands, from one pocket to another.

'Who is able to keep an eye on all this?'

'Other machines.'

'What if they break down?'

'Then we're doomed.'

I looked up to find he was grinning.

'Am I scaring you?'

'Frankly, yes.'

'You ain't seen nothin' yet. Let's go down.'

We came out of the lift into a vast open dealing room, greeted by a soft murmur of voices and discreet phone bells. Just as images of, say, Chicago remain rooted in the Capone era, so the words 'trading floor' still conjure up the screaming

79

bedlam of the eighties; red-faced Essex lads bawling the odds with a phone to each ear.

Today the mood was muted. There must have been two hundred people manning the machines. Some had their feet up reading newspapers, and there were more women than I expected. Twenty per cent, Hall said. He walked me slowly between the long lines of traders, their eyes fixed like rifles on enormous screens. I felt I was reviewing the troops.

'You're in Derivatives,' Hall explained. 'The sexy and dangerous section. Over there is Equity, Fixed Income trades. Regular, steady, boring. In that corner's Research. They tell us if something nasty is cooking in Stockholm or Buenos Aires. Some scam we should know about. But here, this is where the big bets are laid. These are the people you have to watch. Right, Joachim?' A tall young man nodded silently without turning, his hand fixed to a mouse.

'How do you stop another Leeson?'

'That's like asking how do you make a successful movie. If it was that simple, life would be a doddle. There's actually very little to prevent anyone creating a black hole to stash money. Hide it under an impenetrable network of deals, trading at deeper and deeper levels, until the regulators disintegrate looking for it. But it's not the calculating crook who's the real trouble. The real trouble is, statistics show one person in twenty has a gambling problem. That means five per cent of the population are prone to risking more money than they can afford to lose. Hold that thought. Enlarge it to a floor of two hundred traders. In this room there are at least ten who, given the right circumstances, could spin out of control. And all you need is one. It's called the ticket to Argentina,' Hall grinned. 'The wheel spins, you bet the firm on red, the ball drops in black and you head for the airport.'

'I thought regulators were appointed to stop that kind of thing.'

'Regulators are failed traders, Mr Tate. They're only doing the job because they weren't smart enough to work down here. It's like setting a bird to catch a cat.'

'You're depressing me. Maybe my hero should be the villain.'

'Not really. Ask yourself why banks aren't going under every day of the week. Because, as I say, the circumstances, the *conditions*, have to be just right. There are thousands of potential Hitlers running round the world at any given time. But the one who made it did so only when –' he ticked off his fingers, 'his country's economy was wrecked, when democracy had been tried but hadn't fixed things, when an entire nation, which always liked discipline anyway, *yearned* for a strong man to take control, when the rest of the world swooned at the idea of another war, when isolationism was the political ideal and when the universally accepted scapegoats for catastrophe were Jews and Bolsheviks. Take all these conditions and squeeze them together and Adolf Hitler shoots out. If any *one* of them had not been in place, he would never have left his day job.'

As we circulated, Hall stopped to press a shoulder, whisper a word, make a joke to the screen starers. Few responded except to nod. I said they seemed hypnotized.

'Wouldn't you be? They're working with enough money to run Bangladesh for ten years and wondering if they should punt it on the equivalent of which raindrop will reach the bottom of the window first.'

We passed a woman peering into a machine where a Post-it slip bearing a pencilled $224,367,000 was stuck to the top. Hall saw me staring and grinned.

81

'That's her bonus.'

'The women here must have the time of their lives. Five men each, all earning telephone number salaries.'

'Look around. Do you see much fraternizing?' he asked. No. I didn't see anyone speaking who didn't have a phone in their hand. 'Each of these desks is like a confessional,' Hall said. 'You can work touching elbows for six months without even knowing much more than your neighbour's last name. I started off down here. The only person I met socially was way over the other side in Equities.' He pointed across the acreage. 'We'd decide where to go for lunch by e-mail.'

He occasionally introduced me to people, describing one as a Ph.D. in Maths, another as an ex-engineer. They resembled mild-mannered clerks, the kind you see coming off the commuter trains with briefcases and a half-finished crossword. A few had cuddly lion dolls on top of the hardware, others a framed photo of a baby. I was offered boiled sweets while they took a moment to ask about writing films, but I could see their brains remained wired to the phone and if it buzzed, they fought an urge to answer until we moved on.

I recalled to Hall the days when traders were big swinging dicks, on six-figure commissions, buying each other magnums of Krug in the Savoy, jetting to Switzerland for a weekend's skiing. He explained how the balance of power had tilted.

'The juice *used* to be here, sure. Once traders were king. Managers left the room when they came in. Now, it's the reverse. They do their job, fix the deals and go home. Managers retook the high ground when risk control systems came in to monitor what the dealers were doing. They were designed to limit the opportunities for a rogue trader to run riot. When Barings were shown to be so ignorant of what their junior employees were up to that they literally woke up one morning to find they were finished, it brought in so much pressure that now a trader needs permission to pee. Does any of this help you?'

'It's not very exciting. Maybe I can persuade Andree Bruckmeyer to turn the thing into a musical.'

'I'm not a writer,' Hall said as we returned to the lifts. 'But if you want all that yelling and bawling and testosterone, why not backdate your film to the eighties?'

Yep, that would make it easier. What he had told me during the last half hour was depressing. If we were going for authenticity, *Follow the Money* wouldn't even hold up as radio drama. There'd be more action in a film about a supermarket shelf-stacker.

Because of the fifty thousand Tim had negotiated, I felt some sort of application was required. After the adrenaline rush of the deal subsided, after the embarrassment at Jackie's place and the shock of finding she was a switch-hitter (her violent homophobia had, I analysed, been the standard camouflage of a closet gay), I realized I had a serious problem. I was being told to fill two hours of screen time with a thrilling account of how one man sets out to locate an immense amount of money, stolen in a now-you-see-it-now-you-don't flip of a computer key. Plus allotting time for at least two underground car park chases, some raw sex, a bad-tempered boss and a few helicopters. The usual route, when in doubt about whither this kind of plot, is to bring in the expert hacker who says something like "Let's see what happens if—" and shazam, we're on our way. But I did feel I had to come up with something a bit more original, even for people who admired *Before the Dawn*.

Watching the trading floor had been diverting. However,

without the all-purpose hacker, I hadn't a clue how Harrison was going to come out on top.

Back in Hall's office, I outlined my concern.

'Uncountable amounts of money flying around the world at the speed of light. Swarming about like some cosmic sandstorm. Black holes, deep layers of trading, dense smokescreens created by finagling key pressers. However, ninety-nine point nine nine per cent of the cash ends up where it's sent. Point oh oh one doesn't. It disappears into thin air. What are the odds on finding it?'

'Not good.'

'You see my problem.'

'Ah, yes, I understand it.'

He understood it, but he wasn't about to solve it.

'Crime is a mirror of life, Alan,' he said, using my Christian name for the first time. 'Only the unimaginative pay for their sins.'

Was this a snide way of suggesting I should start earning my fee?

'Perhaps you'd like to meet one of our forensic accountants. They'll be full of ideas.'

Christ, *more* research! They'll offer suggestions not even Michael Curtiz could make exciting. ''Well, the first thing we do is spend six weeks going through the printouts—''

'Maybe later.'

Hall peeked at his Rolex and I took the hint.

'Let's get together some time,' he said, guiding me across the Isfahan plains to the door. 'Call me if you want anything.' He took a card from a wallet. 'Use this number. It's a private line.'

As Tim pointed out, you still have to write the bloody thing.

To be a writer, you need two qualities: talent and discipline. One without the other is no good. You can have all the talent in the world but unless you force yourself to sit down and patiently develop the idea that it beams on to your retina, you fetch up like Scott Fitzgerald. On the other hand, remember how Jack Nicholson spent months in *The Shining*, filling hundreds of pages typing nothing but 'All work and no play makes Jack a dull boy' over and over.

I had the talent: after thirty years in the galleys, you can't fail to develop some native cunning. And all I needed to drum up discipline was some pressing bills, an urge to stop the bank writing me clipped reminders. Research is all right as long as it doesn't leave you worse off. I rang my Oxonian quango journalist.

'Easy,' boomed the voice down the line. It was after lunch and the college claret had flowed. 'If the sender's the crook, he'll have the money logged to an address that doesn't check out. 13 Acacia Avenue, Pinner. Something that doesn't leap out as a centre of international commerce.'

'Suppose he sends it to Zurich?'

'Call the bank.'

'The Swiss don't do that sort of thing. Do they?'

'Tell them it's drug money, they'll get the shits.'

'What if the thief isn't the sender? What if it's the one at the receiving end?'

'No problem. Have his orders checked. If the cash was destined to go to the Tokyo Bank of the Obscenely Rich, why isn't the name on his list?'

Hall had said finding this needle in the haystack would be against the odds.

'I need it to be a bit more difficult than that or I'll have a ten-minute movie.'

'Give the investigator some disability.' I heard a belch. 'Make him blind or something.'

'Then he would hardly be assigned the job.'

'Christ almighty, Alan, you're a writer. You have *licence*.'

Maybe the forensic accountant was the route to go. I rang the private number Hall gave me, outlined my needs and he connected me with the FU. They said they would check. When they called back, they said, 'Well, the first thing would be to go through all the printouts . . .'

At the end of ten days, I was still looking at a row of typed questions I'd pinned to the noticeboard above my desk:

> Where is the money?
> How did it get lost?
> Who sent it, or who received it?
> What method did they use?
> WHAT FUCKING METHOD!

Waiting for the answers to drift in through the window, I whiled away the hours by dividing fifty thousand pounds into the number of days I was given to write the screenplay, multiplying the figure by ten, the time I had so far spent on it, dividing this number by twenty-four, the sum of the words pinned on the wall, and working out that to date, I had been paid around £200 a word. This was John Grisham money.

Finally I wrote a note:

> Harrison is on the verge of admitting defeat when he reads in the paper about a young student arrested for hacking into the German Federal Reserve Bank and creating chaos by moving every decimal point 2 places to the right. Nineteen-year-old Kevin Lecroix boasted there wasn't a system invented he

> couldn't penetrate. Out on bail awaiting trial,
> Kevin is approached by Harrison who challenges
> him to find the missing money. Kevin can't resist
> showing off and agrees . . .

That should do it, I was thinking, when the phone rang.

'Hello, here is Andree Bruckmeyer. I am calling to see how you are progressing.'

'Hi. Good.'

'Excellent. Please let me know if I can do anything to help.'

How about a fuck? Or even dinner? I thanked her. Not someone to waste time gossiping, she quickly rang off. Then the phone went again.

'Alan, it's Arnold Hall. How are you?'

'Fine.' He was on a mobile and I could hear traffic.

'Solve your problem with the plot?'

'I'm getting there.'

It was nine in the evening. I wondered why he was calling. Had Andree got him to check up on me? Not likely. She had just done that herself a moment ago.

'Where are you?' I asked.

'Kensington somewhere. I just thought I'd give you a buzz.'

'You want a drink or something?' I felt the introduction of the omniscient hacker was a major leap forward and I deserved a break.

'I don't want to interrupt your work.'

'No one works at this hour. Not writers anyway.'

'Why don't I pick you up?'

I jumped in the shower and the doorbell rang while I was drying off. Parked in front of the house was an American-style stretch limo, white with darkened windows, and a uniformed driver on the step.

'Be right down,' I called. Curtains riffled across the street. This part of Fulham didn't often see these monuments to nouveau vulgarity.

Hall was slumped in the back. Not a tall man at the best of times, his choice of huge offices and lengthy cars made him look like a midget.

'Hi,' I said facing him while the driver reverently closed the door.

'Where are we?' he asked.

'Fulham.'

He was no Londoner. Everybody knew where Fulham was. It starts where King's Road becomes cheaper. The car slid away from the kerb and everyone turned to look as we snaked clumsily through the back streets, taking each corner cautiously, like a coach.

'I'm sorry about the ostentation,' Hall muttered, watching me scan the TV, the cocktail cabinet and the fridge. 'But we deal with people who think this is as classy as it gets.'

'Reminds me of Hollywood,' I grinned. He had a bottle of champagne open and poured me a glass. 'The length of the limo is in exact proportion to the amount of bullshit you are about to hear.'

'Goes for banks too. Boy, does it ever!'

He sounded as if he had had a bad day. And there was I feeling chipper.

'Where do you live?'

'Hotels mostly.'

'Do you have a house somewhere?'

'Yes.'

That was all. No attempt to knit my questions into a conversational scarf.

'Are you married?' he asked after a pause. I told him.

'Anyone in your life?' I told him that too.

'Feel like some company?'

I thought *he* was the company.

'Company?'

'Women.'

'Oh. Well, why not?'

Hall picked up a mobile and pressed one digit, calling a pre-programmed number.

'What do you fancy? Blondes, brunettes? Fat, thin, what?'

I had never ordered women like a pizza before.

'I – er—'

'Gloria, hi, it's Arnold. Need a couple of your specials ... No, I have a friend with me ... Say one blonde, one brunette?'

He widened his eyes at me as he spoke, seeking approval. I shrugged.

'I'll pick them up in ten minutes.' He gave an address to the driver and dropped the phone on the seat.

'Life's much simpler when you're rich,' I observed.

'You think I'm rich?'

'I've seen poorer.'

'You know what I get paid to do?' He began to sound angry, as if I'd upset him. 'I get paid to help people who already have far too much money make a whole lot more.'

'Do you help clients who have too little?' I said, trying to lighten him up. It didn't work. While he spoke, he didn't look at me, he looked out of the window.

'You know the kind of clients we have at CBCI? We have evil men. I'm not talking about a few white slavers or drug barons. They're small beer. I work for men who start wars so they can sell poison gas to both sides. People who hold up famine relief until the UN comes up with the right price. You may read sometimes of aid workers who go missing. There was an Australian a while back in Ethiopia.'

I nodded.

'He made the mistake of telling people he knew what was going on. I know someone who deliberately spreads diseases – cholera, Lassa, Ebola – so he can clean up from WHO. My friend, you can't *begin* to imagine the wickedness out there.'

All right, we're getting serious.

'I didn't see any chains holding you to your desk.' He didn't reply for a moment. When he did, he gave a leer that made it plain he thought I was about as clued in to the real world as a royal.

'What the hell do you know? Sitting at home all day inventing stories.' Another pause. 'I'm sorry. It's been a bitch of a day.'

'I have them too.'

'But you have friends. You have someone to help you forget.'

'Don't you?'

'If I did, would I be forcing you to keep me company?'

The car was edging behind Harrods. Hall took out a couple of capsules.

'Here.'

'What is it?'

'Amyl nitrate. Gives you a hard-on like the side of a house.'

'Thanks,' I said, feeling oddly prurient. 'I don't need it.'

'Lucky fellow.'

He snapped one under his nose and inhaled.

By now the car had stopped and the driver was opening the rear door. Two women climbed in. The first one, the blonde, said: 'Hello, I'm Fiona.'

'Who goes where?' asked the brunette. Hall assigned her to me and she gave a winsome look while gripping my knee to manoeuvre across towards a seat.

'What's your name?' I said.

'Call me Emma.' Emma and Fiona. A couple of Roedean alumni who weren't going to need nine Os and three As to find their niche. As we set off, Fiona immediately tried to jolly Hall along as if she were an old friend, but he hardly took his eyes from the window. She put her hand on his thigh and her lips next to his ear, but it didn't do much. I smiled vacantly at Emma. Apart from a rites-of-passage poke in a Mexican bordello when I was twenty-five, I had no experience of commercial sex. Where you could bend a woman into whatever shape you required without any conversational prologue. Like one of those times when you realize you are dreaming and can control what will happen next. I used to have a lot of them when I hit fifty. You pinch your cheek and don't feel anything, say Christ, it's a dream, then conjure up a nineteen-year-old who will let you get straight into her pants. Then you pray you won't wake up until you've finished. But you always do.

'What's your first name?' Emma wanted to know. She sounded as if she really was keen to find out. I told her.

'I love that name,' she said. 'My brother's called Alan.' I wondered if, come Friday, she'd climb into her Lotus Elan and go home to a stately pile in Wiltshire, where the chaps potted pheasants while the ladies attended to their embroidery.

'He's a writer,' Hall said. 'He can get you into the movies.'

'Oh, I've always wanted to act,' Emma said. I noticed Fiona had her hand into Hall's fly already. 'I loved dressing up when I was little.'

Fiona pulled Hall's erect cock through his pants and gave it a few strokes before moving down between his thighs. Hall lay back, his attention still rock solidly out of the window.

'Have you ever met Sean Connery?' Emma asked.

I shook my head.

'He's always been my dream man. The older he gets, the sexier he is. How about Michael Caine?'

I said I didn't know him either, but I knew a taxi driver who did.

Something else I'd never done was exchange small talk while somebody a yard away was being sucked off. I realized how little first-hand experience I'd had of the louche world I'd written about all these years. Gleaning my information from Continental hotels' in-house porn films, I occasionally puffed up a mediocre story with some group sex antics, but watching it develop in front of my eyes was strangely unpleasant. Fiona's head was moving up and down like a clockwork doll, while Hall, judging from his expression, seemed to be brooding on getting cancer.

Then Emma put her hand in my lap. She was giving me a sweet smile, one that said she had always wanted to make love to a writer called Alan. I felt myself twitch which persuaded her to fumble for my zip. So this is what double dating was.

I leaned over to kiss her but she discreetly moved her mouth away. Of course, hookers don't kiss, I remembered. Julia Roberts said so in *Pretty Woman*. Should I touch her? Run a hand up her leg, fondle her breasts? Or was it just one-way traffic?

Having last experienced sex with a catatonic Jackie, it was refreshing to be given such attention. I wondered what would happen if I turned coy, said I didn't do this on the first night, but by now she had expertly guided my penis through the slit in my boxers and fly and was assuming the position. She and Fiona knelt touching backsides, like a couple of inverted bookends, as they started earning what was clearly an astronomical fee.

Every so often we stopped at traffic lights where the car drew the attention of other drivers, coach passengers and pedestrians. No one reacted, making me feel invisible as I became used to the opacity of smoked glass. After a while I began to wave at them and point downwards, grinning like George Formby.

Conversation naturally dried up. I could have chatted to Hall, but he had his eyes closed and, anyway, what could we talk about? The chances of a secure and lasting peace in Northern Ireland? Eventually he gave a quiet sigh and Fiona tidily pushed his member back and zipped up before resuming her seat. Did she swallow? She must have, unless they went through a grooming course which included lesson five, how to remove the discharge without drawing attention. Emma laboured on with mine, occasionally slipping in some rapid finger movements to hurry things along, but all the time giving the impression that it was coated in the most delicious honey, glancing upwards to let me know she regarded this as a wonderful privilege.

When I eventually came it was with a rush of tingling delight. Like her friend, Emma neatly put things away and sat back holding my hand, gripping it tightly like a child. Which she was. Twenty-one tops, to my fifty-three. Hell, she's making a pile of money, seems to take genuine delight in her work, so stop feeling so *Guardian* about it. Besides, she gave the best head I ever had. By now the car was beyond the city and moving along the M4. I saw the Heathrow exits pass and settled back with Emma's hand in mine. Hall fished out another bottle of champagne from the fridge and handed it to Fiona to open. We drank in silence for half an hour, the car moving off the motorway, penetrating the expensive lush lands advertised as within forty minutes of London. I thought I knew most of the green belt around the city, having played cricket there for thirty years, but Emma's performance had made me inattentive and when I did look out the window, I had no idea where we were. I wondered if I would be able at some point to ask why women in her profession refused to press their lips on mine but didn't hesitate to wrap them around my cock.

Eventually we slowed and the car turned towards a pair of huge iron gates that yielded inwards when the driver held up a remote.

There was no moon and the smoked windows increased the gloom, but when we stopped, I saw a large house. Hall got out and told the driver he wouldn't be needed again. I was looking up at a Georgian façade with Palladian pillars each side of double oak doors. The gardens dropped away in a series of steps giving on to a manicured lawn surrounded by shrubberies. The red-brick pointing had recently been repaired, the window frames freshly painted. Here was a prize example of eighteenth-century English architecture restored with all the sleekness and vulgarity modern wealth demanded – even down to the battery of security cameras that stood like sentries over the main doors.

I still had hold of Emma's hand which took away some of the *froideur* of having Hall pimp me a prostitute. No doubt

94

it was in her training: lesson three, don't make your client feel like a john. For what he's paying he wants you to be romantic, even if it entails dressing like a schoolgirl and shoving a hockey stick up his rectum.

Inside, the house had been decorated much in the style of the bank: black and white chequered marble floor in the foyer, clean, antiseptic colours everywhere. It had the appearance of a movie set, something to be dismantled when the action was done. There was a dispiriting air about the place, produced by throwing ridiculous amounts of cash at what should have been a sensitive recreation of an elegant past. There had been no more care put into renewing this once glorious house than in plastering over a Ghirlandaio fresco.

'The kitchen's through there, the liquor's in the big room,' Hall said, pointing vaguely around before preceding Fiona up the staircase.

'You hungry?' I asked Emma.

'Whatever you want.'

We wandered into the kitchen. It looked like a showroom. Nothing much had been cooked on the gleaming stove, unless the cleaning lady was an obsessive. In the fridge, a few metres shorter than the World Trade Center, was standard wealthy fare: tins of caviar, foie gras and a bottle of Cristal. What the hell, let's be Richard Gere for a while. I popped the champagne and opened the tins. I found a carton of Melba toast, hard-boiled a couple of eggs and diced up an onion while Emma watched. Call me a sentimental old fool, but I felt a cosy domesticity while this was going on. She sensed it too.

'You're married, aren't you?'

'I was.'

95

'You're very easy to be with.'

I resisted the urge to Woody Allen something like "When you're given oral sex five minutes after being introduced, it tends to break the ice." Instead, I tried to sound like we were friends rather than business associates.

'So are you.'

'I like someone looking after me,' she said.

While we waited for the eggs to boil, I drew up a chair.

'I'm not going to trot out the usual questions about your work and stuff. But I am curious whether you have a private life. You know, boyfriends, lovers.'

'Yes.'

'Do they know?'

'About me doing this?'

'It must keep you busy.'

She reached over and squeezed my hand.

'I only work three nights a week.' I covered a silence by finding a bottle of cornichons in the fridge and we munched them until the eggs were ready.

'Did you know, er, Arnold? I mean, have you met him before?'

'No.'

Lesson six: answer questions politely, but don't elaborate. There was both a childlike and a chilly professional manner about her. The way she sought out my hand made me embarrassed, since it was the way my daughter behaved when she was ten. But her so-far-no-further conversation established how good she was at her job. No kissing on the mouth, no swapping secrets, nothing personal. I cooled the eggs under the tap, removed the shells and diced them. We sat for fifteen minutes getting through, including the Cristal, about eight hundred quid's worth of snack. Emma ate without referring to the cost. When we finished she took the plates to the sink.

'Did you see *Fatal Attraction*?' she asked.

'You mean you're going to boil my rabbit?'

She laughed. 'I was thinking about the bonking scene on the kitchen counter.'

Now I wished I'd used the amyl nitrate. She was seriously believing I could perform like Michael Douglas less than an hour after having been utterly drained of my seminal fluids.

'Let's wait a while.'

I wanted to play the relaxed man of the house coming home to a beautiful wife after a busy day selling oil wells. 'Would you like to walk outside?'

The night was still but cool. I put an arm round her shoulders and she put both hers around my waist. For the first time in years I felt at peace. There seemed no reason why I couldn't fall in love with this girl. It was an act, of course it was, but her manner fed my craving for some real feminine attention. I smelled her freshly washed hair.

'You're really nice,' she murmured.

Later on, upstairs, she had a go at working me up for another sprint, but it lay like a newly dead fish in her hand. She tried pornography, describing in detail some of the more arcane practices that clients ordered. She wet her little finger and eased it into my arse, playing gently with the sphincter. She asked me if I wanted her anally. There'd be no problem, she had some lubricant in her bag.

Nothing worked. In the end, she lay out on the four-poster, hands behind her head.

'Do you think you'll get married again?'

From Marquis de Sade to Claire Rayner in a heartbeat.

'Can I marry you?'

'That would be wonderful,' she said, and I swear she meant every word. 'The thing is, I know you're not the kind of man who'd let me go on doing this sort of work. And I wouldn't want to, either.'

'We could retire to the country and grow turnips.'

She brought herself across and lay on me, her hair making a tent around my face.

'That would be marvellous.'

'Then why not?'

'Let me think about it.'

'No, it has to be an instant decision. You think about things, you lose them.'

'You are the sweetest man.'

We cuddled a while then fell asleep. At some point I woke up to find she had moved to the other side of the Emperor-size mattress. I turned on the light to squint at my watch I had put on a bedside table. Three fifteen. Just my luck to have a hard-on. Should I wake her up? That was what she was paid to do, after all. But it seemed so brutal. An elbow in her back and a brief word to get impaled on this. Regular hooker users would have had no such qualms, but me, well, I'd just proposed marriage and been called the sweetest man. When I woke again, it was light.

With the dawn came the recriminations. What was I doing here? Keeping company with a man who treated women like toilet paper. Watching a young girl pretend I was the love of her life and fellate me in a crowded car.

I had turned into the kind of sleazeball I invent in screenplays, the ones who get blown away in the last twenty minutes, whose passing brings hoots of approval from the audience.

Outside, the birdsong was striking up the overture. Normally, the dawn chorus cheered me, made me believe in God and the innocence of nature. Stuff like that. Even in Fulham the local blackbirds produced their own Ode to Joy until the first Heathrow landings steamrollered them into silence. This morning, euphoria was not the response. This morning their songs underlined the melancholy aroused by what I had done. Abused a girl young enough to be my, well, almost my granddaughter. It would have been quite simple to decline Hall's offer to rent a woman. There would have been no embarrassment in passing.

And now here I was, miles away from home, unable to leave until my host felt ready. Who knows, maybe he had plans to haul in a couple of sheep.

Emma stirred and turned over, reaching out an arm. The bed was so wide she couldn't find me. She opened her eyes, crabbed sideways and came close. Her hair retained traces of perfume and I felt an internal plumbing reaction when she slid a leg over mine.

'Hi,' I said. 'Sleep OK?'

'Mnnnn. I had a lovely dream. You and I were living in the country. In a thatched cottage, with roses round the door.' God almighty. 'We had a dog. A gorgeous little puppy. I was *so* happy! What about you?'

'I don't know, it was your dream.'

'No, silly, what did *you* dream about?'

If this had been a script, I'd have answered something like paedophilia, but I said I could never remember. She reached across to read the watch and a nipple brushed my chin.

'I ought to be going soon. I have to be back in London by ten. My mother's coming to town.'

'What did you arrange with Hall? Arnold?' She lay on her

back and stretched, arms above her head, her legs stiffening against mine.

'Nothing. I didn't know he was going to bring us out here. Maybe I could get a taxi.'

The chance to get out appealed. While we'd been decimating sturgeons in the kitchen last night, I'd seen a Yellow Pages.

'I'll call one.'

'Not yet.' She nudged her nose against my ear and her hand fluttered down to my groin. 'Oh, wow, what have we here?'

One of God's little jokes is to give men the best erections in the morning when sex is the last thing on women's minds. Mine came up and pointed the sheets like a tent pole. She crabbed down and gave it some tongue before throwing back the clothes and lowering herself onto it. Whatever guilt I had felt about having sex with young girls melted away. She controlled the rhythm, reaching behind her to massage my balls softly. Then she turned round, holding my penis inside, and I kind of cantilevered up until I was thrusting into her from behind, while she rested her head on the mattress, smiling blissfully. She reached underneath my legs and gently held my scrotum. By now I needed no extra stimulus. When I came it was with a roar, a strangled cry and a feeling that if this was the moment my heart gave out, then my living would not have been in vain.

I fell beside her heaving for breath and she held me tightly. I swear I felt tears on my face.

'Oh, darling, that was *wonderful*,' she whispered. 'Did you feel me come?' Actually no; I was too engrossed in my own *For-Whom-the-Bell-Tolls* earth-moving experiences.

'Yes.'

'I *never* come with clients. You're the first.'

If she was lying, I didn't care.

'You're terrific too,' I said. At times, I can get quite lyrical. 'It damn near took the top of my head off.'

She clung on fiercely. 'It was last night, when you cooked for me,' she murmured. 'I knew then you were something special.'

We lay like this for ten minutes and she told me she wouldn't mind seeing me again, not as a trick, but as a friend. The prospect of getting sex like this on a regular basis suppressed any thought of behaving like an egregious old man lusting after jail bait. I mean, she sounded as if she meant it. About being a friend.

She checked my watch again. 'Maybe you should ring for that taxi.'

I dressed quickly while she watched. She lay above the sheets and I gloried in her nudity. I carried my shoes to the door and tiptoed outside. The last thing I wanted was to wake up Hall.

The directory referred on the cover to Sonning on Thames. I played cricket there years ago. The question was, would Sonning run to a cab service at six thirty in the morning?

It did. The call was redirected to a driver already on the road.

'Where are you?' he asked. I had no idea – wait, there was a letter behind the telephone.

'Rainwood House, Barrington Road.'

'Yeah, I know it. Where you want to go?'

'London.'

'Be about twenty minutes. What name is it?'

'Alan – er, Wilkinson.'

101

The *Breakfast at Tiffany's* mood, the lingering memory of the explosive moment with Emma was worth savouring a while, so I stayed in the kitchen to make some instant. While the kettle came to a boil, mimicking my own recent bodily functions, I fantasized about her; maybe things *do* work out like this. They did for Richard Gere in *Pretty Woman*. They did for Jane Fonda and Donald Sutherland in *Klute*. Not to mention Charles II, Nell Gwynne and a vast percentage of gossip column marriages, when you think about it.

The windows overlooked the drive. As the kettle grew excited, a car came towards the house. I had called only five minutes ago. Some taxi service.

I went to the main doors, nervous that opening them would trigger some Armageddon alarm. Two men got out and walked round to the sunny side of the house. Something went thump, but it was inside my chest. The car was no taxi and these guys were anything but cabbies. They wore trainers and blue jeans, sweatshirts and blousons zipped high to the neck. Dodging round the doorways on the ground floor, I saw their shadows stretching over the carpet in the television room and heard a muffled crunch of breaking glass. As I watched through the door jamb, one of them was using the butt of a gun to clear away the jagged shards until he had enough room to reach through and slip the catch on the sash window.

That proved the system wasn't on.

It proved something else. We were being raided. By men with guns. Upstairs, a young girl was lying naked. Burglars often rape. These two looked just the kind. Thirties, slim, cropped hair and eyes as dead as sharks'.

Why hadn't Hall switched on the alarm?

They came over the sill. I removed my casuals, searching

102

frantically for somewhere to hide. Thieves don't rob kitchens, so I ran back and hid behind the door.

The men knew exactly where they were going and headed for the stairs without a glance in any of the downstairs rooms. By now they were both holding automatics.

My heart started to beat like a car working on three cylinders. What are we meant to do in these situations? Call 999? Find a weapon and have a go?

Reason with them? My hard drive couldn't come up with a single example from the *film noir* file. Wait, hang on. Bogart once confronted two armed men. But he had something they wanted, so they didn't kill him.

Seconds passed. What were they *doing* up there?

Hall mentioned the kind of men he worked for. They've sent hired guns to kill him, I thought. No, they're here to get information. Some megabucks scam. Suppose they threaten the women to make him talk? He'll say do it, they're only whores.

I was standing behind a door, fearful that my heart was going to explode, while a twenty-one-year-old girl was within seconds of being tortured to death.

A woman screamed. A man's voice called out in a fearful falsetto. Then a gun went off. The woman screamed again and a second shot echoed like a howitzer. After that there was no more shouting. The men came out of Hall's bedroom and down the staircase. A smell of cordite drifted with them.

Then Emma appeared naked at the door to our room. She looked sleepy.

'Alan?'

The men's heads swivelled round in surprise. One retraced his steps until he was facing her.

'Where's Alan?' she asked.

The man bent his elbow and shot her at point blank range. She flew backwards into the bedroom.

I just stood and stared. Sweat coldly tickled my forehead. The second man at the foot of the stairs waited for his friend, then they headed back to the open window.

'Hang about,' one of them said, stopping abruptly.

'What?'

'He 'ad *two* hookers?' He spoke in the kind of Cockney you only hear these days in over-the-top TV sitcoms.

'So he were horny,' his mate grinned, replying in broad Yorkshire.

'One was in the avver room.'

The northerner got the drift.

'By 'eck, you mean there's someone *else* here?'

They retraced their steps. The Londoner ran upstairs while his pal went into the living room. A tall closet stood along the kitchen wall. I pulled on the door and a broom fell against my chest as the man upstairs called:

'I fahnd a watch by the bed.'

I felt my wrist. Maxie had given it to me in balmier days. On the back is inscribed 'Alan, Maxie,' with a laurel leaf surround.

'Hers?'

'Nah, a bloke's.'

He came down and handed it to the Yorkshireman who turned it over and read: '"Alan, Maxie".'

'Alan!' the Cockney exclaimed. 'That's what she said. "Where's Alan?"'

They were approaching the kitchen. Cramped inside the closet, I could hear them move around. They came so close, I could hear them breathing.

'This kettle's 'ot. Someone were making coffee. Must have been only a couple of minutes ago.'

'No way he coulda got out, we'da seen him from the car.'

Their feet echoed on the tiled floor. A door opened and closed. Then another. They were looking in the cupboards.

'Shit.'

'What?'

'Someone's coming – outside.'

'It's a bleedin' *taxi*!'

The front doorbell rang. Their feet clattered out of the kitchen. I came out from behind the brooms and peered round the door. One man was speaking into the intercom.

'Hello?'

'Taxi for a Mr Alan Wilkinson.'

'No one here by that name.'

'He called, fifteen minutes ago.'

'You got the wrong address, mate.'

'He said Rainwood House, Barrington Road.'

'Hoax call, John. Someone's giving you the runaround.'

Some muttering crackled through the wire before the driver returned to the car.

I had five seconds to make up my mind.

'Try t'other rooms,' the Yorkie said.

They weren't coming back into the kitchen. Outside, the cab driver was talking into his phone. I padded across the floor, climbed on the counter, opened the window above the sink and squeezed my stockinged feet through. The taxi started. The rest of me followed, and the driver stopped. As I fell, my knee caught the wall. Pain flooded the system, but I held on to my shoes, hobbled to the car and dived headfirst into the back seats.

'Let's go.'

'You OK, guv?'

'Just get the fuck out of here.'

He saw me crouching low in the back, but said nothing as he swung the wheel and headed for the gates. I looked back at the retreating house. My hands were shaking and my heart syncopating. I squeezed my throbbing knee.

'I hope you're Mr Wilkinson,' the driver said, edging into the road.

'Right.'

He was either discreet or someone who'd seen every kind of aberrant behaviour, because he didn't refer to my window exit. Or maybe he was afraid I'd spend the trip telling him the reason. Whatever, I was grateful not to have to invent a laddish account of adventurous adultery. There was too much else to think about.

Like three murders. Three cold-blooded killings. Human beings shot like rats in a cellar. As in all shock, the full effect hadn't yet hit. When the system takes a savage blow, a broken limb, a family loss, an eerie calm often follows. It doesn't last, but for a while you believe you are stoically able to absorb life's punishments. Later, you dissolve. For the first half-hour, it was like that. Just as you say after a car crash, if you'd only taken the other route, waited until the roads were less crowded. But of course you didn't and it happened. If only I had refused Hall's invitation to have dinner, said I don't go in for hookers, sussed out the man's innate seediness. I mean, a Rolex with a Savile Row suit.

But I didn't. I didn't stop Emma giving me a public blowjob. Instead I turned her into a cornball Hollywood romance, a dreamy walk in the garden, an offer to share her life, a *moment*. She must have thought I was fucking barmy.

Now she won't ever think again. Later today, there'll be

a knock on a door somewhere. Her parents will answer. A WPC will gently break the news. Emma – dead? *Shot?* Her job? She told us she was at Lucy Clayton's learning to be a model . . .

'Someone said no one called a cab,' the driver said.

'There was a misunderstanding.'

'I've been there a few times. Usually I get Arabs. Some of them in the full kit. You know, robes, turbans, the lot.'

Marshal your wits. Say as little as possible. When the bodies are found, this man will testify he saw a bloke called Alan Wilkinson come falling out of a kitchen window, yelling, "Get the fuck out of here!"

Concentrate. This is going to be a high-profile case; it's got sex and money. The press will indulge in a piranha-style feeding frenzy. The police will haul in everyone remotely connected with Hall. The show has legs; it'll run and run. But right at this moment, all I could see was Emma flying backwards as someone put a gun against her naked body and fired. The rest of my brain closed down. Trying to assess the implications was like recalling a dream. Everything else just drifted away. We reached the M4 and joined the start of the rush hour into the city.

'London's a big place, guv.' The driver broke a long silence.

'Yes.'

'What I mean is, where exactly do you want to go?'

'Oh, er, Marble Arch'll do.'

Who knew I lived in Fulham? Hall's chauffeur for starters. "I drove him home the night before he died, Superintendent." "Describe what happened." "Well, first of all we picked up a man." "Where from?" "35 Blenheim Road, Fulham. Then, er, some women—" "Who was this man?"

"I believe he called himself a writer, sir. His name? Er, hang on – Tate. That's it, Alan Tate."

Calm down, *think*! You could take the option open to every innocent man: you could tell the truth, for Chrissake. Hall invited you out. He was helping you research a screenplay. He unexpectedly hired two prostitutes and had his driver take everyone to his home near Sonning. In the morning, I wanted to leave, called a taxi, then these two men broke in and—

"Oh, they did, did they? And went round shooting everyone. Except you." "Come on, Superintendent. If I was the killer, would I have rung for a cab? And why would I do such a thing? I'm only a writer. I don't have any clout. Did you hear about the Polish starlet who went to Hollywood and slept with the writer?" This is what my character would say in a film, and get a rueful smile from the copper. But this is real life. Don't believe it? Pinch your cheek. Like in your dreams. If you don't feel anything, breathe a sigh of relief and conjure up a naked girl.

Tell the truth. What's so wrong with that? Because you're the prime suspect, that's what's wrong. Jumping out of a window and telling the cabbie to step on it. "But I was scared, officer, I'd just seen three people murdered." "Why didn't you call us from the scene of the crime?" Because two armed men, men who'd just shot three people down in cold blood in front of my eyes, were gunning for me." "When you managed to escape, why didn't you go to the nearest police station and report this?" "I was er, confused, in, ah, shock . . ."

That's when the cops look at one another over my bowed head. We got him, read his rights. The headlines ticker-taped through my brain. "Writer Accused of Murder. In a plot resembling one of his own stories, 53-year-old Alan Tate was charged yesterday with—" Maxie would be doorstepped. "Ex-Wife of Mass Killer Tells of Unpredictable Moods." The children victimized at school. "One of Father's Victims was Only 21."

You tell the truth, get three life sentences and become the world's most famous miscarriage of justice. When they find this out, say in thirty years, you'll be released with an apology, make a fortune with the book and the movie. Of course, you'll be eighty-three years old, but you'll get your statutory few minutes of fame. Don't go to the police and you'll spend the rest of your life on the run. "Ronnie Biggs Refuses to Meet Tate in Brazil. Wants Nothing to do with Slayer of Young Girls." When you're caught, the prosecution won't have to get out of bed. "Why did you flee?" If you were a rich, black ex-football star in California, you'd stand a chance, but you aren't.

We were climbing the Chiswick flyover. The traffic was backing up.

'Marble Arch is going to take some time,' the driver said. 'You'd be better off getting out and taking the tube.'

'OK.'

He brought the car off the Great West Road and cut through to the nearest underground. There was something unconvincing about his lack of curiosity during the journey, but then he seemed to linger on my face when I paid, as if he were storing the image, registering every feature, right down to the half-inch scar above my left eyebrow where a cricket ball had landed years ago. Photofit are going to love him.

I made a pretence of going into the station and waited until he disappeared before flagging down another taxi. On the way to Blenheim Road, another scene flickered across the screen.

"Mr Tate, the deceased's driver said he picked you up on the night of the murders."

"That's right. Mr Hall rang me out of the blue and—"

"Just yes or no."

"Sorry. Yes."

"Was he a close friend of yours?"

"No. I hardly knew him."

"Why would he pay a great deal of money for a stranger to enjoy the services of a high-class prostitute?"

"He said he was lonely."

"Didn't he hire a woman for himself?"

"Yes."

"Then why did he need you?"

"When he rang, he was only talking about the two of us having a drink."

"Mr Tate – I suppose that is your real name?"

"Yes."

"Why did you tell the taxi driver it was Wilkinson? In our experience, people with nothing to hide don't lie about their identity."

Why *had* I given a false name?

When the children were young, we all went to Los Angeles where I was working. One weekend we drive up to San Francisco and stay at a motel run by what turned out to be the manageress from hell. She scared the life out of everybody. 'You want *another* bar of soap? What are you doing, *eating* it?' When the time comes to pay, I realize I've mistakenly countersigned my traveller's cheques in the space you are supposed to use in the presence of the payee. While I wait my turn to settle the bill, terrified the manageress will

110

call a SWAT team when she sees the mistake, I take a pen from the counter and pretend to write my name, tracing the ball-point tip a fraction above the paper. The manageress sees me and when I tear out the cheque and hand it over, she looks surprised.

'How did you do that?' she barks.

'Do what?'

'Sign this cheque.'

'I borrowed your pen.'

She takes it while my children watch fascinated – Dad's getting told off – and scribbles on a pad. It's red ink, and my signature's in blue. The kids still remember.

I only mention this to show how there are times when a mixture of nervousness, fear and general ineptitude makes us do things that you could never ever properly explain.

Giving a false name to the cabbie was in this league.

I was half-expecting a bunch of photographers to be waiting outside when the taxi dropped me off, and wondered why the street was deserted.

First World War soldiers made the point about living through the carnage of trench warfare, then going on leave to find the family dressed for dinner and discussing the garden. There was no possible way to describe the horrors they'd been through so they didn't try. Instead, they asked about the hollyhocks. After dozing in a bath for an hour, shaving and trying to choke down some coffee, I knew how they felt. The world was perfectly normal, no different from yesterday. The cleaning lady came in, talked about her daughter's new job, the neighbour's noisy dog and asked if I'd seen the telly last night: 'Such language. I hope you don't write things like that.' The phone rang and Maxie reported Lloyd having a cough. Also, her car had failed in

111

the middle of Knightsbridge and what was the number of our garage?

Around ten, I turned on the radio. Northern Ireland, a row in Brussels, a hospital crisis and not enough rain to fill the reservoirs. That was it. By noon there *had* to be word. Hall wouldn't have turned up for work, someone would have rung his house. And he must have had a housekeeper.

'It's twelve o'clock and here is the news. In Northern Ireland, talks are under way to seek a solution to the deadlock . . .'

The phone went and Andree Bruckmeyer asked how things were coming along.

'I hope Arnold was able to be of assistance.'

I waited long enough for her to think we had been disconnected.

'Hello?'

'I'm here. Yes.'

'Oh good. He is such a hard-working man, I was afraid he would not have time.'

Time is something he'll never have again, *liebchen*.

'I, er, was trying to get hold of him, as a matter of fact,' I stammered. 'He isn't in his office. Do you have his home number?'

I heard some papers riffling. 'Wait a minute. Yes, here it is . . .'

A woman answered.

'Mr Hall's residence.'

'Er, Mr Hall, please.'

'He isn't here.'

'Who am I talking to?'

'This is the housekeeper.'

The room began to spin. I sat down.

112

'Are you *sure* he isn't?' I said. Like upstairs, lying in a pool of blood?

'Mr Hall leaves very early to go to his office. You should try him there.'

She hung up.

Could Hall have two houses?

I pressed Redial.

'Hello?' the housekeeper's voice returned, irritated.

'Is that Rainwood House, Barrington Road?'

'Yes. Who is this? Hello – *hello*?'

In *Pulp Fiction*, a character is paid to clean up after a man
gets his head shot off inside a car. He has a reputation for
immaculate work and is the first person killers call when they
want to get rid of bodies, blood and viscera.

The men who carried out the Rainwood House executions
must have seen the film since it was clear that someone had
removed all traces of the massacre before the arrival of the
housekeeper.

Where did this leave me? If the cleaners did their job well,
no one would find evidence of murder. That meant no one
would be questioned, not even the man seen falling out of
the window. So life as I knew it hadn't changed. Had it?

114

One CBCI director and two call-girls wouldn't be seen again. The police would eventually search Hall's house. Suppose they found something, a trace of blood. That would flush out the cabbie and his client Wilkinson, but how could that come back to me? Wait. Shit. The company chauffeur who picked me up the night before.

I'd have to lie.

"That's right, Inspector, Mr Hall invited myself and two women to his house. The next day, he drove us back to London. Time? Very early in the morning. Must have been about seven. I was dropped off first and I believe his plans were to go on to his office. His frame of mind? Well, now you come to mention it, he did seem a bit distracted."

The taxi driver would blow that out of the water.

"That's him. Came out the window, told me to get the fuck out of there. Said his name was Wilkinson."

My only hope was their cleaner was as good as the one in *Pulp Fiction*.

How would Hall, had he not died, have driven us to London? Did he have another car? If so, it would still be in Sonning. He might have called a taxi. Nope; the cops would check. And come up with shoeless Wilkinson. How about we were driven back by some other private car service?

I stopped listening to the news. The afternoon dragged by while I turned in circles, trying to second guess what Hall's disappearance would provoke. Not to mention Gloria looking for two of her specials. The trick was to make sure the cab and its early morning fare stayed out of the frame.

When I eventually turned on the television around six, I vaguely recognized the first images I saw. It was a building. Then the camera zoomed in on a sign: 'CORPORATE BANK OF COMMERCE AND INDUSTRY'.

Panning across to the doors, the viewfinder focused on police carrying out boxes of papers. The newsreader was saying:

'—order was issued shortly after one o'clock to evacuate the premises and a police guard installed on the entrance. A brief statement from the Bank of England said it had revoked CBCI's licence to operate, an order the directors did not wish to appeal. Enquiries failed to confirm rumours that a director had gone missing.'

There followed a short account of the bank's history, which included the fact that most of the stockholders were from Asia and Saudi Arabia.

I left the set on, waiting for something more, a 'news-just-in' coda, but the programme ended reprising the headlines.

Hall was listed as missing. The assets had been looted. The two events have been linked.

I was the last person to see him alive. I would be questioned. Stick to the lie. We drove back to London, girls and all.

If the police believed Hall had scarpered with the money, they weren't going to question whether he hired another car and driver.

Andree Bruckmeyer's office didn't answer. They had probably left for the day. She'd know what happened. What should I tell her? That Arnie and I were getting laid last night? No, don't mention the women. What did it have to do with her? What did it have to do with *me*? I was an innocent bystander, I had almost lost my life and I'm behaving like an accomplice. Establish priorities. You're blameless. Stop sweating, or the scenario about the worst-ever judicial mistake will begin to take shape.

When the phone rang, I jumped so hard I twisted a muscle.

'Yes?'

'The garage said the engine's got real problems.'

'Maxie?'

'How many others do you know with a bum car?'

'It's leased. They'll replace it.'

'Who are "they"?'

'For Chrissake, Maxie, give me a break.'

'What's the matter? You sound nervous.'

'I'm not nervous. I'm just saying I can't tell you anything except call the leasing company.'

'I'm very worried about Lloyd. He phoned to say he's coughing blood.'

'Look, this really isn't a good time.'

'What's so urgent you can't spend a minute talking about your son's health?'

Slow down.

'Nothing, I'm – I don't feel too good myself.'

'They say divorced men die quicker.'

'Do they?'

Maxie was trying to be conciliatory. She knew perfectly well how to deal with the car. And it was evens Lloyd had no more than a sore throat.

'Talk to the doctor. I'll try and stop by in the afternoon.'

'Oh, please, don't let us interrupt your busy schedule,' she snapped, hanging up. When she wanted to, Maxie could make me out to be the supreme deadbeat Dad, drinking away the Giro money while mother and children huddled in front of a cold hearth sharing a tin of catfood.

Lying worried me. Not from any moral standpoint. All of us learn to use falsehoods from an early age and it becomes second nature during parenthood. "Darling, you were marvellous" to the kids after they've fluffed every line in the school play. "You look great" to friends on their death beds. But these weasel words don't get picked over and dissected like the untruths I'm talking about; the ones that lay down a foundation for more lies, building a house of cards that the mildest hiccup could collapse at any moment.

Hall was dead, but only I knew it. As far as everyone else was concerned, he had merely done a runner with a sizeable chunk of a bank's assets. Which meant his chauffeur would be questioned, and he would mention collecting me on the night before his employer vanished. *Ergo*, lying was unavoidable. But keep it to the minimum.

The high concept is a term used in Hollywood to describe a movie project in one sentence. Invented by an industry whose top brass don't or can't read, they are highly regarded by Heads of Development who have been schooled in the soundbite educational system. The idea is to condense the number of words in your pitch to the minimum. For instance, you want to make a film based on the New Testament Epistles. They would boil down to something like 'Dropout carpenter forms religious gang, takes on the Roman Empire, dies.' It's enough for a studio to assess the risks involved in financing a script.

Précising the ingredients collected over the last twelve hours to cook up an alibi, my high concept turned out: a car drives us back to London where I'm the first to be dropped off.

One sentence. No embellishments, no poetic subclauses. So when Rainwood House finds its way into the headlines, when the reporters unearth stuff about Hall's lifestyle: "Orgy Claims in Missing Man's Mansion" – and when a taxi driver describes how he picked up a fare called Wilkinson defenestrating there one morning, who told him there were a number of people inside, the papers would put it down to another sex frolic.

Except the housekeeper said her boss left early for the office. Between the cab leaving and her arrival, everyone had disappeared without a trace. I wished this was just another crap screenplay. When you could wheel on a *deus ex machina*: the miraculous hacker, an extraterrestrial, a ghost.

Less than twenty-four hours ago, I was looking at a wall trying to devise a plot about somebody stealing a fortune. It was a game. Here's fifty grand, come up with a story that'll let moviegoers pass a couple of idle hours. But the game had turned in on itself. Now the task was to come up with an idea to prevent you spending the rest of your life sharing a cell with a horse molester.

My head ached. Normally, I'd have shut down the PC, poured a drink and rented a video. But normally, I wouldn't be recalling stomach-churning images of violent death. I was around sixteen when I saw my first street fight. Before it, I'd assumed that, as in the cinema, a man never used anything but his fists, that if his opponent went down he would haul him upright before continuing. And his hat never fell off. Afterwards, I'd lain awake at night remembering how one brawler kicked the other's face in; I'd heard again the soft squelch of collapsing flesh and realized fists were the last weapons to be used after heads, feet and teeth.

The chauffeur, the housekeeper and the taxi driver whirled round my head, cancelling each idea I had of answering the anticipated questions. In a script, I would junk the one that made the job too complex and start afresh. But all of these were there, written in stone. They were real and had the means to wreck my life.

I left the television on, flicking between news and teletext, but nothing appeared beyond the closure of CBCI and rumours about a rogue employee. 'Rogue' made him sound a buccaneering sort of chap. Errol Flynn was a rogue. Onscreen he leaped about waving a sword, while off it he did the same with his prick. Everyone wanted to be Errol. Rogue traders have brought banks down in the past, but nobody wants to be them, except maybe anarchists. So there are degrees of roguishness.

Hall didn't get anywhere close, not during the brief time I knew him. Only animated when geeing up the traders on the floor, and even then unconvincing, his real character had come through in the limo. Disgusted with his work, needing a chemical to get a stiffy and about as interested in sex as a strip-o-gram.

Something else was going to crop up in the forthcoming enquiries. After finding CBCI coffers contained little more than a few buttons and a dead rat, the police would discover that while Hall had been planning his sensational heist, he had simultaneously been advising a writer on how to steal a billion. This alone should be enough to get me on the chat show circuit:

"Alan, just how similar was your plot to his methods?"

"Very."

"Did you ever consider you may have given him the idea?"

"Well—"

"After all, aren't we influenced by what we see on the big screen? Isn't that a current dilemma we are facing, how real life violence is often only a mirror of—"

"Hey, you want an exclusive? Hall didn't get very far. I saw him gunned down before my eyes. Boom! Plus two

120

young girls. Boom! Boom! You want to talk about real life violence, suck on that, shitface."

Now that really would be interactive Birtian TV.

The only way to move forward constructively was to believe the bodies would not be discovered. Since the housekeeper hadn't found so much as a hair, the killers seemed to be professional and had organized a thorough after-job service. After all, they had factored in the time the housekeeper would arrive for work. Their homework had been immaculate, except for knowing that Hall had brought company back the night before.

So where were we? Hall had called for a car in the early morning which had driven us back to London. The last I saw of him and the two whores was as they let me out in Fulham and drove on God knows where. Use whatever you like: cattle prods, thumbscrews, an evening with Princess Margaret, you won't get any more than that. Am I free to leave, officer? Thank you.

It wasn't until I undressed for bed and my hand went routinely to my wrist that I remembered my watch.

The next morning, all the papers led with the closure of CBCI. By now the rumours had escalated and the tabloids had dug up an old photograph of Arnold Hall that made him look a good deal less than the forty-four years mentioned in his description. The *Sun*'s caption was succinct: 'BANK-BUSTER?'

The broadsheets were more circumspect, reporting only that following information received, the Bank of England had moved quickly to revoke CBCI's trading licence. All employees were to be interviewed during the next few days to establish if there was a shortfall in the company's funds.

Hall was described only as a senior director who had not reported for work and whose whereabouts were not yet established.

Andree Bruckmeyer's phone still didn't answer. Last night, between a series of raddled dreams, I realized she was going to be important to me once the shit began to fly. It was she who had introduced me to Hall. He was *her* friend, not mine.

Surely the number on her card was the company's, not her private line? When I called Directory Enquiries, they said they had no listing for Operfilm. Born out of a hundred bad sixties British films, where red double-decker buses forever circled Big Ben, when Michael Caine was continually insolent to tight-arsed Foreign Office wallahs who lived in immense country mansions but were finally exposed as KGB moles, I started to feel a tingling sensation around my balls.

Only three things ever caused this: the sight of a syringe piercing flesh, the thought of my car breaking down in East Los Angeles. And a belated suspicion that I had been royally set up.

Luckily, the cabbie who took me to Mortimer Street was not the same man who'd done it before as his Mengele tale would still not have received my full attention. I stayed mired in thought the whole way. Stuff like this didn't happen in real life. Whole businesses didn't *vanish*, like the betting shop in *The Sting*. They just didn't. It was true Tim hadn't heard of Operfilm, but he hadn't cared, not after they had stumped up the first payment.

'118, you said?'

'Yes, it's on a corner.'

There was the entrance, no different from last time, with a set of bells next to an intercom. Operfilm had been printed on a slide third from the bottom.

Now it was blank. I rang but no one answered. I checked the others: a solicitor, a PR outfit, an editing room. I tried the PR.

'Hello?'

'Excuse me, I'm looking for Operfilm.'

'We're Reston Associates.'

'Yes, I know. A week ago there was a German film company on the floor below you, but I don't see their name on the board any more.'

The door buzzed open and I walked up two flights to where a young woman was standing apprehensively on the landing.

'They're not here,' she said, rattling the handle of a door that only last week had carried a sign: OPERFILM.

'This is ridiculous. There were people working here. Posters on the wall. They made German films.'

She shrugged. 'Firms come and go all the time in these rat traps. They buy the end of a lease for nothing, trade for a year then bugger off.'

'Did you ever meet any of them?'

'Me? No. You don't come across anyone here. Maybe pass someone on the stairs, but that's all.'

'They spoke German.'

'Well, they would, wouldn't they?'

My confusion was making me talk gibberish. 'Who has the keys to these offices, do you know?'

'No idea. The landlord, I suppose.'

'Who are they?'

'Dunno.'

'Can you find out?'

Her look made it plain she regretted letting me in. She clumped up the stairs and went into her offices while I waited outside. Then she called out 'Langston' and slammed the door.

Langston Properties couldn't even remember if they owned 118 Mortimer Street.

'Opera what?'

'Oper. O-P-E-R. Film. They're German.'

Langston had yet to join the twentieth century. No Hold, no muzak, no infotainment. No microfiche either, since while I waited I heard papers being shuffled and steel cabinet drawers clanging open and shut.

'Hello, caller.'

'I'm still here.'

'No, we don't have any name like that on our ledgers.'

Ledgers.

'Suppose I wanted to look over the premises.'

'Mortimer Street, you say?'

'118.' Another long shuffle.

'There's a solicitor on the ground floor.'

'That's right.'

'They have pass keys to the other offices.'

'Will they let me in?'

'What business are you?'

'Film.'

'All right. I'll ring them and say you're coming. What name is it?'

A pause. 'Tate.'

A secretary had them on her desk when I went back and she led me upstairs. 'I didn't know anyone was on this floor,' she said, unlocking the door.

The rooms were bare except for a few desks and chairs. The walls were clean of movie posters and *Spotlight* photographs. There was no sign anyone had been in there for

124

years. I went into the room Andree had used. It smelled fusty, like an attic. There was the desk where she pulled out the videos of my films.

'You actually say someone was working here last week?'

'Yes.'

She picked up a phone and listened. 'They couldn't have,' she said, holding out the receiver. 'The phones aren't even connected.'

It *was The Sting.* Andree had been speaking German into a phone when I arrived. To herself. All set up for Robert Shaw Tate.

'Are you the police?' the woman asked nervously.

'No.'

'Private investigator, what?'

'I must have got the wrong address. I'm sorry to have taken up your time.'

More than anything, I needed time to think, but when I tried nothing gelled. It was like believing you've lost your wallet. Against a rising panic that some pickpocket was running up thousands on your credit card accounts, you try to remember where you last used it. The restaurant, the wine store, the supermarket, the cash machine. No, it must have been the garage when you filled up – hang on, you picked up the dry cleaning after that. The moment you report the loss, the second after all your cards are cancelled, you find it stuck down the side of your car seat.

I walked the whole way back to Fulham, pausing frequently to marshal my teeming thoughts. Down Oxford Street, sit, across Hyde Park, sit, through Kensington, sit, up the King's Road, sit, squeezing the last drop of juice from the memory lobes.

Someone marked me out to play a fall guy. They knew where to find me and sent along a good-looking woman posing as a film producer. A *foreign* woman. Who knew about my sexual snobbery?

Whoever it was wanted a writer. Post that on the mental storyboard.

Under it, post: Why me?

Because I was broke. I was in no position to refuse. For fifty thousand pounds, I would have paraglided nude into Trooping the Colour.

When Hall devised his plan to loot CBCI, he programmed in a writer, a film writer, whom he would engage to conduct research. It had to be a man who lived alone, who wouldn't turn down a night out with a prostitute. And when he made his move, this patsy would be left as a mammoth red herring for the police. They wouldn't believe *he* took the money, but checking him out would lead them away from Hall and Andree while they fled to a pre-chosen, non-extraditable hideaway. Why me? Because they calculated I would fall for it. And they were dead right.

Hall knew I was in when he rang because Andree had rung immediately prior. No problem getting me into the limo. Feel like a drink? Who would say no to that at nine o'clock on a dull evening? When he suggested hiring some girls, was I going to take offence, make an excuse and leave the fun? We drive to Sonning. Hall takes one to his room, leaving me with the other. We talk, we eat, we go to sleep.

Hold it right there. Hall had already emptied the bank. What would he have done next had the killers not turned up? Found a way to drive me and the women to London while he took off for a private airfield and vanished into the clouds.

126

Then what? The Bank of England hears of irregularities at CBCI, closes them down. Further enquiries reveal theft of an unprecedented magnitude by a man who was last seen in the presence of a writer called Alan Tate.

What were the human imponderables, as they are known in my trade?

Master crook steals the Crown Jewels, but can't resist kissing a portrait of the Queen on the way out, is caught by DNA identity left by his lips. Fog at the airport, escaping fugitive drumming fingers, police sirens jangling.

Hall couldn't have anticipated that I would call a taxi. What would it matter if I did? I remained the last person he saw before he disappeared. I would testify I met him through a German film producer, Andree Bruckmeyer, whose offices are at 118 Mortimer Street. "Well, they *were* there, officer, honestly."

Hall had based his operation on two aspects of the British character.

One, the police would investigate me down to my sperm count, rampage through my life, trumpet my precarious financial state, pointing out that my foreign-born wife lived in a £650,000 house and my daughter attended a £12,000-a-year private school. They'd discover I once earned six-figure sums in Hollywood where I (obviously) frequented cocaine-fuelled parties and indulged my well-known weakness for expensive call-girls. Thus the police found a substitute for the real criminal, whom they knew they didn't stand a cat in hell's chance of catching. For the British tabloid-reading public, a rich, idle pervert made a better villain than some faceless white-collar thief.

Two, and this is where Hall would have scored the ultimate they-think-it's-all-over goal, he knew what would happen next. Having reached a place where the long arm of British law came up a few inches short, he knew he would quickly be forgotten.

Why? Because all he'd done was rob other wealthy gits. Back in the 1970s, a City shyster cleaned out a Lloyd's syndicate and lived openly in American luxury. No one but a few aggrieved names gave a damn. It wasn't a crime, it was a lark. Extradiction didn't extend to larks. Some years later, a security vault was emptied and half the victims refused to come forward to report what they had lost since it would have incriminated them. The public cheered the caper. It was just thieves stealing from each other. And now Arnold Hall had stolen money from other billionaires. What was wrong in that? He didn't loot working men's pension funds like Maxwell. If you must put someone away, what about that brown-nosing writer, the one who likes riding around in fancy cars and cheating on his wife?

By the time I arrived back at the flat, I had reached two indisputable conclusions: one was that my feet ached.

The other was that I had been an utter cunt.

DATE: 29 SEPTEMBER

FAX TO: ALAN TATE

FROM: TIM ROBERTS

Dear Alan,
You have been out all day and you appear to have turned
off your answering machine. I am keen to contact
Andree Bruckmeyer over contracts for *Follow the
Money*. Since her telephone has not answered for the
past two days I wondered if you might know where she
is.

Tim

DATE: 30 SEPTEMBER

FAX TO: TIM ROBERTS

FROM: ALAN TATE

Dear Tim,
You aren't the only one looking for Andree. Her office
no longer exists and nobody has ever heard of Operfilm
at 118 Mortimer Street, including the landlord. I
hope you have banked the ten grand and fear the
remainder may have gone the way of youthful dreams.

Alan

DATE: 30 SEPTEMBER

FAX TO: ALAN TATE

FROM: TIM ROBERTS

Dear Alan,
What are you talking about? The ten thousand is in but
I don't understand what you mean when you say Andree
Bruckmeyer has disappeared. Call me.

Tim

DATE: 1 OCTOBER

FAX TO: TIM ROBERTS

FROM: ALAN TATE

Dear Tim,
It's true. She has ceased to exist. She is an ex-
person. She isn't sleeping, she is deceased. Among
the present, she is a notable exception. In any roll
call she would answer absent. In her case, *cogito* does
not necessarily mean *ergo sum*.

Alan

DATE: 2 OCTOBER

FAX TO: ALAN TATE

FROM: TIM ROBERTS

Dear Alan,
We checked the Operfilm bank account and find it has
closed after processing the ten thousand, so your
Pythonesque explanation probably holds up. What
worries me is that producers usually withdraw *after*
they have seen your scripts, not before. What can you
possibly have done to bring this about? Even more to
the point, what have *I* done to have my calls unre-
turned, and to be conducting this discussion via fax?

Tim

DATE: 2 OCTOBER

FAX TO: TIM ROBERTS

FROM: ALAN TATE

Dear Tim,
It's nothing personal. I am just worried that my phone
may be bugged.

Alan

DATE: 2 OCTOBER

FAX TO: ALAN TATE

FROM: TIM ROBERTS

Dear Alan,
I think it may be time for you to take a rest and seek
medical advice.

                                                    Tim

In *An Englishman Abroad*, Alan Bennett has the exiled spy
Guy Burgess ask what is the point of having a secret if nobody
knows you have it. He's right. When someone lowers their
voice and recounts some devastating gossip about a friend,
begging you to keep shtum, your first reaction is: "Blank is
going to *love* hearing this."

However, that is in a different league to keeping the knowledge of three murders under your hat.

Hall thought he had everything figured out. How to steal
the money, cover his tracks and escape. He missed only one
trick; he didn't consider being killed by a partner who decides
the whole loaf is preferable to half. Clearly CBCI's assets
were gone, or they wouldn't have been closed down. Whoever ordered his murder copped them. Who would that be?
Only one name came to mind:

Andree Bruckmeyer.

Hall completed the theft, sprinkling the cash around the
world in the manner he explained to me in his office. He
tells her it's done and to complete the final moves. Call the
patsy. She rings to make sure I'm home, and he collects me.
The plan moves into endgame.

Except Andree had seen *Double Indemnity*. Designing
woman cheats on her accomplice. An old tale, but one that
never fails to draw the punters.

What she couldn't have foreseen was that Hall would pick up a couple of women. That was clear by the surprise shown by the gunmen she'd hired to kill him. 'Hey, there were *two* hookers—' They were not expecting someone else in the house.

But they *must* have been. They knew *I*'d be there. She would have told them to leave me alone. After all, I was the crimson herring, the diversion, the false lead, the aniseed to distract the bloodhounds. Why kill the girls? Who knows? They had shown their faces? For target practice, fun? Had Hall wanted them dead when he and Andree drew up the original plans? If not, why did he pick them up at all? Could he not have stuck at my company? "Hey, Alan, feel like coming back to my place? . . . God, is that the time, why not crash here and I'll drive you back tomorrow?"

What if the hookers were Andree's idea? Make a killing a massacre. Why? After all, they only needed me as a belated witness to an alleged shooting of someone whose body is never found. A story the police would suspect as a cover for Hall's disappearance, a fiction supported by this bankrupt writer who'd say anything to make a buck?

My balls started to contract again. I was being set up. But on a scale I had never imagined until now, until Andree assumed the Moriarty mantle. In the manner in which mathematicians claim they solve the riddle of centuries, Fermat's Theorem say, I was suddenly and momentously overwhelmed by a lateral thought, a realization that seemed so pure, so simple that I wondered how I hadn't guessed it before.

Hall would shortly turn up dead. His body would be found. And I would be the prime suspect, not merely of being a rich man's poodle, but of being his killer.

That's what Andree's charade had been working towards. Why she had wanted me in the first place. Hall thought it was to distract the cops. Andree knew it was to pin his death on. Who better than an airhead scriptwriter hired to develop some cockamamie idea that would draw him close to the mark? As Louis B. Mayer once so accurately remarked: 'What does he know, he's only a writer?'

She had told the shooters to put on an act and pretend to look for me. 'Alan!' That's what the Cockney yelled after he shot Emma. 'She said his name was Alan.' While they were banging kitchen drawers, I remember thinking at the time: they're looking for me in the *fridge*? Among the *crockery*?? And in the taxi, wondering why, when they must have seen the open window, they didn't follow? She'd told them to make sure they scared the living daylights out of me, that when I took off, I had to believe I was running for my life. She wanted me out of there fast so they could clean up before the housekeeper arrived. In that they succeeded. I'd shat bricks in that broom closet.

Andree ordered the house to be cleaned because she didn't want the housekeeper to find Hall; that would have been too soon. First the wild-goose chase, her exit, then have him fetch up in a shallow grave somewhere, maybe under his laburnums.

With my watch. 'Alan, Maxie'.

Andree Bruckmeyer, the thinking man's Barbara Stanwyck. Alan Tate, the Fred MacMurray *de nos jours*. I was duck *à l'orange*. When the doorbell rang, I didn't even need to look out of the window.

'Mr Alan Tate?'

'Yes.'

'Detective Inspector Tarrant. This is Detective Sergeant Woodrow. I wonder if we might have a word?'

They came in, filling the flat, glancing at the floors and ceilings like chartered surveyors, making me feel like John Reginald Halliday Christie: "You got me, gents, the bodies are in the walls—"

'Might I ask if you know a man called Arnold Hall?' Tarrant led off.

'Might I ask what this is concerning?' I said with a genial smile. Obstructing justice was the last thing I wanted to imply.

'It's concerning a Mr Arnold Hall.'

'I met him once or twice.'

'Once or twice?'

'Yes.'

'No. I mean, was it once or was it twice?' Tarrant repeated slowly.

I have written enough police shows to know this wasn't the correct procedure. Somewhere, yellowing in a bottom drawer, was a Directive to Writers giving chapter and verse on Proper Investigating Methods.

'I believe you're meant to start by explaining the enquiries you are engaged in,' I said.

Woodrow had his nose up close to the noticeboard above my PC, and the paper listing the rhetorical questions about the plot.

'What's this, sir?'

'My work.'

'What work would that be?'

'I'm a writer.'

'"Where is the money?"' he read out. '"How did it get lost? Who sent it, or who received it? What method did they use? What fucking method!"'

He turned towards me and raised an eyebrow.

'They're notes for a script.'

'Can we get back to Mr Hall?' Tarrant said.

'Can we get back to my question?' I persevered.

'You didn't ask one.'

'I said you were obliged to explain the reason for your enquiries.'

'That isn't a question, sir, that's a statement. I'd have thought a writer would know that.'

Woodrow was back eyeballing the noticeboard.

'"Where's the money?" What money?'

'Money stolen in a fictional story I'm writing,' I answered evenly. Jesus, why hadn't I taken it down? I knew the police would be round. Four days had passed since CBCI closed. They would have interviewed the chauffeur and got an account of Hall's last trip.

'We're enquiring into the whereabouts of Arnold Hall, an employee of the Corporate Bank of Commerce and Industry,' Tarrant said, in a speak-your-weight tone. 'You may have heard this institution was recently ordered to stop trading. We've reason to believe that you and Mr Hall were acquainted and wondered if you could throw some light on the matter.'

'I went to see him to research this story. I saw him in his office on –' I flicked through a desk diary – 'the 16th of September at 11 a.m. He gave me some general information and showed me around their trading department. I left some time before one o'clock.'

'And the second time?'

'The second was three or four days ago when he rang and asked if I wanted to have a drink.'

'So by now you're friends,' Tarrant said. The DS was bent over papers lying on my desk.

'More acquaintances.'

'What's your definition of the difference?' Woodrow asked, without looking up. Nice double act they had going, making me turn awkwardly from one to the other. Someone once answered this question by saying you fucked the wives of acquaintances but never those of friends, but these two didn't give the impression of wanting to kid around.

'I suppose it's a matter of degree,' I said. 'But I would never call anyone a friend if I'd only seen them twice in my life.'

'Did you go for this drink?' Tarrant took up the verbals.

'Yes.'

'Where did you go?'

You know perfectly well. 'As a matter of fact, we ended up at his house in the country.'

'At Sonning on Thames.'

'I believe so.'

'You aren't certain.'

'It was near Sonning.'

Woodrow picked up a sheet of typescript and read out: '"Harrison is on the verge of admitting defeat when he reads in the paper about a young student arrested for hacking into the German Federal Reserve Bank."'

This wasn't going anything like the way I'd anticipated, and that was because I had neglected to hide the notes that came as close as you could get to a blueprint for knocking over CBCI.

'So your story, the one you're researching, is about robbing a bank, is it?' said Tarrant, holding out a hand to Woodrow for the paper.

'That was why I went to see Hall.'

'Give you some tips, did he?'

'Inspector, may we, as they say, cut to the chase? I met Hall on two occasions. What else can I tell you?'

'He took you to his house.'

'Yes.'

'What time would this have been?'

'We got there about ten, eleven.'

'You went in his car.'

'Yes.'

'And he brought you back here afterwards.'

'No.'

'How did you get home, then?'

'I mean no, not right away,' I stammered, hearing the ice start to crack under my skates. 'I stayed the night and – I stayed the night.'

'I see.' Tarrant nodded, then looked puzzled, as if a thought had just occurred. 'Why did he take you all the way to Sonning for a drink? There are enough pubs around here, aren't there?'

'Yes, but after I joined him, that was what he suggested. That we go to his place.'

'For a drink.'

'I didn't know it was in his mind, but we picked up a couple of women.'

'Oh. Friends of his, were they?'

How indiscreet had the chauffeur been when he got to this bit?

'They were call-girls.'

'Prostitutes,' Woodrow said behind me. 'Might as well call a spade a bloody shovel, right?'

'Then he drove you all to his house.'

'His driver did.'

'Ah, he had a driver.' As well you know, you transparent

137

plod. How else did you find out where I lived? Don't hold your breath about making Superintendent.

'Yes.'

'So he stayed the night as well and drove the lot of you back the next morning.'

Here we go.

'No, not the same one,' I said.

'Hall had a *second* chauffeur?' Tarrant asked, widening his eyes at Woodrow. These two were about as spontaneous as Bob Hope.

'All I know is, a car turned up the next morning around seven.'

'Can you tell us anything about this other driver? Or the car.'

I pretended to think. 'No, not really. It wasn't a limo and he didn't wear a uniform like the other one.'

'Can you recall anything Hall said to him?'

'Not beyond telling him where to go, no. It was very early. There wasn't much conversation at all.'

'I expect you were knackered,' Woodrow said. 'What with the tarts and everything.'

'What happened when you reached London?' Tarrant asked.

'They dropped me off first here. I've no idea where they went after that.'

'The girls,' Tarrant said, tugging his earlobe like Bogart. 'Where did you pick them up?'

'I'm not sure exactly. It was somewhere behind Harrods.'

'How did Hall organize them?'

'He called from the car.'

'It was his idea?'

'Yes.'

'He just guessed you were in the mood for a bit of how's yer father,' Woodrow said, breathing on my neck. I didn't turn round.

'He suggested them, and I didn't say no.'

'Course not. After all, he was paying.'

Take another breath, let it out slowly.

'That's right.'

'So,' Tarrant went on, smiling now. 'After he dropped you, that was the last you saw of him.' I nodded. 'I see. Well, thank you for your help, sir. We may need to check one or two things with you later. You're not going anywhere, I hope?'

'No.'

Woodrow gave a look that said, "Think you're smart, don't you. Well just you wait, sunshine." Like most detectives, he was indistinguishable from a professional criminal; the same hard-eyed gaze, lumbering walk and resentment that I should dare to answer back. I led them out.

'So you're a writer,' Tarrant said, relaxed and easy now the business was done. Wait for it: 'Anything I might have seen or read?'

'I shouldn't think so,' I replied, opening the door. 'I'm not famous.'

Woodrow swivelled his head as he passed, 'Who knows, sir, that might change soon.'

After they left, I sat for a long time. It had been an effort to keep in mind they were only looking for a bank fraudster. All the while, I was trying to blot out the gunshots, the screams, focusing on the need to say nothing that implied he was dead.

I had presented myself as a hanger-on, part of that grotesque world who trail around after the rich, freeloading on

139

their yachts, at their parties, sharing their whores; whose entire social credibility rests on a nod of recognition from a royal, who actually strive to get themselves a mention in Nigel Dempster. Not a pleasant thought, but at least I hadn't come across as someone terrified of being arrested for murder. Although, when I mulled it over, I wasn't sure which was worse.

Then there were the screenplay notes. I knew the cops would come round, yet I hadn't given a thought to shredding them. Had this been fiction, it would have been the first thing I'd have the hero do. After all, heroes are supposed to be smart. Could they *seriously* be taken for plans to loot CBCI? Come on, officer, *really*!

It wasn't the police I was concerned about. It was the thought of having a five-thou-a-day QC look over his half moons in the Old Bailey and fillet me with a contempt honed at the finest public schools: "Would it not be true to say, Mr Tate, that in exchange for expensive prostitutes and invitations into circles not usually accessible to people of your background, you used your knowledge of criminal behaviour, having written on the subject for much of your life, to assist Hall in fleecing his employers? Is that not precisely the reason he asked you to research this so-called film?"

Never forget Oscar Wilde. Steaming along in the witness box on an ocean of wit, he hit the iceberg of one question from Carson: 'And the boy Grainger, did you ever kiss him?' Wilde saw another laugh present itself and explained that he did not, because the lad had been ugly. He never recovered.

What iceberg was waiting for my bows? The notes about hacking into banks? It was too late to burn them now. Woodrow and Tarrant would want to know where they had gone.

Circumstantial evidence they might be, but men have been hanged on less.

Learn from Wilde. Don't ruin everything for the sake of a joke.

But the Bruckmeyer scenario frightened me. Hall's body would be found, and the police need look no further than the man who fell out of a window of the deceased's house and told a taxi driver to, how did it go again? 'Get the fuck out of here!'

When I'm stuck in traffic, instead of waiting for it to disperse I will cut down the first side road and drive miles through back streets in the belief that I'm making progress simply by being in a state of motion. Trying to be active fills most of our days. I've known film producers fly to Los Angeles for one meeting. They come back shattered, believing they've performed a marathon session of hard work, when all that's happened is they've sunk endless food and drink in first class, stayed in a luxury suite, and attended a ten-minute discussion, during which nothing was resolved.

The following day, I wished I had some vacuous trip to give me the same satisfaction. I left the flat only once, to load up on newspapers. I spoke to no one for fear of betraying what I knew. The answering machine filtered all calls and I took only those unconnected with my nightmare.

Maxie rang to say Lloyd had tonsillitis. Tim tried once and I felt his displeasure in the curt demand to return his call. But I daren't. Once the talking started, I wouldn't stop. What's the point of having a secret if . . . ? Everything would spill out and I would compromise myself more times than a menopausal MP.

What I did was read every paper and listen to every hourly newscast for fresh revelations about CBCI, which turned out to be next to nothing. Hall was mentioned briefly by the tabloids, who were turning him into a folk hero, but gradually the bank's collapse was moving through the inside pages to the business section. Having nobody to doorstep, the hacks moved on to stalkers, mugged pensioners and lesbian parents. None of them came down Blenheim Road, which meant the police didn't think it was yet in their interests to hand over my name.

Finally, I went out. I rented a car and drove to see Maxie, reminding myself I hadn't told her about the Operfilm assignment, worried that if she knew I was coining it, she'd go berserk with the plastic, most of which I was legally required to settle.

I had rarely involved her with the nitty-gritty of my job. When producers dicked me around, I kept it quiet. Being American, she was likely to fling a brick through their windows, and I couldn't afford to have a crazy wife on my CV. Far better to do things the English way; pretend you weren't seething with rage, adopt a breezy manner and write a letter saying you hoped one day to work with them again.

She had changed the gate combination and I waited until she pressed the release. Even when I reached the doorbell, I had to wait a full minute before she appeared momentarily.

'I'm on the phone.'

I went into the living room and heard her say: 'Are you contagious? Can you still go to lectures?'

Lloyd. Or was she doing an Andree and talking to herself just to prick my conscience? 'Your father's just come in, do you want to speak to him? No, of course, you're right, rest your throat as much as you can. 'Bye, darling, and take care. Love you.'

'How is he?' I asked as she hung up.

142

'Not good. The college doctor agrees he ought to come home. I mean, way up there in Durham—'

When Maxie first arrived in England in midsummer, I took her to Nottingham to see where I had grown up. She insisted on packing long johns, convinced that anywhere north of Hampstead lay under snow nine months of the year.

'How's Sophie?'

'Fine.'

Maxie preferred sons. Daughters reminded her of the problems she had given to *her* parents, which forced her to admit that there was a time when she too had been a terrible pain in the arse. Once, when she was complaining about Sophie's ingratitude, 'I spent all fucking day shopping with her for clothes and she ridiculed every suggestion I made, right in front of the assistants,' I said surely she had treated her mother exactly the same way, and she'd yelled, 'Yes, but I'm a damn sight nicer than my mother!'

'So how are things with you?' she asked without sounding at all interested. 'Do you want tea, coffee or what?'

'Cup of tea'll be fine. They're OK.' Just a few corpses, the cops think I busted a bank, nothing special.

While she blundered nervously in the kitchen, making what should have been a simple task into a major performance: 'Only teabags, I know you hate them, and I'm out of sugar, I never use it' – I wondered why I thought coming round would cheer me up. I also wondered if there were any men in her life. Lloyd and Sophie were away, and none of the Neanderthal neighbours had ever entered her guest list. Life must be pretty barren. When I say men, I mean sex.

'It's good to see you,' she said. 'Is there a reason?'

'You sounded worried about Lloyd.'

'I was.'

143

'And I wanted to see how you were getting along.'

'This is it,' she said, spreading her arms to embrace the kitchen. 'What did you expect?'

'You never liked it out here. You always said it cut you off from civilization.'

'It does, but what do I want civilization for these days?'

She had tried to write a sitcom years ago, and it was full of lines like that. When it was turned down, she decided television couldn't handle intelligent dialogue. I told her she had learned the first principle of life. She never tried again, and when anything of mine was shown, she spent the time wincing at lines and reminding everyone they weren't even funny the first time she'd heard them. The trouble was, they were lines that weren't meant to be jokes.

'Are you seeing anyone?'

'What, you mean men?'

'I mean anyone.'

'Like who?'

'You know, Maxie,' I sighed, 'when you rang, I honestly thought you were hinting for a bit of company. You know what to do when the car packs up. It was like asking me how to set the washing machine.'

The tea went into the living room on a tray. One cup.

'It's boring as hell out here,' she said, leaving me to pour. 'And I've been getting scared lately.'

'What about?'

'In the sticks, no one can hear you scream,' she said.

'I did suggest selling.'

'I know, but I thought, the kids grew up here. Maybe they'll want it when we go. But lately I can't get either of them to come anywhere near the goddam place. Sophie has

144

some boyfriend in London and Lloyd, well, Durham may as well be Greenland.'

'What boyfriend?'

'Rides a motor bike and deals crack, knowing her.'

'I thought she was meant to be in school. I thought teachers were supposed to be *in loco parentis.*'

'I've been getting some funny phone calls lately,' she said, letting the kiddie talk die.

'What kind of funny?' An imaginary floorboard creaked.

'Not the ha ha. Just – odd. It goes, I pick it up, no one's there. Or someone says they're checking the line. Yesterday, a man asked where you were but rang off before I could give him your number.'

'How many altogether?'

'Half a dozen maybe.'

'Did you ring the engineers to see if they *were* checking the lines?'

'No.'

'When was this?'

'Couple of days ago.'

I rang and they confirmed yes, they had been doing some routine repairs. 'The rest were silent, except the man who wanted me?'

She shrugged. 'Maybe it's nothing.'

'Look, you really should think about selling,' I said. 'Get a flat in Chelsea or wherever. Rejoin the human race.'

'Yeah, maybe I'll think about it.'

Meanwhile, from the moment she had mentioned funny calls, I was thinking of my watch and its inscription. They knew Alan meant Tate. Tracing Maxie would be a doddle. But why would they want to?

145

'These silent calls. Could you hear anyone breathing on the other end?' She glanced over, suspicious.

'You seem very interested. What do you think they were, some female for you? Someone you'd told if a woman answers, hang up?'

'There's no one like that.'

'There was the Kraut.'

I stood up. 'I'll ring Lloyd and Sophie. And if you decide to sell the house, let Richard know.'

She came across, cutting me off at the door. 'I'm sorry,' she said, tried to continue, then burst into tears. In all our married years, I had rarely seen her weep. For a moment, I was grasped by a thought that she had some terrible news she'd been bracing herself to relate. Something about the children, something unbearable.

'God's sake, Maxie, what's the matter?'

When I tried to pull her into my arms, she resisted. 'I'm so – so – miserable! I can't – can't think! I can't think straight – I—'

I yanked her towards me and this time she didn't strain against my tight embrace. We stood a long while before she stopped shaking.

'Things have been getting out of hand. I don't seem able to cope any more. You spend years up to your neck in children problems, then they leave, along with your husband – it all gets so fucking bleak.'

'You must leave this house. It's become a morgue.'

Easing gently away, she found some Kleenex. 'I don't suppose there's any chance you might want to move back,' she said, not looking at me. 'I don't mean, I don't mean, you know – just use one of the spare rooms.' She paused. 'The worst is the nights. I wake up and think I hear things.

146

I force myself to walk around, to stop feeling scared. I know there's no one out there, no axe murderer, it's kids' stuff, I know, but your mind takes off on its own.'

So now there were two of us, both scared, both lonely, both facing nightmares. If I stayed, she would lose hers, but gain mine. If I left, I'd never stop worrying that her fears were justified. That there *was* someone out there. Someone with a watch in his pocket and murder in his mind.

'I've a couple of things to sort out first,' I said. Her face stiffened in the way a face does when hopes are dashed. 'But I'll be back. I promise.'

On the drive home, I couldn't stop thinking about the way she had dissolved. This wasn't some passing mood. She was disturbed in a manner I hadn't seen before. Even when Lloyd had balanced on the brink of life with meningitis, she had presented a stern resolve while we sweated through the days and nights. Only when the crisis was over did she let go, and that was relief. What I had just seen was despair.

Silent phone calls, a man who asks for me but doesn't wait to get my number.

And a watch bearing our names in the hands of two contract killers.

DATE: 5 OCTOBER

FAX TO: DI TARRANT, METROPOLITAN POLICE, NEW
            SCOTLAND YARD

FROM: DS MORRISON, THAMES VALLEY POLICE
            HEADQUARTERS, KIDLINGTON, OXFORD

Sir,

Re: Arnold Hall, Rainwood House, Sonning

I am confirming my telephone call of today's date
reporting evidence given by Thomas James Willoughby,
taxi driver, employed by Kwik Kabs Car Service, Sonning on Thames. At 10.05 this morning, Willoughby
spoke to the sergeant on duty at Sonning Police
Station. He said that having read about the missing
financier Arnold Hall, and learning that he lived at
Rainwood House, Barrington Road, Sonning, he wished
to make a statement concerning events that took place
on 29 September when he received a call from Rainwood
House at 6.15 a.m. to pick up a passenger. The man
gave his name as Alan Wilkinson and said he wished to
be driven to London. Willoughby states that he
arrived at the house at 6.30 and upon ringing the bell
was informed by an unseen male there was no one there
of that name. He returned to his vehicle and was about
to leave when a man leaped through a ground floor
window and told him to 'get the fuck out of here'. He
confirms the passenger gave his name as Wilkinson. He
was ordered to drive to Marble Arch, but as they
approached London, the traffic was heavy and he suggested that it would be quicker to complete the journey by underground. The passenger agreed and
Willoughby dropped him at Ravenscourt Park tube
station. He says Wilkinson was in his fifties, medium
height, brown hair and well spoken. Having picked him

148

up in unusual circumstances, he made a note of the man's features and is confident he could recognize him again.

The housekeeper at Rainwood House, Mrs Janet Gaunt, has stated that she arrived for duty at 9.30 a.m. and found no one in the house. She said Mr Hall always left for work before she got there, and she had no reason to be concerned until she heard that he was missing. She said it was not uncommon to find evidence of guests having stayed overnight, but on this day the only bed used was Hall's. His wardrobes and bathroom still contain all his personal effects but to date, his passport has not been located.

Mrs Gaunt added that a small window in a ground floor room had been broken but since the latch was in place and there was no sign of robbery, she had not thought it suspicious at the time.

I await further instructions.

N. MORRISON, Detective Sergeant,
Thames Valley Police

A week had passed since I stopped shaving my upper lip and the shadow of a moustache developed into soft bristle. The effect created was of a provincial town clerk with thwarted ambitions. A dab of Cherry Blossom dark tan gave it extra body. I debated whether to dye my hair, but decided this would make me into an out-of-work character actor or a closet gay, and the idea was to direct attention away, rather than towards me.

A military helicopter collision sent the press haring up to Scotland and the coverage buried CBCI. A sentence here and there gave no impression the police were breaking a leg to find Hall.

When I returned from Maxie's, I drew five hundred out of a cashpoint, packed as much as I could cram into two suitcases and moved to a bed and breakfast in King's Cross, an area behind the railway station that made Fulham look like Beverly Hills. Every man over fifty looked like me, and I took lessons on the right sort of splay-footed walk to use while wearing a Fair Isle jumper under a tatty raincoat.

My first floor window offered a front row circle view on the local street life, a sluggish ballet of underage tarts, pimps and drug pushers. Dozens of writers have made careers bringing this traditional urban scene to prime time, venturing through with hidden cameras and tape recorders to locate the new folk heroes of television drama. They paid the going hourly rate to sit in pubs over vodka Ts, gathering research on how to deal with a punter who wants you to shit on them.

Where I stayed, there wasn't much of a bed and less of a breakfast. I seemed to be the only guest not on the game, judging by the bedspring symphony, interspersed with cries of pain, that broke out regularly on all sides around the clock.

When I checked in, the landlady was first surprised then suspicious that I wanted the room for more than an hour: 'You do know where you are, dear?' she enquired. 'I don't want you complaining about what goes on here.'

My good woman, I'll have you know I have been given a seeing to by the most expensive whores in the land.

'This will do fine,' I said when she showed me the room, letting her think she had a man of mystery among her PGs. There was no demand for identity, everything was settled in cash and, taking a wild guess she wasn't a movie buff, I signed in as Joseph Gillis, the hard-up writer who befriends Norma

Desmond in *Sunset Boulevard*. I felt an affinity. Who knows in which swimming pool I'll end up dead?

There was little future, I decided, in staying at Blenheim Road. The two cops, I forget their names, Debenham and Freebody, would have been back the moment they heard the tale of the kitchen window vacator. Alan Wilkinson would rapidly morph into Alan Tate and I'd be faced with "So what was that about driving back to London with Hall and the girls and what were you specifically referring to when you told the driver to get the fuck out of there?" They would see my moustache and, in that witty police way for which our boys in blue are famous, remark that a *Jurassic Park* mask from Woolies would have looked more convincing.

In Fulham, I was chopped liver. I wasn't a whole lot less in King's Cross; maybe the meat before it hit the grinder. The odds were better on England dominating Wimbledon, chess, flamenco dancing and the European Union than on tracing Hall's assassins.

In films, an innocent man tries vainly to clear his name until despair finally overwhelms him. He climbs the parapet on Waterloo Bridge, seeking relief from a hostile world, and prepares to jump. But in that last second the moon, momentarily emerging from behind a cloud, lights up a passing taxi. He sees the face of the man he's been seeking, the one who can clear him, the real criminal. There is a medium close-up, leading to close-up to extreme close-up. The Bernard Herrmann music thunders as he realizes Where There's Life, There's Hope. He descends the parapet and walks away with a step that turns into a march, then a swagger, sending a joyous message to the audience that as long as you don't quit, you will surmount overwhelming odds. And he will carry them along to the final reel when he flings the villain at the feet of the detective who has been obsessively hunting the wrong man for years and says, "Here, I'm making a citizen's arrest."

All I had to do was get from standing in the window of the King's Cross knocking shop to this final scene in the next two weeks.

'Hello, Maxie.'

'What the hell have you been up to? The police have been here.'

'What did you tell them?'

'Tell them? *Tell* them? What do you think I told them? I told them you don't live here any more and to fuck off.'

'Did they?'

'Not before trashing the whole house. They started in the attic and worked down. One of them carried a battering ram, the kind they use in drug busts. I was terrified. What's this *about*?'

The telephone box was papered with whores' business cards, photocopied photos of women with huge tits and arses, and it stank. Just when English youth stop vandalizing phone booths, they start wanking off in them before these icons.

'Do me a favour,' I said. 'The car's got a mobile. Get it.'

'Alan!'

To show I wasn't kidding, I slammed down the receiver. In the time I estimated she needed to reach the garage, I had decided that Cindi with her Asian looks and offers to show me Nirvana was the one I'd call. Still that foreign snob thing. I rang the mobile number and Maxie's voice returned. Unmellowed.

'—think this is some kind of *movie*? Who are we this week, James fucking Bond?'

'You can bet the cops have bugged the phone,' I said.

152

'Why? Why would they bug my phone? Why are they looking for you? What have you *done*, for crying out loud?'

'If you'll just shut up for a second. Let's meet.'

'You can't tell me now? On my untapped mobile? What did I have to go and get it for?'

'I'll be in Regent's Park. In the rose gardens by the fountain. You remember how to find it? Come into the Inner Circle by the York Gate—'

'Yeah, sure, carrying a copy of *Time* magazine. What's the password?'

'Very droll, Maxie. It must be obvious even to you something is seriously up.'

'How do you expect me to get into town? The car's bust.'

'It got you home, it'll get you to the train station.'

'What if it won't start?'

'Try it.'

'You mean *now*?'

'I'll hold on.'

She said something I didn't catch and went inside the house, keeping up a commentary: 'Here I go, looking for the keys. Oh yes, here they are in the wooden bowl beside the door as usual. Now I'm turning round and going to the garage . . .'

I heard the car door open and the engine turn several times. Start, *start*!

Then it roared into life, the revs screaming.

'OK, OK, it's going!' I yelled. 'Now get to the station – Maxie, can you hear me?'

The engine settled to a purr. 'Tell me one thing,' she said.

'What?'

'Why should I give a shit about what you've done? We're not married any more.'

'Because of things that go bump in the night,' I replied, and rang off.

It would take her an hour to Victoria and a taxi to the park another twenty minutes. I walked down Euston Road practising my new persona. Laurence Olivier, I think it was, who said to get into a new character he first of all found an appropriate pair of shoes. The kind he reckoned such a man would wear. Acting from the feet up. A middle-aged failure reduced to living in a cheesy boarding house behind a main-line station required dirty suedes. The type you see on MCC members, the ones who wait half a lifetime to join a club simply to be able to wear its tie. This end of town didn't lack second-hand clothes markets and I soon found the right prop. Lord O. was dead right; scuffing along in them, I *was* that ex-major in *Separate Tables*. I assessed the effect in shop windows and I prayed to God a car wouldn't draw up and Juliette Binoche would wind down the window and ask directions.

When the police passed, I looked away. If anyone did give me a glance, I worried they'd read a description of a famous missing writer and connected it with my one and only tele-vision appearance, fifteen years ago on a morning talk show to plug *Before the Dawn*. This was before the film had been released, when it was still regarded as a success.

London parks have changed over the years. Once they were the stamping grounds for uniformed English nannies, wheeling Rolls-Royce-style prams and greeting one another in booming tones copied from their employers. Nowadays, they were more likely to be cheerful Portuguese girls in torn jeans. It's rare to hear English spoken at all. On hot days, there is a feel of Lebanon; black-robed women picnicking,

Ferragamos peeking out below the hemlines, while their menfolk talk with their hands beside the lake. On Sundays, while the natives stay in watching Italian soccer, the entire foreign community empties into these great greenswards to enjoy gardens the British have long taken for granted. If there's any sport being played, it's more likely to be softball.

Which is why I like parks. You have the pleasures of London without having to endure the English. Someone should show Paris how to do the same with the French.

Queen Mary's Gardens were still in gloriously prime condition for early October. Maxie and I used to meet there in the pre-children years, when she worked in Baker Street, and we'd bring deli sandwiches and coffee. She it was who first instilled in me an admiration for my own country when she would gaze entranced at the flowerbeds and marvel at their splendour. Embarrassed, I'd mutter about the odd priorities of British youth who tore up cinema seats, trashed high-rise ghettos, yet for some reason left public gardens alone, but the reluctant truth was I felt a sense of pride. She said every country had its own sentimental attachments; the French for their food, Italians their penises, but to venerate gardens was the mark of a superior civilization. When I reminded her Lord Melbourne called them a dull thing, she dismissed him as your standard upper-class cretin.

Now, as then, the cast of sedentary characters remained mostly the pensioned, although there seemed more solitary young people around. Nobody gave me a second look. I was just one more unemployable fifty-year-old with nothing better to do in his life than sit alone thinking Is This All There Is Left?

There were several benches around the central water fountain, each occupied by one person. It's an unwritten English

155

rule that you never choose one already occupied. Even with three feet of space in between, you are invading someone's privacy or, more probably, making them nervous that you're a flasher. Far better to walk endlessly about, even if your feet are blistering, than act like either a foreigner or a pervert.

This observation came to mind when a young man sat on the end of mine. Not having anything to read, I stared ahead. He crossed and uncrossed his legs a few times before placing an arm along the back of the bench. I lifted my chin and gave the sky a panning shot that ended a couple of feet above his head. He was smiling.

'Nice, innit?'

English? Speaking to a stranger? Oh, shit, that can mean only one thing.

'Very.'

'I always like this time a day,' he said softly, and nudged a few inches closer. 'People leavin' work, you know, lookin' for summing to do of an evening.'

'Yes.' Another sideways budge. By now, his fingers were near my neck.

'I ain't seen you here before. Come a lot, do you?'

'No.'

'You from London?'

'No.'

'I know London like the back a me 'and.' He held out a palm under my nose and turned it over, grinning. 'If you want, I could show you round. I like showing people round.'

What else could I have expected, wearing stained suedes and a shoe-polish-enhanced moustache?

'I know some great pubs,' he went on and I felt his fingers brush my ear. 'You know, where certain types go. People with the same interests 'n' that.'

'Really.'

'You're a bit shy, aren't you? I like shy fellas. I hate those who come on like, you know, Tarzan.'

For Christ's sake, Maxie, where *are* you?

'What's your name?'

'James.'

'Mine's Eric.' He held out a hand and when I took it, he held on to my fingers. 'They call you James or Jim?'

Thank God I never forget a good comic routine. Rowan Atkinson, was it?

'No,' I said. 'Most people call me sir.'

'Sir?'

'Those of a lesser rank. Senior officers use my full title. Chief Superintendent Pinkerton, Regional Vice Squad.'

His hand left mine and his body left the bench. There are moments when it pays to possess total recall of trivia. Most of us become tongue-tied in embarrassing situations, only thinking of the perfect response hours later, and spend the rest of our lives waiting for a second chance to use it. But to make a career of recycling other people's dialogue, which is the art of cinema writing in a nutshell, you get to collect all kind of snazzy repartee. The trick is to have it ready when it's needed.

Maxie appeared, gazing about with a hand over her eyes like Cortés clocking the Pacific. She caught sight of my wave and marched across. It didn't look as if her mood had improved. She was frowning. Then I realized she was wondering if she had made a mistake, that I was someone else. When she knew I wasn't, she performed a startled recoil that Stan Laurel used.

'*Alan?*'

'Hi.'

157

'What have you *done* to yourself?'

'Damn. You recognized me.'

'You look ridiculous.'

'Like the shoes?' I pointed them towards her, wiggling my feet. I stood up and she took a pace back. Or maybe she was just afraid passers-by would assume she was actually friends with this wuss.

'We're going to stroll around,' I said, 'and you aren't going to say a word until I've finished.'

She listened in silence, well, almost in silence while I told her everything. Well, almost everything. I left out the actual amount offered by Operfilm – it had stopped at ten thousand anyway – and I glossed over the events in the limo. Yes, I explained, weak as I was, I didn't object when Hall hired a couple of women, but nothing happened, nothing carnal, since I realized after years of a good marriage, my virility with other partners had faded to almost nothing. That was the only time she interrupted:

'Just cut the crap and get on with it.'

When I reached the shootings, she stopped dead. *'What?'* From there to the end didn't take long.

'And that's it. That's why the police are looking for me.'

'Not for murder,' she said. 'They only want to ask you about this guy whatsisface.'

'And why I came flying out of his house, out of his *window*.'

'You're meant to be the writer. Think of something.'

'I did.'

'What?'

'I told them Hall found another car to drive us back to London.'

'Why did you do that?' she said, with a look I knew well. When I pretended to sign those traveller's cheques in San

158

Francisco. And when I was pruning the upper branches of a plum tree and managed to saw off the one I was straddling. Complete incomprehension.

'I don't know. Like Steve McQueen's story in *The Magnificent Seven*, it seemed like a good idea at the time.'

'Wait, wait, wait, wait just one goddam minute here.' Whenever she began a sentence this way, I knew I'd overlooked a plain and obvious fact. 'Good *idea*? What was wrong with telling the plain *truth*?'

'Sure, that I witnessed a triple murder. By a couple of contract killers. Guys who never get caught. Leaving me to shit in a bucket until I'm ninety.'

'What beats me is why you didn't get in the taxi, drive to the nearest police station and report it. You wouldn't have had any residue on your hands or your clothes to prove you'd fired a gun. They'd have no reason to suspect you. Why didn't you?'

Christ, she was right. I didn't know why. The moment I dived into the cab, the thinking side of my brain had shut down.

'However,' she went on, 'that's water under the bridge. You didn't and that's that. Right now, the cops don't know anyone was killed. But you didn't have to tell them a pack of lies about Hall driving you back the next day.'

Didn't I?

'You could still have stuck to the truth most of the way. This sleazoid took you to his house with some prostitutes for an orgy. And that's what happened. But early in the morning, you got disgusted with what was going on, or just plain tired, and you called a taxi to take you home. Why didn't you say that?'

'And the phony name?'

159

'You gave the driver a false name because – because you had your reputation to think about.'

'Why did I come out through the window? And tell him to step on it?'

She was fazed for about a second. 'The door was locked and you couldn't open it and, well, you wanted to leave quick rather than say prolonged goodbyes – shit, Alan, so maybe you had to lie a *little*, like saying you were disgusted with screwing whores, or you had a reputation that needed protecting, but if you *had*, you wouldn't right now be hiding from the cops, and they wouldn't be pulling our house apart or bugging the telephones. Or anything. But –' she sighed with real weariness, 'you didn't and that means you'll probably spend the rest of your life looking like you do now, a total asshole.'

She ran her eyes from my moustache to the suedes.

Once she told me what I ought to have done, it all seemed obvious. Men go to sex parties, get tired, call cabs, use phony names. None of which was against the law. The police would realize it wasn't me who stripped the bank and see just another dirty mac who'd had enough for one night.

'How was I to know it'd turn out like it did?' I said. 'I'm just not used to seeing people massacred. When I reached the taxi, I thought the papers would have the news by lunchtime.'

'Pretend it's a screenplay. Cut to man leaping out of window into cab. "Get going, fast," he says. "You Wilkinson, the guy who called?" "No, my name is Tate. Wilkinson is inside waving a gun around. I think he's been dropping acid."' She saw my expression. 'God almighty, you used to be better than this.'

'I used to be a bigshot. I coulda been a contender.'

160

'The trouble with real life is, you can't rewind,' she said and for a moment she squeezed my hand.

'Seriously, Maxie, what am I going to do?'

At this point, her inspiration dried. She gazed over the ornamental lake.

'I guess you turn yourself in. What have they got on you? Hall is missing. They don't know he's dead. You lied to protect him while he was taking off for Tierra del Fuego. You're an accessory, that's all.'

But she didn't sound as if she believed herself.

'They may never find him,' I said. 'And they may find I never got a dime. But while they're looking, no judge is going to let me walk further than Brixton exercise yard.'

She drew a deep breath and shuddered slightly. 'You tell kids lying never pays.'

'Got anything else to make me feel good?' I asked, wishing she would touch my hand again.

'Yeah. What about the killers? They must still be looking for you.'

I hadn't pitched her my Bruckmeyer scenario and I was too tired to do it now. And anyway, that would mean mentioning my watch and, as Gerald Ratner found out, there were some things best left unsaid.

'I wish.'

'You wish what?'

'The way I see it is, I hope they find Hall's body—'

'Are you *crazy*?'

'—then all I have to do is get hold of the shooters and prove it was they who shot him and not me. Easy-peasy.'

Maxie said nothing for a full ten seconds and when she did, she smiled wanly: 'I hate to say this, honey, but you're right.'

She said she'd call Richard to see how I stood legally, was it inevitable I'd be held on a charge severe enough not to warrant bail. 'Lawyers have a wider view of things,' she said, trying to cheer me up. 'Like doctors. You think it's cancer, doctors say it's indigestion. You think you're facing twenty years, the lawyer gets you community service.'

'Maxie, I didn't do anything. Not even to warrant community service.'

'You looked a gift horse in the vagina,' she said. 'Next time, stay home.'

She asked where I was staying and when I told her, she asked if King's Cross was my idea of a hair shirt. All I could say was they do it in the movies. 'You know, go and live on the wrong side of the tracks.'

'Even with that stupid moustache and second-hand shoes, the idea that you, with your Oxford accent and a tendency to ask for the wine list in McDonald's, could drop out of sight in King's Cross, is a bit like Prince Charles taking his slappers to Butlins.'

'Where do you suggest I go?'

'Hide in plain sight. Check in at the Savoy.'

'You have all my money.'

'I deny that. But if you need some, I might be able to find a few quids.'

All these years, and she still can't get English slang right.

'The Savoy?'

'Wherever.'

'Movie people use the Savoy,' I pointed out.

Then she said the cruellest thing since she told me I was too old not to wear a tie: 'So what? They've been avoiding you for years.'

*   *   *

162

When we parted, I was reminded of calf love. Having a girl say she doesn't want to see you again can devastate a sixteen-year-old who's just found something more complex than masturbation. The reason why boys of my generation started drinking was because it was what Bogart did in *Casablanca* when Ingrid Bergman stood him up at the Paris railway station. We all wanted to be Rick, who turned to drink after his life was shattered by a woman. We swore never to let anyone hurt us again, not ever, and started downing the hard stuff by the gallon, hoping one day she would, of all the gin joints in all the towns in all the world, choose the Hop Pole in Beeston, Notts to walk into. Except Bogey never threw up after a few Shippos while trying to belch the alphabet.

Maxie kissed me, avoiding my mouth and said, 'Look after yourself.' The taxi pulled away and she waved through the rear window. My throat closed. Women tell men to look after themselves when they've decided that's it. It's worse than saying good luck, because there's pity in the words. They conjure up a picture of – how did Rick put it? – a guy standing on a railway platform with a comical look on his face because his insides have been ripped out.

She was right about the disguise; it had to go. To hide in plain sight or, as we say, full view, had merit. Sooner or later, my landlady was going to wonder why I stayed in her house, since I never brought anyone in to paint my balls with lipstick or piss in my mouth. She would think I was weird and notify the police.

On the bus back, I caught sight of an inside page of the *Evening Standard*. A small headline read: 'Missing Writer Sought by Police.'

Please, make it Salman Rushdie, I prayed, but there was my picture. It had been taken on holiday in France ten years

163

ago and had stood on Maxie's side of the bed. The police must have nicked it. Comparing my reflection in the window, I wasn't worried anyone would point me out there and then, but reading the account later, I realized my room for manoeuvre was shrinking to a cubby hole:

> Police have released a photograph of 53-year-old Alan Tate, a freelance scriptwriter they wish to interview in connection with the missing banker Arnold Hall. They stress they have no reason to believe Tate, who has not been seen at his rented Fulham flat for some days, is involved in the collapse of CBCI, but wish to eliminate him from their enquiries.

'Eliminate' had a sinister ring.

The Operfilm cheque for nine thousand, shorn of Tim's percentage, had reached my account. Yellow Pages listed a small hotel behind Hanover Square, and the single room rate had dropped since the tourists were starting to go home.

Years ago, I adapted the memoirs of a criminal who had stayed on the run for some time after taking part in a sensational prison escape. Television calls these hybrids fact-based drama. After his recapture, he put together an account of his adventures. Usually nothing has happened to him except months of boredom indoors, his brain rotting away on daytime chat shows and Australian soaps. However, by the time a publisher's editor is done, his story becomes a non-stop saga of thrills and spills and narrow escapes. Movie rights are sold, but after Tom Cruise and Stallone pass, it usually fetches up as a straight-to-video or a TV mini-series starring Jane Seymour. What makes them saleable is a craving by audiences to know the events actually happened. They get a charge reading over the end titles that "Bernard Sloman is currently serving twenty years in Illinois Correctional Facility. Detective Bronowitz was cleared of fabricating evidence but resigned from the police force. He is now a chicken farmer in Idaho and lives alone. Irving Homer is reconciled with his family and between reading for a law degree, advises youngsters on how to avoid a life of crime."

Anyway, Irving said in his book that not until he convinced himself that he was *not* a fugitive, but just a regular guy going about his business, did he stop worrying that he was attracting attention. He said he learned not to hide his face from a cop, but to go up and ask him a question. Not to sit in the backs of bars wearing dark glasses. David Janssen played The Fugitive for years on television, and he was always looking at his feet. Irving said he wouldn't have lasted ten minutes on the lam.

So I took off the moustache and threw out the suedes. I needed to alter my appearance, but it had to be done properly.

Living most of my life in London, I'd come to be known by a number of people. Hiding in full view of everyone precludes those who would recognize you. What was the point of going into the Groucho to be met with a chorus of "Hey, Alan, why aren't you in Paraguay?"

A Berlin producer told me about using Peter Falk in a film when *Columbo* was the highest-rated show in Germany. Comics impersonated him everywhere, copying the glass-eye stare, the cigar and dirty raincoat. One free weekend, Falk had asked how he could travel round the city without getting mobbed. The producer called in a make-up artist who turned the actor into someone his own family wouldn't have identified, giving him the anonymity to go where he liked unmolested.

I had met a few make-up people over the years. These days they hung around Pinewood, waiting for a big budget American production. One was shooting now, something about Anna Karenina, keeping the entire British film industry temporarily away from the Job Centre.

Among them was Wendy Phillips. She had done a great job on *Before the Dawn*, making the actors so unrecognizable that she saved their careers after the film bombed. They still send her flowers every Christmas.

The Pinewood exchange put me through.

'Hello, sugar! Do you know the police are looking for you?'

No, Wendy, I just got back from Mars.

'That's what I want to see you about.' I played on the knowledge that in her younger days, she'd been busted for hash and held an exaggerated view of police brutality. She wasn't likely to fink on me. When I gave my address, she whooped with laughter.

'What a sense of the dramatic,' she boomed. 'You should take up screenwriting.'

'Bring your box of tricks,' I told her.

A big woman, Wendy. A shade under six feet, she'd have been on first call when they remade *Amazon Women Meet Godzilla*. No one was certain about her sexuality, which was almost inconceivable in the fishbowl of film-making. Some men swore they'd slept with her – 'Like throwing a sausage up the Blackwall Tunnel' – but when you rang her home, the machine said neither Wendy nor (fill in a woman's name) were in right now, but . . . What was important, though, was she was as fiercely loyal to her friends as she was scurrilous about her enemies. And she catalogued me as a mate. We had first met at Elstree Studios where she'd been kind. Writers are treated like shit on a film set, forever being yelled at for getting in the shot or tripping over cables. Women take pity on them. You can get laid a lot if you look persecuted.

'Well, would you look at that,' she said, peering out of the window at the street. 'Which one is Lynda La Plante?'

I told her what I'd told Maxie and she listened with a good deal of sharp intakes of breath and whispered expletives.

'Shit and derision! What you gonna do?'

'Make it up as I go along. But I can't, looking like this.'

She sat me next to the window and undertook a close inspection, feeling my nose and stroking my neck. It felt quite sexy, her breath cooling my cheeks.

'What sort of effect are you looking for? Quasimodo or Chippendales?'

'Is there a sort of middle ground?'

'It's always easier to make up old than young,' she explained, pinching a jowl and wiggling it. 'Trouble is, prosthetics need regular topping up.' Her debate was with herself and as she examined my hands and plucked at my hair, she muttered on about shades and dyes. 'Stand up.'

She moved round, prodding my gut, straightening my shoulders and tilting my chin.

'Clothes,' she announced. 'Different clothes will do it better than any makeover.'

'What do you mean?'

'Magritte reckoned the secret of life is, if you're an artist you should dress like a civil servant and vice versa. He said it confuses people's preconceptions. You're a writer. You dress like it. Shitty. I never met one yet who spends more than ten minutes shopping for clothes. Do you have any money?' I said a bit. 'Let's get down to Savile Row.'

'You're kidding.'

167

'The coppers are looking for a scriptwriter.' She emphasized the word as if it were ethically somewhere below critic. 'So you have to appear to be the chairman of Burmah Oil. A Daimler and driver wouldn't come amiss.'

'I said I had a *bit* of cash,' I muttered, counting four hundred and some change after paying the deposit on the room.

'Tell you what. We'll cut your hair. Right now, you look like Beethoven.' While I stared in a mirror, she snipped and primped and combed, making it shorter than since I was a boy. When I complained, she pointed out prison barbers took the Foreign Legion style as their starting point.

Actually, she made me look younger. Not by much, but when I stuck out my chin, the wattles vanished. She tinted a section but changed her mind, saying it would turn me into Ronald Reagan. From her holdall she produced a variety of spectacle frames, dropping them briefly over my nose, but rejected each with a disapproving twitch.

'They make you look a prat.'

'Maybe the chairman of Burmah Oil *is* a prat.'

'Don't interfere. I'm playing God here. Creating a man in the image of my ideal.'

'What's your ideal?'

'I was seventeen years old when I saw him. He was in his forties, peak of condition. Wore a hand-stitched suit, grey pinstripe, fabulous Italian cut, pinched at the waist. He wore gleaming black shoes, sculpted around long thin feet. His hair was grey at the sides and swept over the ears like swan's wings. When he moved, it was on the balls of his feet, lightly like an athlete. There were lines round his eyes that said dissolute when required. Piano-playing fingers manicured to perfection. There was a scar under his chin and his nose was slightly off centre, suggesting he might have boxed in his youth. When he looked at me, I was transfixed by his gentian eyes. I couldn't breathe. All I wanted was to lose myself in his arms and be carried away from a hostile world to a place where he would fight dragons for me. As he approached, my knees trembled. It was as much as I could do to stay upright.'

'What happened?'

'What happened was he was stepping out of a taxi. He tripped and stamped on my foot. Broke a metatarsal. Never even stopped to apologize.'

'And that was it?'

'Yes. But I've never forgotten him. His image has ruined more than a few relationships. Whenever someone treads on my foot, I think of him. I can still smell the Old Spice. And now I have a chance to reinvent him. If I'm successful, you may have trouble controlling me.'

While she talked, I watched her in the mirror. There wasn't the flicker of a smile. People who spend their lives creating make-believe become serious fantasists. I wondered if I ought to ask if she was kidding, but decided against introducing suspicion into what was either the most poignant tale of infatuation I'd ever heard, or the most bathetic. She slung her holdall over a shoulder and marched to the door, saying:

'OK, kid, let's go to work.'

We went shopping. We hit a row of department stores before settling on a men's department Wendy decided she could dominate. I stood silently by, like a reluctant schoolboy with Mummy while she collared the assistants, frightening them out of their bored aloofness. They couldn't supply her fast enough with different suggestions.

'Oh, for God's sake, man, *green*? What are we trying to do, turn the poor sod into a *leprechaun*?'

They quickly came to like her. There wasn't a straight in the place and they saw in her the dominatrix figure they all secretly aspired to be. Had a man tried her manner, he'd have been abandoned after two minutes holding a tie and a pair of shoes that pinched. Recognizing that rarity, a customer who had firm ideas what they were looking for, their senior man Geoffrey took charge, flicking a tape measure around my neck, up the leg, down the arms and elbows, tutting at my waist.

No one addressed a single word to me.

'We could let the trousers out an inch or two—'

'That would mean going double-breasted. He's too wide already.'

'Of course, he could try the tweed—'

'Put the blue on him again, but wider stripes—'

The final image started to take shape. Wendy went away and returned with a furled umbrella, placing it in my hand the way window dressers arrange their dummies.

'Geoffrey,' she commanded. 'A titfer.'

We traipsed through to Hats. Wendy said she didn't want to spoil the ship for a ha'porth of tar. 'Having come this far, we don't want him crowned like a bank manager.'

'Absolutely not, madam.' He fished out a box and revealed a curly brim trilby. 'We find this is popular among the more raffish of our peers.' Wendy lowered it on my head like a coronation.

'Yes . . .'

'Only the upper classes could carry off something like that,' Geoffrey said, adjusting the level a fraction. 'Anyone else would look like a bookie.'

Wendy put an arm round his shoulders. 'Geoffrey,' she announced, 'you're a miracle worker.' This made him blush. 'I want to see the manager. I want him to know you are the jewel in his crown. I'll never shop anywhere else, ever.'

What I may have thought never came into it. I was left staring in the mirror at someone I wanted to throttle. But she was right; the one thing I did not look like was a writer.

'Now you could check into any hotel in the world,' she said after I settled the bill which saw my cash flow dry to a trickle, 'and you'd have everyone fighting to wipe your arse.'

We weren't quite finished. Returning to the B & B, she used a grey tint to fleck the hair around my ears before announcing that yep, this was as close as she'd get to the man who broke her heart and her foot when she was seventeen.

I packed the suitcases and when I checked out, Wendy slung an arm round my neck and said loud enough for the landlady to hear:

'Petal, I haven't had a rogering like that since I took on the All Blacks rugby team. And not even they topped it off with a foxtrot.'

We took a cab to Hanover Square. Wendy gazed at her creation with all the pride of a parent who has just seen her son collect a Speech Day prize.

'Remember, you're a toff. Don't smile when you want something. Expect the world to do your bidding and it will. Writers want to be loved. They overtip and start every complaint with "Sorry". "Sorry to mention this, but you've just taken my seat." You now look like the Lord Chancellor on the way to have tea with Queenie. Behave same.'

We drew up outside the hotel and Wendy told the driver to wait. She led me to the door, pointing at the taxi when a commissionaire came forward and he hurried to unload the cases.

'Now, before I go,' she said, 'is there anything else you'd like me to do?'

'You've done so much already,' I stammered. 'I can't begin to say how grateful I am—'

'I was just wondering how you intend to check in here.'

'I reserved a room on the phone.'

'I mean pay for it. I couldn't help noticing your wallet's gone anorexic.'

'I've got a debit card.'

'I see. You'll sign in as the Marquis of Fuckingham and hand across a card reading Alan Tate.'

'Oh.'

'Hotels have newspaper shops, dear. Papers currently offering large rewards to anyone spotting you.'

'Jesus, my characters never had this problem.'

'Then you better start thinking like them,' she said, leading me inside by the elbow to Reception. 'You have a reservation for—' she turned to me and I gave the name I had used on the phone.

'Phillips.'

She lingered only a moment to register my lack of imagination. 'Mister Phillips is working for my firm and we shall be taking care of his bill.' She handed the clerk her credit card.

'Very good, Miss, er, Phillips.'

'Miz to you, young man, and let me hasten to add there is no kinship between your guest and myself. My company refuses to countenance nepotism.'

'Of course not, Miss, Miz, madam.'

He moved along the counter to swipe the card.

'Couldn't you have said Sebastian Melmoth or something?'

she muttered. 'I thought writers were meant to be imaginative.'

'Only when they're paid.'

When the reception clerk returned her card, she said loudly, 'After you've settled in, come round to the office and meet the team.'

Then she shook my hand, pushed through the revolving doors and was gone. For the second time in two days I felt depressingly alone.

She was right about the newspaper shop. It stood across from the lifts. While I waited, I looked at the latest *Evening Standard*s piled next to the till.

There was a headline on the front page over the right-hand column.

'MISSING BANKER – BODY FOUND'

DATE: OCTOBER 10

FAX TO: MORT DELANNOY, MOVIELINE INTERNATIONAL,
            LOS ANGELES

FROM: ELAINE MORGENSTERN, c/o SAVOY HOTEL,
            LONDON

Dear Mort,

Prepping *Anna Karenina: The Prequel* is proceeding on schedule at Pinewood. This contact concerns another matter.

You may recall an English writer called Allen Tate we used on *Unspeakable Behavior*. If you check with legal, you will find the reasons why we eventually exercised cut-off. Apparently Tate is now being hunted by the British police in connection with the killing of the banker involved in the CBCI thing. While I have been in England, I have closely followed this story and want to share my thoughts with you about a possible scenario. Here are the facts as of today's date:

You will recall CBCI invested heavily in our 1991 project *Gulf Guys*, later retitled *Satan in the Desert*. You no doubt read *Time* magazine's account last week of what happened to them, so I'll fast forward to the latest twist.

Tate was apparently hired to write a film about a billion dollar bank theft using modern technology. He was advised by Arnold Hall, a CBCI senior director. He was the one listed missing until his body was found beside a freeway two days ago. He had been shot once through the heart.

The night before he disappeared, he and Tate went to his home with two hookers. Tate tells the cops Hall drove him back to London the next morning but a taxi driver swears he picked up a man calling himself Alan Wilkinson leaving Hall's house in panic through a window. The word is Wilkinson was really Tate, and here's where the plot thickens. Tate has now also disappeared. As they say over here, he 'scuppered.' Although the British police are talking only about wanting him to help with their enquiries, everyone says they reckon he either killed Hall himself or knows who did. He was meant to be working for a German film company that it turns out never existed. I spoke to that snot of an agent of his, but he wouldn't say anything except that he's taken our cut-off of Tate to the WGA.

Mort, here's the pitch: a writer is researching a bank heist. Then the bank gets robbed in reality, and he becomes the prime suspect.

The writer starts living his own scenario!

I think it has terrific potential and we should get a script written ASAP. CBCI is going to play big for a long time and all the major studios will shortly jump on it. We don't need to go expensive. Get some kid fresh out of film school. I know we're not likely to get a deal with a story set in England, but we could put it anywhere. I'm thinking Silicon Valley. We could still keep the Arab bank angle and have Tate played by Keanu Reeves. You know, stupid.

I'll keep you posted on further developments. England's an island and once they seal the air and seaports no one can get out. Anyway, what we know of Tate's smarts, he isn't going to stay free long.

Just one point on *Anna K.* Could you have research check the Plaza, New York, was built in the period prior to the Leo Tolstoy original material? We can of course use any New York hotel for where Anna's parents bring her to learn English, but product placement thinks it would be constructive to use the

Plaza since everyone's heard of it after the Neil Simon movie.

I really *miss* L.A.! The English weather sucks and they drive so fast, I'm back on Prozac. What I'd give for a decent farmer's market. Vegetables here are sold with the dirt on.

Miss you all like crazy,

ELAINE

My picture had returned to the front pages and they'd stopped using the 'eliminate from enquiries' phrase.

The press have smart ways to make points without upsetting their legal departments. Where would they be without the word 'admit'? 'While stating that Tate was not a suspect in the murder, a police spokesman admitted recent events have increased the urgency finding the 53-year-old scriptwriter.'

First I'd been described as an author, then film writer, now scriptwriter. What was next, scribbler?

There were few moments of comfort wearing my new disguise, but one was the relief at the chasm between how I looked ten years ago on a Brittany beach, and how the public saw me after Wendy had finished. I gradually gained enough confidence to behave as if nothing were wrong. I wandered round the hotel, thinking myself into the role of a Swiss businessman, chatting to the barman about *fussball*.

Reading biographies of the stars, you come across passages about how, when they were unknown, they'd practise by taking to the streets dressed as a panhandler or a busker. Repeating to myself that I was auditioning for the part of an international tycoon, and developing a guttural accent, it became increasingly easy to keep up the pretence, although when someone replied in German, I had to explain that actually I was Romanian. Wendy's diktat about behaving as if the rest of the world was only there to serve my needs worked like a dream. I walked around with a swagger, gave orders to the staff, left out please and thank yous, and occasionally even flicked my fingers. Out of character it might have been, but, by God, it produced results. No one told me to wait my turn, or to find someone else because they were busy. Everybody *jumped*.

A day passed before more details came out about the body found beside the A34. Yes, it *was* Arnold Hall, director of the collapsed CBCI. A report described how a motorist had pulled over for a rest and discovered the body, naked and partly decomposed, leading a pathologist to conclude it had lain there for up to ten days. He had been killed by a single shot to the heart at point blank range, but further enquiries were needed before the police would confirm whether it was murder or suicide.

Oh sure. Racked with guilt, Arnold took off his clothes, walked forty miles to the A34, went into a lay-by and put a gun to his chest. A gun some wild animal had subsequently carted away.

The tabloids were off and running. Sex, money and murder all in one. The bank was hardly referred to. What *was* mentioned, and in every paragraph, was the mysterious man who had leaped from Hall's window telling a taxi to 'get the f★★★ out of here'. A man calling himself Alan Wilkinson, a name similar to that of the television scriptwriter Alan Tate, now the target of a nationwide hunt. From needing to be eliminated, I was now a target.

When I was younger, I used to go to Los Angeles once a

year, check into a hotel and wait for my agent there to arrange meetings. With little on my CV but *Assignment Berlin*, my days weren't exactly helter-skelter, and hours were spent sprawled across a bed surfing forty-six TV channels all showing the same programmes. Actually, one channel *was* different. I clicked into an old movie where all the men wore tails and the women stood like esses, and their houses had ceilings so high, you would need an air balloon to reach the curtain rods. I thought I had two stations superimposed, because between the characters' dialogue a disembodied voice whispered things like 'He goes to the window . . .' 'She sees the smoking cigarette on the desk . . .' 'The door slowly opens behind them . . .'

It took a while to realize I was watching television for the blind.

What I learned then, and what I was reliving now, was the stultifying effect of idleness. Waiting for something to happen could be a description of all our lives, but waiting for it banged up in a room designed only for sleeping can bear down so hard on your brain, you can soon become seriously deranged. Closing your eyes to discover what it's like to watch television without sight is a sure way to reach the very edge of sanity. Dressed like someone about to give a maiden speech in the House of Lords, unable to think of a single constructive idea on how to escape from a nightmare, was enough to pitch you over it.

The only direct human contact was when the maid asked if she could clean up. When she did, I'd grab the phone and do an Andree, talking to myself about deadlines and contracts and flights to Zurich. Or I went downstairs to ask about limousine services, heliports, block bookings to *Phantom of the Opera*. I'd wave to imaginary friends beyond the main doors and hurry outside, making as if to embrace complete strangers.

Walking round Mayfair, a solid depression returned. I thought about Maxie, how she must be half out of her mind, but I was too scared to call. Had those night sounds been only her imagination? Were there really people out there with her name on a list? And why? What reason did anyone have to go after my wife? My ex-wife. Should I have Tim contact her? How could I do that without revealing where I was? He read the papers. He knew I was no killer. He'd realize I had to stay out of sight until things were sorted out.

I called the Groucho and said: 'Could Tim Roberts call Maxie and see if she is OK?' Anonymous enough. But then what? 'And leave a reply to be picked up later by one of his clients. He'll know which one.'

Meanwhile, there was 35 Blenheim Road. I had only removed two suitcases of clothes. There remained almost everything I held dear. Pictures of Sophie and Lloyd, my books, my PC, my *life*! I was still the tenant; I still had the keys. When fugitives say the trick is not to act like one, did that mean having the chutzpah to call in home and collect the mail?

I took the tube to Fulham Broadway and cut through the back streets to the flat. To complete the toff effect I carried the umbrella, which had a few kids' eyes drifting after me. When I say kids, I mean six-foot teenagers on mountain bikes who took a moment off checking cars for mobile phones.

The house was halfway down and I walked briskly along the other side, the umbrella at slope arms like Steed in *The Avengers*.

A policeman stood in the doorway of number 35. Was this the time to test the ask-him-a-question theory? Maybe not. I passed, giving a twist of the neck anyone might make and continued until I reached a roadsweeper collecting the first of the autumn drop.

'What's going on?'

'Dunno. The coppers bin inside all day. Took things out.'

Took things out? Why would they do that? What were they looking for?

'Who lives there, do you know?'

'Ha'n't a clue.'

The local TV news at six thirty gave the answer. I was in a pub and the set was built in above the counter. There were soccer photos all over the walls and on big match days a hundred fans tanked up here, and vomited outside.

The newsreader led off with the usual definite-article-challenged headlines: 'Murder Victim's Watch Found in Fulham House . . . Good evening. Police investigating the murder of CBCI banker Arnold Hall have found his Rolex watch at an address in Fulham.' Shot of the house and the bobby. 'Police say they are anxious to trace the man who has been living in the flat until recently.'

Hall's *watch*? In *my flat*?

'They have named him as Alan Tate, fifty-three, married with two children.'

Two more slips down the greasy pole. Earlier, I'd no longer been a scriptwriter but a *television* scriptwriter. Now, I didn't even merit a trade at all. They showed the picture taken on Quiberon beach again, a happy tourist without a care in the world. What had happened was we'd been staying near what the French call a *plage sauvage*. After the kids had settled down with their buckets and spades, we realized the local custom was for the women to go topless. Maxie refused point blank when the first women to pass by were around

180

eighteen, but then a woman in her sixties had appeared carrying a rubber dinghy with her husband, and the children shamed Maxie into lowering her brassiere straps and then, in stages, slipping it off. For a few minutes, she stayed with her arms crossed, like Vanessa Redgrave in *Blow Up*, but gradually became emboldened enough to lower them, one at a time. Five minutes later, she was frolicking in the water and I was storing up photos for the family album. When she saw what I was doing, she gave a shriek, snatched the camera and took the shot currently being beamed into every household in Britain.

Someone behind said, 'That's Blenheim Road.'

Two young men were holding lagers. 'There was a police car outside all morning.' I turned and gave them my full face.

'What were they after?' I asked.

'Summing about that bloke they found dead on the A34.'

'Where's Blenheim Road?' I asked the barman.

'Outside, up on the left.'

When I was a child, murders were rare and people talked about them all day long. Nowadays they were so common, they needed something weird to attract attention. One body does not a story make. Hall would have to wait until they found the two women before he went prime time.

Andree Bruckmeyer must still be around. She wouldn't trust anyone else to plant the watch. Knowing I needed a motive to kill Hall, she worked on the well-publicized fact that I was broke and left something worth twenty thousand.

Patricia Highsmith wrote a story called *Strangers on a Train* that was made famous by the Hitchcock picture. The plot explored the idea that since motive is the reason most killers are caught, if two people each had someone they wanted

181

dead, all they need do is swap murders. No motive, no conviction; two perfect crimes. Andree had plugged the one gap in the theory that I had killed Hall. She gave me a motive.

History groans with the weight of conspiracy theories. Since the Kennedy assassination, they've sold millions of books. Jack couldn't have been shot by one redneck acting alone, it wasn't possible. It also wasn't commercial. Watergates, Irangates, a stream of juggernauts rolled by clogging up months of TV time with cheap-to-make programmes which pulled in huge audiences, a broadcaster's Valhalla. When an Australian ex-Prime Minister went missing, presumed drowned, the story sold was that he had been a double agent and *swam* to China. Jobbing authors relocated to Swiss hillsides on the strength of books probing papal bankers, Stalinist defectors, Churchill's secret deals with Hitler, Supreme Court justices with Ku Klux Klan roots, Errol Flynn's Nazi connections and an endless list of MI6 chiefs who turned out to be KGB implants. Elvis was living with James Dean in a Witness Protection Program because they were both on death lists, having information about the extent of Jewish Mafia influence in Hollywood.

You don't have to restrict yourself to the present. Does anyone know what happened to Christ's body after it disappeared? I mean, resurrection – per-lease! He had been working for the Romans as an agent provocateur and they fixed it so he only *pretended* to die on the cross. They shipped him to Provence where he lived to eighty.

My response to all this garbage had always been dismissive. Humans are simple-minded organisms, barely capable of pissing and chewing gum at the same time. Maxie had a brother who hit the news some years ago when he was caught in Gorky Park trying to proselytize Muscovites to the American way. Pre-glasnost Soviet police accused him of espionage and for a few weeks the papers debated if it were true. Maxie wrote a letter to the *New York Times* saying her brother couldn't possibly be a spy since he was incapable of retaining more than one thought in his head at a time. She illustrated this by saying if she sent him into town to buy a light bulb, then asked if he could pick up a pint of milk, he would return with one or the other, never both. He was released within a week and many people believed it was on the strength of Maxie's letter, which made him out to be a moron. He never completely forgave her, even though he made a fortune with a book and on the lecture circuit.

I subscribe to the bulb-or-milk theory of human deviousness. When in doubt, choose the simplest explanation, even if it won't bring you worldwide sales.

Or rather I did, until they found Hall's Rolex in my flat.

There were two possibilities: Andree planted it before the news broke about CBCI, certainly before the police called round to quiz me on Hall's whereabouts. All she had to do was wait until I left and flip back the front door catch, since I never double-locked.

Or it was the police. From all the conspiracy talk over the last few years, the accusation of faking evidence was the most often proved. Think of the Fours, the Sixes, the Ninety-sevens released because of tainted forensics. CBCI was news because it involved big money. Now murder. The cops, realizing it wasn't going to drift away as they had hoped, decided to find a goat. Who better than that writer, the one who fell out of Hall's window. He had to be guilty of *something*.

183

Or there could be a link between the two. Since Bruck-meyer now owned the same kind of money you would have if you went around China and got every single Chinese to give you a pound, what detective was going to refuse a fortune to collect the watch from a left luggage locker along with Hall's clothes, and 'find' it in Tate's flat?

Whatever. The bottom line was that nobody was going to believe me when I protested my innocence. Nobody. The nation was united in hatred of someone the press detailed as hanging around corrupt financiers in order to take part in orgies involving innocent young girls.

The hotel receptionist passed across a message along with my key. Wendy wanted me to call. It had started: 'Alan, look, I only agreed to help because I honestly believed you couldn't possibly have done these terrible things, but this *watch*—' I delayed the moment by ringing the Groucho. Yes, Mr Roberts did leave a note. Shall I read it out? It says Maxie is worried and could you contact her soonest?

She answered her mobile on the first ring.

'Alan, where are you?'

'Never mind that, what's happening?'

'What do you mean what's happening, *you're* happen-ing, for Chrissake, you're all over the papers, TV, everywhere . . .'

'Are you OK?'

'You mean apart from the hundred reporters hanging around the gate? I took the main phone off the hook days ago.'

'So there are people around the house.'

'Day and night.'

Suddenly I was grateful for the press.

'Listen, I can't talk long. I just wanted to hear your voice.'

184

'Well, you're hearing it. And it's wanting to know what you're going to do.'

'I haven't got a clue.'

'You don't think you ought to turn yourself in?'

'What good would that do?'

'The longer you run, the more it sounds like you, well, you know. Remember O.J.'

'I prefer to remember *Les Misérables*,' I said. 'Or *The Fugitive*. People have got used to cops getting it wrong.'

'How did the watch get there?'

'Obviously it was planted.'

'Who by?'

'Someone who wants me to take the rap.'

'I didn't know people said "take the rap" any more. Can they tap mobiles?' she asked anxiously. 'What about Squidgygate, and I-want-to-be-your-tampon?'

'Yours is digital, they were analogs. You're tap proof.'

'Are you still wearing that awful moustache?'

'No.'

'Oh, hon, what are you going to do?'

'Don't keep asking that. I'm pretty certain the Kraut's behind everything.'

'The one you picked up in the bar.'

'You're going to tell me there's a lesson to be learned here.'

'No. No, I wasn't.'

'If I could *find* her, let them know it was her put me on to Hall. Then—' Then what?

'Then what?' Maxie said, reading my thoughts.

'I don't know.'

'How long before they come across the two women? I

185

mean, if they found him beside a main road, they aren't exactly *hiding* the bodies, are they?'

'Do *you* think I should give myself up?' I asked, and there was a pause that gave her answer. 'You do, right?'

'As you said, it could be ages before there was a trial. You'd spend years in prison, and even then . . .'

'Even then, what?' I caught the dying fall in her voice. 'Even then I've got no case.'

'Lloyd and Sophie rang.'

'What did you tell them?'

'I said it's all a terrible mistake.'

'What did they say?'

'They both reckon you were set up.'

'They *did*?'

'Although Lloyd did say you shouldn't have fallen for it.'

'He's absolutely fucking right.'

'And Sophie was a bit upset about the, you know, the sex stuff, the prostitutes.'

'Love, I have to go.'

'You will keep in touch.'

'I promise.'

Sophie imagining her father in bed with a couple of girls almost her age brought on a wave of depression that made it impossible to keep talking. Squeezing a tear of consolation from the call, I was relieved the journos were doorstepping. I meant to ask if she had had any more silent calls, then remembered she said she'd taken the phone off the hook.

I lay on the bed a long time, switching around the news programmes. When the phone buzzed, I was dozing.

'Get my message, sugar?'

'Wendy – yes. Sorry, I must have dropped off.'

'Who stuck you with the Rolex?'

186

'I'm working on it.'

'Listen, I've been going over what you told me.'

'*Please* say there's something that doesn't add up.'

'There's something that doesn't add up.'

'What?'

'When the gunmen were pretending to look for you, it was to get you scared, so you'd run like shit. They weren't going to kill you, because you were the patsy.'

'Right.'

'They weren't to know you'd called a taxi.'

'Can't see how they would, no.'

'So they assumed you'd hoof it down to the road and hitch a lift or something.'

'Where're we going, Wendy?'

'They *also* couldn't guarantee you wouldn't find the nearest phone box and call the police. I mean, they had no way of knowing you wouldn't.'

'*I* don't even know why I didn't. I never even thought about it until Maxie pointed out it was what any normal person would have done. All I can think is, my brain just froze.'

'Never mind why you didn't. What I can't figure out is *their* POV. They have you haring off down the road, that was their orders. But now what they have to do is move three dead bodies, and a gallon of blood, then clean up as if nothing's happened. They knew when the housekeeper showed up, but they *must* have factored in the shorter time it would take the police to come, had you rung them right away. I know when you get burgled, they take their time. But surely, three killings would put a firework down their panties, and the killers'd know that.'

'Maybe they saw *Pulp Fiction*. Had a Mr Wolf call.'

'Travolta and Jackson didn't have a deadline,' Wendy persisted. 'Your fellas did. And I'll tell you, shoogs, call me houseproud, but *I* wouldn't contract this job out. I wouldn't risk someone else leaving a thumbprint or a speck of blood. There were three people shot to bits. You don't just run a Kleenex over the bedpost. Remember *Psycho*? How long it took Norman to clean the shower after he'd sliced up Janet Leigh? *Hours*.'

While she talked, I started to wonder why they went to all this bother, have me run off, become a scapegoat? Why not do what a million B-movie plots have done? Kill Hall, the women, then me; wipe the gun that shot them and place it in my hand. Shove some LSD down our throats to complete the picture of a man who goes berserk, then kills himself. Why get any more complicated? I wanted to keep Wendy on the phone, test it out on her, but a wave of weariness flooded my system, swamping vocabulary.

'I know this isn't getting you very far, sweetheart,' Wendy was saying, 'but I was going through the scenario in the bath and—'

'I'm glad you called. I need contact to stay sane.'

'Keep going over it,' she said. 'From the moment you met this tosser to when you jumped out of his window. Make like you're in a Beirut basement.'

'Or the Château d'If.'

'Hey, Edmund Dantes got out of there in the end. And you know how? Because he *thought* about it.'

When she rang off, I tried what she suggested. At least it gave me an occupation.

Starting with Bruckmeyer's call shortly before Hall's. The arrival of the limo, picking up the girls. He had pressed only one digit on the phone. I remembered thinking at the time, he's got a call-girl agency pre-programmed like the rest of us might have our home, the bank. Where was that phone now? With the police, surely, since he left it in the car. That means they'll have traced Gloria, been told Emma and the other one, her 'specials', haven't been seen since.

That's supposing Hall had rung an agency. Suppose Bruck-meyer was Gloria, suppose she'd arranged the women – where's this leading?

Needing a fall guy, he picks me up, having already booked the whores, and we go to his house. Then what happened? Emma and I wake up in the morning, she says she has to be back in London, so I say I'll ring for a taxi. She says no, not yet, and works me over for twenty minutes.

It was all about timing. I go downstairs, she nips next door and lets Hall know and he contacts the men outside loading their guns with blanks and waiting for the word to start the charade. In they come, bang, bang, have me running for my life. We're back to *The Sting*. After I leave, Hall and the girls spit out the blood capsules and hug each other for a job well done. He pays them off and heads for the airport, while the police listen to a terrified writer's hysterical account of a mass murder. They drive round, find nothing and tell him to stop wasting their time. Later, when CBCI collapses, its coffers emptied by the missing director, they come back and order him to go over everything again, slowly. By which time, Hall is a needle in a worldwide haystack.

Except Andree is working on a rewritten scenario. She exchanges the blanks for real ammunition and the killers sprinkle the bodies around the Home Counties.

She waits for me to come home and calls, expecting an account of the massacre and how, mysteriously, the police found nothing. She'd probably explain it by saying Arnold was notorious for his practical jokes.

However, I hadn't gone to the law, so when she does ring, she only hears me say things were fine. She'd have been momentarily puzzled, and then realize I haven't reported it. I ask for Hall's home number and she gives it, knowing I expect to hear the bodies have been found by the housekeeper.

If this is what Wendy meant about the therapy of recall, it wasn't working. I didn't feel any better at all, especially when I remembered it took Dantes twenty years to figure a way out of the Château d'If.

Maxie had said she would talk to Richard. I rang both her phones but neither one was connected. The vacuum was driving me nuts. It was like in the early days, before *Assignment Berlin*, when Tim would tell me he had given a producer my name for a job and was waiting to hear. I'd sit by the phone all day long. If I needed a crap, I'd pull it as near to the lav as the restricted cord in those days would permit, then sit, holding pre-bunched toilet paper in case it rang in mid-strain. When it sometimes did, I'd fall sprawling, trousers around my ankles, to hear someone asking for Maxie.

I could not simply lie there thinking in circles. Like being stuck in traffic, I needed to move, to *do* something.

So I rang Richard at home. Before he picked up, I cut the call, programmed in 141 to prevent him tracing me and redialled. In *The Godfather*, Marlon had said trust no one.

'Hello?' A child answered.

'Er, is Mr Nixon there, please?' Who was this kid? Richard's children were grown up. There was a pause, then approaching feet.

'Hello?'

'Christine?'

'Yes, who is this?'

'It's Alan.' There was another pause. 'Alan Tate.'

The receiver clunked down and after more heel-tapping, Richard came on.

'Alan?'

'I'm sorry if I scared Christine,' I said, although her lack of any response had made me fume. After all these years, she acts like I've got leprosy.

'You didn't scare her. She was just surprised.'

'Did Maxie talk to you?'

'Yes.'

'Did she ask about what, er, what chances I had?'

'Yes.'

'Is there any reason you can't talk?'

'Christine's sister is here with her kids.'

He was giving me the bum's rush.

'What did you tell Maxie?'

'Why don't you ask her?'

'Her phone's off the hook.'

'Oh.' There followed a further hiatus. 'Where are you?'

'I'd rather not say.' Two can play at this game, you bastard.

'I understand.'

'Richard,' I said, making it clear I was getting exasperated by his evasions. 'Do I turn myself in? Yes or fucking no.'

I heard him breathe deeply. 'That's something only you can decide. If you feel you can determine your innocence by going to the police, then you should consider it. On the other hand, the longer you stay in hiding, the more difficult it'll be to argue your case. If you think circumstances are against you, then you might wish to—'

'Circumstances *against* me? You mean if I think I won't get away with it?'

'I did say it was not a good time to discuss this.'

'Richard,' I said, measuring my words quietly but really wanting to burst his eardrums with a shriek of rage, 'it may be a bad time for you, having company and all, but I'm currently wondering if I'll soon be working out the best way to hang myself with a prison blanket. All I want are a few words of advice. I'd like you to put your professional manner aside just for a second and talk to me as a friend.'

'What you want to know is,' he said, his tone remaining as steady as a spirit level, 'what are your chances if you give yourself up. '

'Yes.'

'Maxie said you became involved with this man Hall through a writing job. She says you went with him and some – some other people . . .' He muffled the speaker for a second and called out, 'I'll be right there,' before resuming, *sotto voce*: 'Whatever happened, the circumstantial evidence seems against you. The prosecution can't make a case on that alone, but you have to be aware it makes things difficult.'

'How difficult?'

'A man is murdered and you're seen running out of the house. Two weeks later, you report to the police. As I told Maxie, this is what you *should* do. Staying on the run only makes things harder for anyone to believe your side of the story. Alan, despite what you read, very few innocent people are convicted of murder. There's only one truth, so you can only tell it one way.'

'You're saying I should give myself up.'

'As your lawyer, I have to. Otherwise, I'm obstructing justice.'

'Fuck me, Richard, we're on the phone, not in the sodding Old Bailey.'

'Unless you have a reasonable chance of finding who set you up, continuing to hide serves no purpose at all. I will obviously represent you all the way.'

'I don't have a bloody clue where to find Andree Bruckmeyer.'

'I have to go now,' Richard said. And he went.

There wasn't much else he could have said. Thirty years' friendship notwithstanding, a lawyer can only give legal advice, and his was to give up. What grated was the way he put a family gathering before my problems. While I resumed the prone position, he doubtless went back to Snakes and Ladders. Damn, I forgot to ask if I'd get bail before such time as they were ready to charge me with murder. Maybe they didn't need to wait.

Thoughts of Oscar Wilde returned as the night dragged on and sleep kept its distance. Sitting in the Cadogan Hotel, pissed on hock and seltzer, his friends telling him to catch the ferry to France. Wilde refuses, seeking a glorious drama to enhance his life, a moment that would top anything he could produce on the stage. But real life was no script to be rewritten according to audience reactions. How would I fare inside? One thing I knew for certain, I would never be able to write 'The Ballad of Brixton Gaol'. I would never be able to write anything more creative than 'Help!' on the wall.

Eventually I fell asleep, waking a couple of times to ward off a swarm of hovering demons. At one point, I thought I'd give it one more chance and pinched my cheek to see if it could just remotely be a dream after all.

When the telephone buzzed, I jerked awake and squinted at the red numbers on the bedside alarm. It was almost ten.

With the heavy curtains closed, it still seemed the middle of the night.

'How're we doing?'

'Wendy.'

'Just checking in. What's new?'

'I've decided to give myself up. I spent all night trying to find one thing I had going for me,' I said. 'Came up with zilch.'

'You want any money?'

'What for?'

'Run off some place. Where did Lord Lucan go?'

'He had influential friends. All I can do is tell the truth and hope for the best.'

'I guess so.'

'You don't think it's a good idea.'

'All I know is, I couldn't spend one night in a jail.' I heard the shiver in her voice.

'I'll be all right,' I said without conviction.

'Let's have lunch first,' she suggested. 'Somewhere nice. We'll get arseholed.'

'On hock and seltzer.'

'On *what?*'

'Sounds like a good idea.'

'I'll get a table at Bibendum. One o'clock.'

'See you there.'

I showered, ate breakfast in the room, put on my toff's gear like a matador dressing for the corrida, and went out.

London was warm, the skies clear, as an Indian summer gave a final encore. I wandered down to Piccadilly Circus and cut through Soho to the Groucho. I debated going in. Wilde had been on my mind during the night and I, too, wanted to produce a last flourish. Let everyone see the famous fugitive before they picked up the *Evening Standard* and read I had surrendered. Putting talent into my work, but genius into my life.

How long would my fellow members talk about me? There's a Tony Hancock sketch where he imagines himself dying. What would his mates say down the pub? "Hear about old Hancock? Gone and snuffed it." "Go on, he never did, well well – right, 301 is it, middle for diddle, off you go, Charlie." He sums up his epitaph as "He came, he went, with nothing in between." When he really did decide to kill himself in some godforsaken Australian hotel, I wonder if he reprised the routine.

By now, I was equating arrest with death. What would I miss? Cricket, wine, sex, the first breath of spring, the sweet melancholy of autumn. I won't be around to see the children graduate, fall in love, watch them edge along the pockmarked road to marriage and parenthood. Won't be there to tender advice and wait for them to ignore every word.

My world will shrink to an overcrowded cell with nothing to think of but the terror of the next moment, the fear of mindless violence, the stink of men. Looking forward only to a monthly visit from Richard, who'll feel bound to say the appeal stands a good chance, and I'll pretend to believe him while planning to choke myself to death on toilet paper.

Since I had never been inside a prison, all I had to go on were movies. *The Criminal, Birdman of Alcatraz, The Shawshank Redemption*: brutality, pathos and buggery. Oh, sure, there was that TV series *Porridge* to make it all sound a bit of a lark, but I didn't count on sharing with the likes of Ronnie Barker.

Since this was my last day of freedom, I decided against

the Wildean route in the Groucho and instead set off to walk all the way to the restaurant, which lay across Hyde Park in South Kensington. I would store up the memory of each step to dwell on later, as Wendy had said, when I was banged up in the equivalent of the Beirut basement.

I returned to Piccadilly and walked past BAFTA and Fortnum's towards Green Park. At the Ritz, I paused to let an enthusiastic doorman march across to a slowing Bentley Continental. The car was a beauty and I lingered, curious to see who would come out. The commissionaire opened a rear door, saluting, and a middle-aged man emerged before turning to offer a hand.

He pulled out a young woman. As she straightened, her long dark hair fell away from her face. While a bellboy hurried out pulling a luggage trolley, the couple entered the hotel. I made sure by studying her profile until she disappeared, but there was no mistake.

It was Emma.

DATE: OCTOBER 18
FAX TO: ELAINE MORGENSTERN, SAVOY HOTEL, LONDON
FROM: MORT DELANNOY, MOVIELINE INTERNATIONAL,
            LOS ANGELES

Dear Elaine,

As I told you on the phone, everyone has shown great enthusement over your concept. We have given it a working title of *Losing the Plot*. Initial response from Warner's and Fox is positive but you may want to note what was said in terms of sales potential. They see it more as *The Firm* (the Grisham/Cruise movie) meets *Terminator Two* than Rick Moranis plays *The Wizard of Oz*. Latest research shows morons are still beefy box office particularly with the teenage market, who see them as role models, but video sales don't exploit the re-view market. People only see Keanu Reeves once.

What you are pitching is the idiot-in-a-box scenario. How does he get out? Who do we root for, the good guys or the bad? Warner's suggested Tate is Jim Carrey and we go for SFX like *The Mask*. Fox were keener on Whoopi Goldberg, using spiritualism like in *Ghost*. Either way you have to lick the problem that the hero is a klutz, which means either upgrading his IQ if he is to star, or making him a child molester so the sympathy's with the cops. Get Morgan Freeman on his case. Warner's said Denzil Washington is looking for material, so maybe Denzil is framed by white supremacists. We could go any which way. Meanwhile, look into this guy Tate's background. Does he have a wife, a family? Maybe talk to his agent again and say we'll pay the rest of his *Unspeakable Behavior* deal if he can come up with usable information.

On *Anna Karenina*, I looked into The Plaza and find

197

it opened in 1889, which makes it too late. Why not have Anna stay with the Vanderbilts? They had mansions all over Fifth Avenue, and with their foreign name, it makes sense they might have known Russians. The main thing with these historical movies is to make them accessible to a modern audience, so why not have the writers work up a scene where Anna makes friends with one of the Vanderbilt girls and they end up sharing a bed. You know, innocent girls stuff that goes a bit far, sexually. So when Anna goes back to Moscow she knows where to find her clitoris. We thought it would make a change to have Americans teach Europeans a thing or two instead of it always being the other way round. I mean, there were thousands of Vanderbilts, so they must have screwed like rabbits, right?

We are still aiming at a PG rating, so tell the writers not to get too French and have the girls losing their bracelets.

Sorry to hear you can't get sanitary food in England. I'll Fedex a month's supply of tofu.

Everyone here sends love and kisses.

MORT

They were met in the hall by a manager who shook the man's hand warmly and said, 'A pleasure to see you again, sir.' When Emma was introduced, he bobbed his head.

I sidled through the doors and watched them bathe in the VIP treatment that continued all the way to the lifts, omitting the card-swiping and registration rituals. Two large suitcases came in carried by a bellboy.

It was now or never to test Magritte's theory. I walked briskly to the lifts and when one arrived, followed them in.

Emma took her companion's hand and leaned against him

198

as she had once leaned against me. No one even glanced in my direction.

'Are you hungry?' the man asked and she snuggled into his chest.

'You know me, I was born hungry,' she giggled.

'Then we'll have to do something about that,' he replied, putting his arm round her when the doors opened.

I waited for the bellboy to ease out the cases, by which time Emma and the men were halfway down the corridor. When they turned a corner I broke into a trot to see them waiting by a door which the manager was unlocking. As they moved inside, I hurried on past and noted the number: 367.

My knowledge of luxury London hotels had been gained down the years through meeting Hollywood hucksters. The Ritz was a favourite with them and I was certain I had once been in 367 talking about a Sidney Sheldon. As I skimmed past, I glanced inside, but all I saw was a vast array of flowers on a sideboard next to a silver champagne bucket.

When the bellboy emerged, he was holding a tenner. The manager backed into the hallway, wished them a pleasant stay, and closed the door.

My head had not stopped thumping since the moment I had recognized Emma.

The last time I had seen her, she was being flung backwards from a bullet in the chest. If the shooter had missed, he had meant to. More likely he used a blank. But even blanks can wound at close range, so he must have aimed off.

Vertigo. She was Kim Novak, and I was a catatonic James Stewart, the required murder witness. Andree Bruckmeyer was not cinematically illiterate after all. What had happened in that film? Stewart only *thought* she was the woman who'd

199

led him to the belltower, where she had supposedly fallen to her death. When he realizes it *is* her, he has to discover who did die and why.

No help there. Emma was the same woman who'd screwed me in the limo and later at the house. So she must have rehearsed her death scene in advance. She was part of Bruck-meyer's plot. The one in which only Hall had not been told of the pink pages which had him really killed instead of pretend. He was Cavaradossi. Scarpia falsely promises Tosca that if she puts out for him, he'll make sure the firing squad uses blanks on her lover at his execution. Meanwhile Hall believed he was Alec Guinness in *The Captain's Paradise*, bribing the executioners to shoot the officer in charge.

What are you *doing*? In suite 367 is somebody who framed you for murder, and all you can do is think of what films it reminds you of. Behaving like someone only able to relate to the world by parading his Trivial Pursuit movie know-ledge. Who can't give a view on the Middle East problem, but if you want to know who did Bette Davis's hair in *Now, Voyager*, look no further.

For the fiftieth time, I reflexed a glance at a bare wrist, then asked the hall porter the time. Half-past one.

Christ! Wendy.

'Hello, you have a table for a Miz Phillips. Is she still there?'

'Are you the friend she's waiting for?'

'Yes.'

'She was getting worried about you.'

'Not pissed off?'

'I think she ought to explain her precise state of mind. Hang on a sec—'

'Are you OK?'

'I'm sorry.'

'I told you never to say sorry. Where are you?'

She said she'd be over right away. She gave the impression of enjoying herself. Make-up artists may be treated better than writers, but the job satisfaction isn't what you'd call consuming. Once you've put the slap on the actors, there isn't much else to do except touch it up every so often while they complain about the lines, the lights and the director. Wendy was someone who actually *envied* the writer, seeing them as the creator without whom no one would be crawling out of bed at 5 a.m. to go to work.

For a month or two, it is true we're pampered. When you start the script, producers are constantly calling, inviting you to lunch or LA: "The weather's great out here, come and get a tan." Meaning, come where we can keep an eye on what you're doing. You want a research trip, no problem. The film business must be the only one in the world where, if you say you want to gather local colour in South America, you're told fine, three days should be enough. Actually, with speedboats and helicopters, it often is. While you're working on the first draft, you're given carte blanche. What do you need? A bigger PC, food, girls, boys, coke? Just as long as you deliver on time.

Once you do, the party's over. Rewrite demands are abrupt, verging on hostile. After that, silence. You are the classic fuckee. They've had their way, they don't call, they don't write. No premiere tickets, no mention in the publicity, and when the film comes out, three other names have somehow become attached to yours on the writer's credits.

There is an upside to this, however. If, usually *when*, the movie fails, the actors, the director and the producers may have trouble finding new work, but nobody can remember who wrote the turkey. On the whole, I prefer to miss the premiere, and if anyone does notice my name, to hide behind the usual excuse that every line was rewritten by somebody else. Thus, I don't go down with the rest of the ship and have the chance to repeat the experience all over again. Michelangelo and Mozart would have agreed that the main object of producing art is to be paid. Dr Johnson said only fools write for any other reason than money, and he wrote a whole fucking *dictionary*.

I apologize, but I get worked up when I think how poorly creative people are treated. We have to make a living, like anyone else. All right, some of us might get six hundred thousand dollars a week to put a few jokes into *Waterworld*, but it often means rising before eight and plagiarizing other scripts until sometimes way beyond six in the evening. No one said it would be easy. There are no free lunches in Hollywood.

'So fill me in,' Wendy said, walking me through to the Ritz bar. 'I'm a bit pissed since I felt obliged to finish the bottle I ordered in Bibendum.'

We ordered sandwiches and coffee and I told her about Emma.

'You're absolutely positive it was her? All cats look alike in the dark.'

'It's her.'

'You never forget the lips, right?' she grinned. I hadn't detailed the goings-on in the limousine but she was aware the vagina is the last orifice whores are required to bring into play.

'Who's she with?'

'A wealthy john with a Bentley Continental.'

'Any ideas?'

202

'I don't suppose this reminds you of a film.'

'*Vertigo*,' Wendy replied. 'With one difference.'

'What?'

'Kim Novak couldn't get rid of James Stewart by calling the cops. This one can. And will.'

'She knows I'd tell them she was involved,' I pointed out.

'In what?'

'Killing Hall.'

'She wasn't the one jumping through windows. All she did was get paid to blow off a couple of bozos. After she finishes, one of them, Alan "call me John Wayne" Tate takes out a gun and shoots the other. That's the story I'd tell, if I were her. And why should anyone disbelieve it?'

'So it's not *Vertigo*.'

'No. It's something called real life. There's no good-guy-always-wins here. Like Peter Finch said in *Network*, in the real world Kojak doesn't always get the villain.' She noticed my face obeying the laws of gravity and smiled. 'Look on the bright side, sugar. You've got a damn sight more going for you than when you woke up this morning. I assume you've changed your mind about surrendering.'

'Yes.'

'Good. You have a lead. Don't waste it.'

'I'll try not to.'

'Tell me how you reckon this Emma can improve your situation.'

'She must have been paid a fortune to go along with murder.'

'If she knew it was on the agenda when she got the job.'

'She can be leaned on,' I said. Wendy gulped her coffee.

'In what way?'

'Look,' I said, lowering my voice when the barman arrived

with the sandwiches. 'This girl is top of her profession. By appointment to Her Majesty. No handjobs behind the bike sheds for her.'

'Do I detect some kind of point emerging?'

'But one thing she's not is street smart. I'm guessing she's from a good family who don't know she's on the game. And they'd all have a mass coronary if they found out.'

'Because she's called Emma and speaks naicely, you assume she must have a duke for a dad?'

'I'm saying it's one way to go.' Her expression was drawing wind from my sails. 'Jesus, Wendy, what other way is there?' She fiddled with a spoon and looked at me closely, adding a smile. 'What?'

'I'll bet you've never treated a woman badly in your whole life,' she said.

'Maxie.'

'Oh, you beat her up?'

'No, of course I didn't.'

'Alan,' she went on, her voice softening to a tone you normally hear only in intensive care, 'I'm not trying to pry, but would it be true to say you spent a large part of your youth losing women you fancied to other fellows?'

'I had my share of failures, I'm not ashamed to admit it. Why?'

'And did these women eventually come back complaining how awful their lovers were? How they'd been stood up, ignored, knocked about, generally treated like shit?'

'Sometimes.'

'And did you cook them meals, listen to their problems all night and let them sleep in your spare room?'

'Do I detect a point emerging here?'

'And as soon as they were back on their feet, they gave

you a hug, said you were their bestest friend in the world, then went off to find another sadist. The point is, you poor sod, you're a good man and, as every woman knows, good men finish last. They never get served in a crowded pub, and they can't get a taxi in the rain.' I had to glance in the bar mirror to boost my morale. At least I still *looked* like a captain of industry.

'So, with this little scrubber,' she continued, sharpening her tone, 'the one who was paid to fuck you over in more ways than one, this bitch who has the power to send you away for ever, you think if you ask her nicely, she'll burst into tears, say she's thoroughly ashamed of herself and *confess*? Is that *all* you've learned about women?'

'What would you do?'

'I'd find out where she lives. Then I'd force my way in and punch her hard, below her belly button. While she's gasping for breath, I'd take a blade and hold it on her face and tell her that without her looks, she's sewage. I'd remind her no one is going to pay five hundred an hour to be serviced by a hooker who's missing a nose. And since it's unlikely she can fall back on a Ph.D. in nuclear physics, her options for alternative work are not several.'

I listened, wondering how much any of us know about one another. While she was speaking, she appeared to be enjoying her violent images. You know how when someone cuts you up on the road, you spend a few minutes fantasizing about forcing him over a cliff? That's how she was amusing herself.

'I get the drift.'

'But could *you* do it?' she demanded, treating the question more as a philosophical dilemma than a test of my resolve.

I've written a dozen sadistic villains and itemized their actions in stark detail. But to do it for *real* . . .

'If I had to.'

'Do you believe in capital punishment?' She picked the smoked salmon out of her sandwich and chewed on the pieces.

'No.'

'A man breaks into your house, rapes and kills your wife. What do you think should happen to him?' I hesitated and she told me: 'You'd want him handled by an Elizabethan executioner. The ones who were trained to disembowel a victim and show him his entrails while he was still alive. You'd personally like to tie him above sharpened bamboo and watch while the wood grew and pierced his scrotum. You'd—'

'Right.'

'Personalize any moral problem and you revert to savagery in a blink,' Wendy said. 'Liberal jurists make laws with their heads. The best ones have no wives, no lovers, no children to distract them. So, when we have a gorgeous young woman, on the threshold of life, who probably said you made her come like no one else . . .'

I couldn't help it, I reacted. 'Ah, I see she did. Then carving Donald Duck on her tits is out of the question.'

'I can't imagine doing it.'

'Close your eyes. You have a son, right?'

'Yes.'

'Your boy is Arnold Hall. This whore leads him into an ambush and stands aside while two men blow his brains out. Hold that thought. Hold it in your mind. Now tell me again what you couldn't do.'

I opened my eyes and saw she was smiling. 'Back to

206

the jungle, sugar,' she said, sliding off the stool and gathering her shoulder bag. 'Why do you think we've survived a million years? Because we knew how to fight dirty. Come on.'

We returned to the foyer where she asked directions to the internal phones.

'What is the first thing we need to know?'

'Where she lives.'

'And how do we do that?'

'Follow her.'

'Hey, you're *good*.'

'Cut it out, Wendy.'

'What do we do when we get a new job?' she asked, speaking like a nursery school teacher. 'When we need to understand the people we're writing about?'

'Research.'

'Who she's with, and how long he's staying. Unless you plan on camping out here.'

'The hotel isn't about to tell us.'

She pointed to the house phone: 'You know his room number.'

She watched me bite the inside of my cheek. It was a lifetime habit, sparked by nervous thoughts. People move their seat on a bus when they catch sight of my facial contortions. I knew what she wanted me to do, but this sort of stuff had never come naturally. When I was an undergraduate, a friend was able to spend hours on the phone, keeping up an outrageous pretence with ease, and I envied his inventiveness. He once rang me, pretending to be the VD clinician he knew I had been seeing about a dose of non-specific urethritis. He said my latest test had shown some surprising results. For instance, it was clear I had recently engaged in sexual relations with a rabbit: 'We've never seen the myxomatosis virus in the human system before, Mr Tate . . .'

I'd call someone with a broken leg and get as far as 'This is the Victor Sylvester School of Ballroom Dancing and I'm pleased to announce you have won six free lessons,' before dissolving into giggles.

'Just remember, it's your life in the balance,' Wendy was saying.

I asked for 367, mentally rehearsing: Good day, sir, sorry to bother you, this is reception. I was just checking how long we'll be having the pleasure of your company. May I just confirm, could I, er, confirm how you spell your name? Jesus, suppose it's Smith.

The operator said there was no reply. Of course, she said she was hungry. They were at lunch. I replaced the phone with relief.

'OK, what now?'

When I shrugged, Wendy said, 'In your stories, the gumshoe would sweet-talk a chambermaid into giving him the key and he'd search the room. In a suitcase, he'd find a book of matches with a telephone number written on the flap, which would amazingly turn out to be her home number . . .'

'Leave off.'

We sat in chairs with a view of the front entrance.

'The chances are she won't recognize you.'

'She didn't in the lift.'

'What would you have done if she had?'

'I – don't know.'

'You would have put on a thick foreign accent and told her charmingly that unfortunately zehr vass somm mistek.'

'Right.'

208

'If I recall correctly,' she continued after a while, 'men like to put it in and wiggle it about in the afternoons. So they'll come back from lunch and spend an hour or so playing hunt the salami. After which, he'll have a nap while she goes shopping.'

Something said she wasn't getting this from old films. 'You reckon?'

'Just a guess. So we don't need to go traipsing around after her. What is important is to find out when sugar pops leaves and she goes back to her drum.'

Drum. I hadn't heard that since *The Sweeney*. Wendy had worked a lot on 1970s television series and picked up the lingo. Why a flat became known as a drum was anybody's guess. Probably coined by a writer one night in the bath and foisted on the public as authentic villain chat. I wrote several episodes for a series about London conmen where the main character was forever coming up with elaborate rhyming slang: "Give me a gin and Philharmonic, squire," or calling his wife Her Indoors. People wrote in to say they remembered their grandfathers saying these things when, in truth, the series creator privately admitted making them all up. Fiction soon becomes subsumed into truth once it passes through a TV screen as drama. It affects actors as well. Men playing tough guys get beat up in bars. Louise Brooks said the trouble with Humphrey Bogart was that, after eleven at night, he thought he was Humphrey Bogart.

I once dramatized the life of an Englishwoman who lived in France during the Nazi war. At the same time, a journalist was researching her biography. He used to pass over tips, saying don't bother to ask about her late husband. Whenever he mentioned his name, she'd change the subject, saying Gaston didn't do anything in the Occupation. Well, you can't have a series without a romantic hero, so I invented all kinds of Scarlet Pimpernel exploits for him; nipping in and out of Germany, helping Jews escape, shoot-outs at Swiss borders and so on. We were obliged to send the scripts to her for approval and she raised no objections.

Some time later, the journalist asked what I had done to her. He said having written off her husband as best left unmentioned, he was now hearing how Gaston risked his life every day. He said it was clear she believed this to be true. The woman was sharp, intelligent, and even in her seventies ran a large business. But she'd read my scripts and accepted my inventions as fact. When truth conflicts with legend, John Ford said, print the legend.

'I'll find out,' I said. 'Leave it to me.'

We sat there like 'tecs in a dime novel hiding behind newspapers until shortly after three o'clock when the pair returned. Faces flushed, hands entwined, they chuckled their way to the lift. A receptionist handed the man a note which he stuffed away unread.

'You're in luck,' Wendy said, standing. 'They've been at the Bolly. He'll be less cautious.'

I have a condition called ectopia. The heart suddenly starts to syncopate. The doctors say it's a muscle thing, nothing to worry about, but when it first started, I thought I had only weeks left. Usually, it's brought on by excitement and the familiar uneven rhythm began as we crossed to the phones.

'367, please.'

'Don't say sorry and keep it short,' Wendy said.

'Yes?'

'Reception here, sir.'

'Yes?'

210

'Just verifying when you'll be leaving us. I seem to have lost—'

'Tomorrow.' His voice dropped to a barely audible whisper and he hung up quickly.

'He's leaving tomorrow.'

'What time?' She stopped me calling again by taking the phone: 'Don't get over-confident.'

She asked for the front desk and said, 'I have a package for suite 367 and I want to make sure it reaches the party before he leaves tomorrow . . . noon? Thank you.'

'You didn't learn all this painting actors,' I said and she grinned mysteriously.

'A girl has to make a living the best way she can.'

What Emma would or wouldn't be able to do to help me wasn't discussed, but we both knew she was a slender thread. Was any professional criminal going to confide in a prostitute hired for a walk-on part in a multi-million-pound scam? "Here's my address in case you ever want to do lunch . . ."

Wendy was pleased we at least had a break and so was I, especially coming as it did, on the way to the scaffold. If nothing else, I could march Emma to the company chauffeur. He must have noticed what went on behind him as he drove to Sonning. Drivers never miss a trick. When they take you to a film location, they'll list precisely and accurately who's banging whom. One told me couplings became typecast during a shoot: 'The head stuntman always has it off with the hairdresser, the focus puller shags the continuity girl – it's all about status.'

The more I thought about it, the more the limo driver became my lifeline. He could verify it was Hall who rang *me*. If I'd been planning to kill him, would I have left it to a million-to-one chance he would ask me out for a drink?

'Nothing's gonna happen till tomorrow, sugarlump,' Wendy said, heading for the entrance. 'I have stuff to do.'

'How's *Anna Karenina*?'

'Chaos. They ordered five tons of fake snow for the troika sequences, then discovered there wasn't a troika to be had this side of Warsaw, so the director now wants them on bikes. He says it's what people remember most about *Butch Cassidy*. Somebody as we speak is writing a song called "Snowdrops Keep Falling on my Head". I *adore* Americans. Their can-do thing is truly inspirational.'

'When do they start shooting?'

'Why, want some rewrite work?'

'I never read *Anna Karenina*.'

'Nor's anyone. The writers ran the Garbo movie to get the plot,' she said as she kissed my cheek and left.

I could fall in love with someone like Wendy. Until now, I never realized friends really did rally round when you hit trouble. I'd always been sceptical when they said things like "If there's anything I can do, anything at *all* . . ." I wondered how they would react if you said, "Well, until I get sorted out, I'd be grateful if you'd look after my children, pay their school fees, let me stay a few months, use your car and oh, twenty grand wouldn't come amiss."

But Wendy was special. I hadn't seen her in ten years and anyway, our paths had only crossed a few times. Anyone ringing me on that basis would have me struggling to end the call, terrified they wanted money.

What she said about not pulling punches induced a queasy doubt. What if it came to nose-slicing? Think Lloyd. Emma caused my own son to be mutilated, maimed, killed. Now how do you feel?

It still didn't work. There would come the moment when

212

you said to yourself, I am now deliberately going to hurt this person. Was I capable?

I hovered about the Ritz for a while, mainly because there was nothing else to do. I realized I was becoming obsessed with seeing Emma again. Wendy said they would fuck for a while, but I didn't want to miss them coming out. I read a paper, wandered round the hotel shops, ambled about the foyers, looking every inch a luxury hotel lizard.

When she did appear, she passed by only a couple of yards away, stopping at the hall porter to ask whether some tickets had arrived. He checked and shook his head, promising to chase them up, and she went out.

Ignoring Wendy's caution about unnecessary surveillance, I followed her. The commissionaire asked if she needed a cab but she declined and crossed the road, nipping in and out of the traffic, raising a couple of laddish honks. I kept pace on the other side as she headed towards Piccadilly Circus. I guessed her sights were on Old Bond Street and glowed when she proved me correct and went into Ferragamo. I watched through the window as she spoke to an assistant who showed her to a seat and went away, returning with several shoe boxes. She tried on a couple of pairs, walked up and down a few times, but came out without buying.

Next stop was Tiffany across the road. Growing more confident, I went inside and followed her to the first floor where she circled the displays, calling someone's attention to a silver money clip. While the assistant answered her questions, I edged along until I was standing behind her. The proximity sent a frisson of fear down my back. If she turned, she would be looking right into my face. Would she remember? Of all the tricks in all the joints in all the world, she has to walk into the one she recognizes. I forced myself to stay there while she changed her mind about the clip and asked to see a cigarette lighter. Was she buying her john a *present*?

'May I help you?' a voice said and I turned. So did Emma, but all she saw was my back.

'Zank you, but I am jost, how do you say – broosing?'

'Browsing,' the assistant smiled and moved on. Encouraged by my success, I stepped up to the counter alongside Emma and said in my best Conrad Veidt voice:

'Pliss, may I see . . .' and pointed to the clip, while Emma was flicking the lighter wheel and asking:

'Do you have one in gold?'

'I'm afraid not, madam.' She gave it back and walked away. I dickered a moment with the clasp then put it down.

She toured the more expensive displays downstairs before returning to the street. When I came out, she was heading towards Regent Street. The sequence in Tiffany had left me breathless. I had stood close enough to smell her hair. I'd handled an item she had just put down, and she hadn't sussed me. What purpose all this had served, apart from boosting my confidence, I couldn't say. But I had flirted with danger. I was no longer behaving like a fugitive. In fact, for the last few hours, I'd forgotten I was one. As we moved through the fashionable Mayfair thoroughfares, I felt I was filling out my role. Head up, look at the policeman straight in the eye. Bogey never skulked in *The Big Sleep*.

She went over Regent Street into Soho. I tagged behind, keeping her bright red belt in view. She went inside a shop that catered exclusively for left-handed people. Golf clubs, scissors and stuff. The place was too small to reprise the Tiffany two-step, so I waited up the road where the peep shows began.

'Full frontal pussy inside,' a lad called out. When I told him I was a dog man myself, he didn't laugh.

She took some time and when she emerged, she was carrying a gift-wrapped box. So the Bentley Continental was a southpaw. As she walked away, juggling the present and her purse, a slip of paper fluttered unseen to the pavement as she walked away.

It was a credit card receipt made out for £17.50 and signed M. Burnside.

Now she was vanishing in the early rush hour crowds. I put on some speed and followed her all the way back to the Ritz.

M. Burnside. Maybe Wendy knew how to gouge an address from a name and a credit card number.

I filed the receipt idea away. I'd known for some time I needed to replace the old matchbook clue device since almost everyone had stopped smoking.

Emma, or M. as she now became, approached the hall porter who gave her an envelope and his wishes to enjoy the show. I saw her take out two tickets before the lift devoured her.

What now? Go back to my own hotel? The adrenaline was flowing too fast for that. I was on a roll. In a single day, I had found not only the girl who played a star part in my nightmare, but her real name. Also, Watson, it surely did not evade your notice that her companion was left-handed.

There was more. He was well known at the Ritz, receiving the kind of attention usually reserved for Hollywood royalty. M. was clearly his regular partner, whom he took to lunch and the theatre, not the usual perks for a hooker. They were relaxed with each other, although, as I had discovered, M.

215

could put the Pope at ease. What with this avalanche of useful information flowing into me, I was not in the mood for a lamb cutlet and an evening of CNN describing the weather in Texas.

It was five o'clock. West End theatre curtains rose at eight. Would they eat first? Not after their long lunch. On the other hand, apart from a salami roll, I'd had nothing since breakfast. A distant chink of crockery indicated tea was being served along the hall. I chose a table that gave a view of the main doors and ordered the full monty: lapsang souchong, crustless sandwiches, cream cakes and preserves. Nearby were two elderly Americans indulging in an act they would never dream of back home: filling themselves with killer cholesterol two hours before dinner.

Elsewhere, professional women were giving power teas. The hand that rocks the teapot calls the tune. Instead of smiling grimly at lunch while the waiters handed their male guests the wine list and the bill, here they were in command, and the men waited like boys around nanny as she asked for information on percentages and minimizing below-the-line overheads.

An hour later, my bladder was bursting from a gallon of lapsang. I paid and went to the lavatories. When I came out, M. and her john were disappearing through the Arlington Street side exit, where the Bentley was waiting. A doorman closed them inside, leaving me with the embarrassing prospect of having to say to a taxi driver the most overused words in the history of the cinema: follow that car.

That was assuming a taxi could be winkled out of the rush hour as easily as Rock Hudson managed in his Doris Day comedies. The Continental turned into Piccadilly towards

216

Hyde Park, while I panicked on the kerb. The doorman saw me and said, 'If you aren't going far, sir, you'll do better to walk. They've closed the underpass.'

A traffic subway ran under Hyde Park Corner and when the police closed it off, usually because of some bomb scare, the whole area ground to a halt. Like now. I saw the roof of the Bentley marooned, going nowhere, with blue lights flashing ahead and cars trying to U-turn. M. was looking through the rear window and the driver was making helpless gestures behind the wheel.

Then his passengers got out. I turned and bought a paper beside Green Park tube station and when they passed, the man was saying, '—leave it till next time, darling—'

They strolled back past the hotel and on towards the Circus. She led him inside the Criterion restaurant, where she pointed at the decor in the rear section, implying he hadn't been there since it was changed some years ago. They sat in the front area and ordered drinks while I remained outside. There had to come a time, I decided, when M. would realize that everywhere she went, there always seemed to be some bloke in a pinstripe and curly brim trilby hanging about. Wendy's warning had been not to overdo the surveillance thing because you might blow it, and this tart is your only lifeline.

While I waited, I constructed a Sherlockian profile of her friend. About fifty, expensive suit, immaculate shirt, quiet tie. The Continental clued in his status. Rolls-Royces were bought mostly by Arabs, who painted them sky blue and gold-plated the radiator mascot. Mercedes meant Croydon carpet manufacturers, Jags and Daimlers dull chairmen, while Porsches carried City hucksters.

A Bentley said serious old money. Especially his, an E

217

registration from the sixties. (KHJ 508E, should you be wondering if I'd made a note of it.)

What kind of man comes occasionally to London, bringing two large suitcases to stay only one night, and hires the same call-girl? When he passed me at Green Park, he sounded at ease, unlike the clipped, nervous whisper he'd used on the phone. It was the voice of a well-educated Englishman who didn't need to put on airs.

His complexion gave the impression it was regularly exposed to foreign climates; nothing gaudy, no George Hamilton sheen. What else had Wendy described when she spoke of her ideal man? Long, manicured fingers. Hadn't noticed, but let's assume they aren't miner's hands. Expression dissolute when required? Employing top-price whores answered that one.

While I loafed around Eros, I found I was coming to like the man. If I had his bank account, I would probably go the same route. I wondered if M. was planning to have him murdered too.

They stayed until almost half-past seven and I tagged behind them as they ambled through the crowds up Shaftesbury Avenue. So they weren't seeing *Phantom of the Opera* in the Haymarket, thank God. I was relieved since, not wanting to hang about the street until they came out, I had decided to see their show, and apart from not being a founder member of the Lloyd Webber fan club, I was certain *Phantom* would have had the usual round-the-block queue for returns.

They crossed into Chinatown and weaved through to Charing Cross Road. They must be going to the opera at the ENO. I hoped for their sakes it wasn't *La Traviata*. Tarts dying of consumption might be a bit hard for these lovebirds to swallow. A friend told me about having to console his

218

grief-stricken grandmother, whose beloved husband had suddenly dropped dead while they were staying in a hotel. Desperate to find something to stem her tears, he turned on the television. *Fawlty Towers* was showing. The episode where Basil has to sneak a corpse out of one of the rooms.

But they didn't head for the Coliseum. They walked instead into Great Newport Street and stopped at the Arts Theatre Club. A poster was advertising a limited season by the Berliner Ensemble of Schiller's *Mary Stuart*. Three hours of cod English history in German. And guess what, there were a few tickets still available.

Why was I doing this? They'd still be at the Ritz tomorrow morning. They weren't about to run off to Gretna Green, if eloping couples still did that. Why not go back to my room and get a good night's rest?

The question still hadn't been answered by the time I took my seat four rows behind them amid a mostly German-speaking audience.

Ninety minutes is long enough to resolve a whole slew of private doubts, and by the interval I knew why I was sitting here, chuckling along with the rest when an occasional joke surfaced in what sounded like an interminable frosty dialogue between two women, Elizabeth Tudor and Mary, Queen of Scots. I was here because I'd become terrified of being alone. To be alone meant brooding on how hopeless the situation remained. The entire nation was looking for me, a murder suspect, and here I was thrilled to bits that I had run into a woman who could affirm my innocence, but by doing so, would incriminate herself. Wendy might have waxed lyrical about torture, but I knew, if I thought about it in the silence of a hotel room, there was more likelihood of a woman becoming American president than of M. turning herself in because I had once made her a plate of snacks and asked for her hand in marriage.

They stayed in their seats at half-time talking animatedly. Occasionally glancing across while the first act dragged on, I noticed they were rapt in attention, catching every nuance of the script. At one point, M. clapped when one of the women said something that had my neighbours drawing in their breath. They obviously weren't sharing my thoughts, which revolved around why Schiller chose these two women to make a play. They never met in real life. There had been a spate of dramas a few years ago in which playwrights had projected ideas via unlikely partners. Marilyn Monroe and Einstein, Dali and Freud. Some worked, others collapsed under their own pretensions. Maybe Schiller started it all with these two. The German tongue, however, is suited to anger, and the performers kept their audience, minus one, in complete thrall.

Then, halfway through the second act, a thought suddenly intruded that snatched my attention from the despair I was trying to keep at bay. It must have been prompted by the bludgeoning effect of the language, but I suddenly wondered whether they and the last person I had heard speaking it were acquainted. I wondered if they knew Andree Bruckmeyer. I even began to wonder if she was in the audience.

The curtain finally dropped and the actresses took their bows before a reception that emulated a Nuremberg rally. People stood, American-style, clapping and calling and glaring down at me for staying in my seat. Eventually exhausted, the audience shuffled to the exits. I stayed in the middle, head down in case Andree was there. I hadn't been conceited enough to think M. would recall one face among so many clients, but I was pretty certain Bruckmeyer wouldn't forget the man she cultivated to play the biggest fall guy since Adam.

When they emptied into the street, I was loitering across the road in a queue waiting for a minicab service. They were talking, gesticulating, clearly still fired up by what they had seen. Surely no one could be *that* impressed by Schiller unless their first language was German. I was competent in French, but an evening at the Comédie Française didn't exactly leave me holding my ribs. They stood by the doors a few minutes as the last of the audience came out and dispersed, but no Andree showed. Then M. linked her arm through his and they strolled off, still talking up a storm. I trailed them along Charing Cross Road, into Shaftesbury Avenue, then across to Dean Street. The whole day had been like something out of Chandler and by now I was comfortable in the gumshoe role, pausing when they did, using shop windows and bus stop timetables.

Until, after crossing Old Compton Street, they went into the one place, apart from ladies' lavatories and Ascot Royal Enclosure, where I was unable to follow.

They went into the Groucho.

DATE: OCTOBER 19

FAX TO: MORT DELANNOY, MOVIELINE INTERNATIONAL,
           LOS ANGELES

FROM: ELAINE MORGENSTERN, C/O SAVOY HOTEL,
           LONDON

Dear Mort,

Things are stuck here. You may have already heard
about the great snow fiasco. Five tons of crystals were
dumped at Pinewood when one of our people – a Brit, of
course – signed for it on behalf of Anna K Productions
pleading ignorance of the decision to cancel the
order after the troika no show. Dealing with Brits is
like talking to mentally challenged farmboys. I used
to think they were so polite. All that please and
thanks and do you mind awfullys, but now I found this
is their way of putting you down. When they want to
insult you, they pay a compliment. 'Well done' means
'I never expected someone from Hollywood to know that
two plus two equals four.' 'How brave' means you're
a complete asshole and 'clever you' says you're a cretin. If you tell someone: 'I was reading some Dosto-
evsky the other day,' they say 'well done, how brave,
what a clever person you are.' Meaning absolutely the
opposite. They have towns called Maidenhead, would
you believe!!! And Slough. It's my guess all the scene
shifters come from Slough.

Anyway, we've nixed the troika and got some bikes,
which research swears were used in the 1860s. Kevin
has been on to Chris de Burgh's people to get him to
write a 'Lady in Red' type song suitable for pedalling
Russians. We wanted it to be spring, but now we're
stuck with the fucking crystals and have to use them.
Kevin's talking about having Anna bike around a snowy

222

Tsarist Russia with serfs and shots of grinding poverty, while we see her thoughts of skyscrapers and the Statue of Liberty. Old corrupt world images contrasted with new freedom and hope. I think it's a great concept.

About *Losing the Plot*. I had someone research Allen Tate (it's *Alan* by the way). Apparently, he's known around Pinewood and I came up with the name of a woman, Jackie, who he left his wife for. Guess what, she is working under (and do I mean *under*!!) Marti Van Allen. Marti's over here dyking around on some vet series (not the Vietnam kind, animal doctors) and I spoke to her briefly this morning. She says she has a story about Tate, she's actually met him, but didn't want to tell me on the phone. She and Jackie are coming here for lunch. I expect to have more to tell you later.

Meanwhile the cops continue to look for him and he gets a mention most days in the papers. Nobody is in any doubt that he did it, although his motives aren't clear. Hall liked to throw wild parties with coke and hookers and they think maybe Tate went berserk. Sounds just like home, don't it?

Can't you haul your ass over here? I'm dying for some decent conversation. I've no idea who's in and who's out at Disney, what's happening at Fox, etc. I can get CNN in the hotel but it's all east coast shit about people I never heard of, or Bosnia. Mail me some entertainment tonight or hard copy videos, even the *National Enquirer*. Something a girl can *believe*!

Failing that, send Brad Pitt. The kind of action I'm getting, I'll end up on the end of Marti's dildo.

Love me,

ELAINE

'Holy shit, where are you?'

'I'm sorry to ring so late, but I need help, I need it quick, and you're the only person I can trust.'

Always be nice to your agent.

'What do you want me to do?'

'Can you come to the Groucho?'

'You're in the *Groucho*?'

'Outside. Tim, I'm really sorry about this—'

'I'll be there.'

Inside, the nightly show was on full volume in the main downstairs bar, jammed with the core of the London glitzerati all looking as if they were about to explode.

The club had been going since the middle eighties and soon took off as the place to be seen. Not heard, not during the 6 to 11 nightly meat market, when the decibel level reached Concordian proportions, but that didn't matter since no one was listening. The founders had formed it as a protest against the men-only rules at the older Pall Mall mausoleums, and succeeded beyond their dreams. If you had the stamina and a craving for the louche, there was every chance you could end the evening with tinnitus, a belly gargling with Dos Equis and a partner next to you waiting for romance to kick in. Also, unlike the traditional London clubs, it served terrific food, stayed lively until the small hours and had a minimum of elderly pooves seeking young men's opinions on the works of Heironymus Bosch.

Looking through the windows, my breath clouding the glass, I felt like Woody Allen in *Stardust Memories* when he is in a train full of zombies, gazing across the platform at one bursting with partygoers, and wondering why he was never where there was any fun.

Was the Groucho moving centre stage in the drama? Andree recruited me here, where now a Germanic pair were visiting. Coincidence? There are no coincidences. There are only conspiracies and determinism. Your life has led you to a spot where you suddenly see your ex-partner and their lover. But so have *their* lives, whether you bump into each other in Soho or Sidi Bel Abbes. Somewhere a puppeteer pulls a string and you move. Andree Bruckmeyer, through M. and her current client, through Schiller, through me to this upmarket ale house. Le Carré had never seemed so plausible.

A taxi stopped and Tim got out, shoving me into a doorway.

'You and your research,' he said. 'How many times have I told you, writers are supposed to make things up.'

'There's a couple inside. She's twenties, long dark hair, wears a grey jacket and matching skirt. Carries a red Chanel handbag. He's fiftyish, smart dark blue pinstripe, sun-tanned. Her name is Burnside, first initial M. I *have* to know who he is. Maybe he's a member, maybe they've met other people, I've no idea. They've been inside half an hour and probably came to eat, so they're likely to be in one of the restaurants upstairs.'

'Stay out of sight,' he said, looking at his watch. 'The pubs are closing. There'll be quite a few people around, and you have a decent price on your head.'

'How much?' I asked, and managed a thin smile. I watched him go inside, sign the book and press through the crowd to the stairs. I crossed the street and looked up at the lighted first floor windows. My clothes smelled stale. The walking, the day's tension, had made my bones ache. It was getting harder to repress the feeling I was only treading water until I was caught. So I learn his name? Is that enough to shout shazam?

225

A screenplay would have put Andree in that theatre with M. and Burnside. Ignoring one another during the performance, something would be exchanged, a word, a note, before they hurried off in opposite directions. Please, Tim, come down and say you saw them, and guess what, they were with the disappearing Kraut, whatsername again . . . ?

The swing doors revolved and out he came, striding past, making me trot to catch him up.

'Did you see them?'

'Yes.'

'And?'

'He's a member.'

'What's his name?'

'Burnside.'

I stopped dead. Someone slammed into my back and swore. 'So's hers.'

'So you said.'

'I thought he was her latest trick, and it turns out they're *married*?'

He urged me to walk on since we were blocking the pavement and people were pausing to stare.

'They may be,' he said. 'But I doubt if it's to each other.'

'What do you mean?'

'Because I heard her call him Daddy.'

I stopped again. The hell with onlookers.

'Jesus wept. It's *Chinatown*.'

'No, that's across the road.'

'Incest. Faye Dunaway and John Huston.'

'So that makes you Jack Nicholson,' Tim said. 'If you remember, he had his nose slashed for butting into their business.'

'They're staying in the same suite at the Ritz.'

226

'There are more things in heaven and earth, Horatio—'

'Tim, they screwed this afternoon.'

'You saw them?'

'No, but they had a boozy lunch, they were hanging around each other's necks . . .'

'You know where they're staying, when they eat and have it off. Is there anything you *don't* know about them?'

'Yes. How they can follow three hours of Schiller in German.'

'So now it's wartime spies. Shall I go back and yell *Achtung!* to see if they click their heels?'

I tried slowing his pace. He was six three and I was having to run to keep up.

'Tim, your vanishing Andree Bruckmeyer was German.'

'Not mine, white man, *yours*.'

'Didn't you tap her for another deal?'

'We talked.'

'Now she's disappeared.'

'It's not unknown in this business.'

'Do fly-by-nights usually pay ten on the nod?'

We came to an empty Indian restaurant and he led me inside.

'We just need a drink,' Tim said to the waiter.

'You have to eat. It's the law after eleven.'

'OK. Bring whatever you've got left over in the kitchen along with a couple of pint lagers.'

We sat down. For a moment he fiddled with the edge of the tablecloth.

'Look, somehow you've got into a shitload of trouble,' he said, avoiding my gaze. 'I don't quite know what to say.'

My heart went ectopian. My old friend and financial life-line was about to resign the account.

'I've never had a client before whose only press coverage has been as a murder suspect. So, take a deep breath and try to explain just what in fuck's name has been going on.'

I was getting good at pitching the story. First Maxie, then Wendy, now Tim. It felt like Hollywood.

American producers don't read. What they want, as with children, is for you to tell them a story. "Once upon a time, there was this serial killer . . ." They listen in silence while an assistant makes notes. When you've finished, they show they have a total recall of everything you've said, every word. Had they *read* it, they wouldn't have stayed with the plot beyond the second sentence. The richest screenwriters are the ones who spin the best tales. I've heard them. You can hear a pin drop and when they're done, the studio development exec. is wiping a tear and reaching for his cheque book. They are perpetuating the ancient tradition of the roving storyteller, reciting the same tale down through the generations. Go to the Djna El Fna in Marrakech and hear for yourself.

While I honed my pitch of the last week's incidents, avoiding any 'Oh, before that, I should have saids', Tim listened, while wolfing down a plate of monosodium glutamate the waiter brought with the lagers. The only distraction I had was wondering where he put all the food. Here was a man who kicked off with a breakfast that never contained less than two fried eggs and a half pound of bacon and/or sausages, business lunched most days and spent evenings slicing through four courses plus cheese. And yet he looked like an anorexic Ichabod Crane. By the time I came to the moment I rang him, the curry had gone and he was mopping the remains of the sauce with a fingertip. I assumed he had already eaten one dinner that evening.

228

'Why didn't you tell the taxi to take you to the police?'

'That's been asked before.'

'Who by? Who've you told?' I mentioned Maxie and Wendy.

'Wendy who?'

I explained how I came to be looking like an ad for a building society.

'She's right. You don't look like any writer I've ever known.'

'You're the only person besides me who ever saw Andree Bruckmeyer.'

'I quite fancied her, as a matter of fact. I don't suppose you banged her?'

'No.'

'Did you try?'

'No.'

'You could have. You're divorced now. You can do anything. Except break the windows.' We smiled at the shared joke for a second. 'OK,' he said, calling over the waiter, 'let's take it step by step.' Tim asked if they had any samosas and the lad nodded, first turning round the door sign to Closed. Outside, we could hear jangled shouts. His radar warned of drunks approaching whose evening wouldn't be complete until they'd hurled racial abuse and vomited a vindaloo.

'You know this berk and the tart are related. What now?'

'I don't know, but it's a start.'

'A start for what?'

'I'm not sure.'

'Let's get this clear. You've been wandering around, looking like a queer peer, sitting through a play in German, yanking me out of bed to go into the Groucho, all for reasons you can't quite put your finger on.'

'Bruckmeyer hired the girl, so perhaps she can lead me to Bruckmeyer,' I said without much conviction.

'Don't hold your breath.'

'The alternative is turn myself in and rot on remand, during which time everyone forgets I exist.'

'The point seems to be how are you going to get to Kraut One?'

'The middle act is always the hardest to write.'

'You could tell M. you're in the movie business and if she plays her cards right, you'll make her a star.'

'That's your way, is it?'

'Believe me, it works.'

The drunks passed, looking like the Droogs in *A Clockwork Orange*. One rattled the door and, finding it locked, slammed a fist against the glass. When I glanced over at the waiter, he'd been joined by an Indian in cook's whites holding a meat cleaver. When the voices outside receded, he returned to the kitchen.

'I wonder if Daddy knows his poppet is supplementing her allowance,' Tim said. 'And if not, what she would do to stop him finding out.'

I had not mentioned Wendy's way to pick her brains, but said there might be a problem in persuading him to believe it. After all, who was I but a desperado ready to say anything to get off the hook? I was dismayed to hear him agree.

'Yeah, and how much would she know anyway?'

I said I could take her along to the chauffeur, who would support my version of the high jinks in the limo.

'What high jinks?'

At twenty, I'd have proudly detailed every moment of the trip to Sonning. At fifty-three, these things don't carry the same swashbuckling brio.

'There was a certain amount of, er, professional activity on their part, the women.'

'And the driver saw it in his mirror?'

'He could have. In any event, he certainly wouldn't have mistaken them for chartered accountants.'

'OK,' Tim drawled, biting into the newly arrived samosa. 'You tell her if she doesn't bail you out, you'll tell Pop she's on the game.'

'It sounds thin.'

'Especially since all she has to do is open a window and shout, "Officer, he's over here."'

'You said let's take it step by step. What's the next?'

He pointed to my samosa and when I shook my head, speared it.

'I can confirm there was a woman calling herself Andree Bruckmeyer who hired you to write a film, and who put you on to a contact in CBCI to help with the research. It's a start.'

'*If* I give myself up.'

'That would certainly help.'

'You could tell them even if I don't.'

'Actually, the police rang a few days ago,' he said, wiping pastry flakes from his mouth. I stared.

'What did they want?'

'They found out I was your agent and they wanted to know if I'd seen you.'

'They searched the house.'

'I know. Maxie said.'

'That's where they got the picture that's in the papers.'

'You're lucky it doesn't look anything like you.'

'It's ten years old.'

'You've aged since then.'

231

'Mostly in the last couple of weeks.'

He downed the rest of his lager and wiggled the jar to get another. 'Oh, by the way, a friend of yours also called.'

'Who?'

'Elaine Morgenstern.'

'Never heard of her.'

'*Unspeakable Behavior*?'

'What about it?'

'She offered to complete payment on your contract.'

'What happened? The WGA threaten to blacklist them?'

'No, she said it would be in exchange for information.'

'On what?'

'On you.'

'*Me?*'

'Apparently her outfit, Movieline, are developing a project about a writer who gets caught up in a real life murder—'

'They can't do that.'

'They're doing it.'

'Already, I'm a Movie of the Week? Can she do this, I mean *legally*?'

'You're not in much of a position to sue.'

'What did you tell her?'

'I said she should get in touch with the prime source. You.'

'Who will they make the killer?'

'I thought your first question would be who's playing your role,' Tim said, attacking another pint of lager.

'TV movie?'

'What else?'

'Jane Seymour. Mother of mercy, is this the end of Rico?'

'I'll string them along until they pay what they owe, then pull the plug.'

Morgenstern's move didn't really come as a surprise. I've been hired to write treatments of sensational cases that were still in the courts. A starving man doesn't wait for his friend to die before he starts carving off the flesh.

Tim watched me gaze at my lap. 'Cheer up,' he said. 'We're not done yet.'

'*We?*'

'I am duty bound to do the best for my clients.' His clients. That was a relief.

'I tell you, Tim, I honestly thought you were softening me up for the elbow.'

He pulled a card from his wallet and waved it at the waiter. 'Are you mad? I aim to beat Movieline to the draw. If anyone's going to write this story, *you* are. Oliver Stone is looking for another true life story of blood and guts. This sounds right up his alley.'

The next morning I arrived at the Ritz around eight and called Burnside's room. When he answered curtly, I hung up. He's there, but what about her? Maybe she said her goodbyes last night and went home. In which case, I was down the longest snake back to Start.

The day hadn't opened well. All my underwear was used up and I had to pull on yesterday's pants. My groin chafed from the pavement pounding, and the suit needed a clean. All in all, I felt like shit, far from the man who used the world's luxury hotels as homes from home. The hall porter gave me the fish eye, and when a bellboy clipped my toes with a luggage trolley, all he said was 'Mind your backs'.

I bought a paper then ordered coffee and croissants in the breakfast area. When I didn't see my name in print, the day looked a smidgeon brighter.

233

A minute later, M. came in followed by Burnside and they sat at the next table. I lifted the paper and turning the pages, caught a glimpse of her face and his back.

M. appeared subdued. The spirit they shared last night was absent. Neither spoke, and when I peeked again, he was reading a typed letter.

'Anything wrong?' she finally said. He stuffed the letter away.

'No, not really. They're getting worked up about the yen, that's all. I have to go back for a meeting.'

'Do you absolutely *have* to?'

'I must, darling. I'm sorry.'

'I hate goodbyes,' she said softly, sounding close to tears.

'How do you think I feel?'

'This always reminds me of school.'

'When you come out, we'll have a week in Gstaad.'

I was seized with an impulse to lower the paper. What would happen if, looking over her father's shoulder, she saw me? I blocked out the scene. I wouldn't move a muscle, just keep my eyes steadily on hers. A sort of Banquo's ghost. She would look, look again, then frown. I still wouldn't react until she realized who I was. What would she do? Run? That would lead to Daddy learning what she did in her spare time. She'd go pale. Her father would ask if she was ill. She'd shake her head, but her cup would tremble and he'd become alarmed. No, no, I'm fine, really, well, maybe I'm coming down with something. He would notice her eyes fixed over his shoulder and turn in his seat, when I would hoist the paper.

It would make a terrific scene. A flavour of Brian de Palma out of Hitchcock, bringing the audience forward in their seats. Like the man rising from the bath at the end of *Les*

Diaboliques, or the hand coming out of the ground to grasp Amy Irving's ankle as she places flowers on Carrie's grave. Be a great part for a woman. Her reactions – shock, conceal-ment, guilt. Who could do it? Susan Sarandon twenty years ago. Nowadays, they're all dollfaces.

I decided I wasn't ready for my close-up yet, Mr De Mille, and kept the newspaper at full mast.

She was asking when she could come out to see him and his reply was evasive, as if he didn't want to be pinned down. 'I may be away in November.'

'What did it really say? The letter.'

'I told you, dear. The Japanese are making waves—'

'It was from Dr Angstrom. Wasn't it?'

'It's absolutely nothing to worry about.'

'So it was from him.'

'You seem to know more than I do.'

'Daddy—'

'Move your bag.'

I heard a chink of china as the waitress brought their food. Dr Angstrom. Medical. He's ill. Wait. Germans call everyone Doctor. With a K.

'Can I read it?'

'No, Maddy, you can't.'

M for Maddy. Madeleine?

Silence lengthened until:

'Please don't sulk,' he said, annoyed. 'I'd like to stay longer, obviously I would, but I simply *can't.*'

'That's what you used to say when I was at school.'

'I have to work, or you wouldn't be able to afford Chanel handbags.'

'I don't need Chanel handbags.'

'Fine, give it to Oxfam.'

Turning pages, I saw she was holding a handkerchief to her nose. Her father stretched out a hand and squeezed her arm. 'Don't, Maddy, please. Didn't we have a good time last night? I certainly did. I loved every minute.'

She blew her nose and ran the corner of the handkerchief carefully along the rim of her eyes. 'When's it ever *not* going to be business, Daddy? When's it just going to be us, being together like other families?'

'Because, unhappily, we're not like other families.'

'Whose fault is that?'

'Mine. All mine. But there's nothing I can do about it, I'm afraid.'

'There is. You could quit.' He didn't reply. 'You could resign.'

'Yes, I could.'

'But you won't.'

'Mad-dy,' he said, his tone moving from penitent to critical within the two syllables. 'You may think this is like being at school all over again, but I don't. You're twenty-three, and I'd prefer to treat you as such.'

'What's so important you can't stay one more day . . . ?'

'I really don't wish to discuss it any more.'

It was apparent he had only just broken the news he was leaving, using the letter as the excuse, although he knew yesterday when I pretended to be from reception. His whispering was now explained.

Why didn't one of them say something to give a clue what his business was? Where did he live? Switzerland, Germany? He could resign, but he wasn't about to. Unless the Bentley was rented and the Ritz a perk of a well-paid job, he was drowning in money. All I could gather from their breakfast spat was that he liked his work and wasn't going to chuck it in to please what was manifestly a spoiled brat of a daughter.

But what did he *do*? Trouble with the yen. Banking? Venture capital? Funding mega crime? A hint might build a bridge to Bruckmeyer, to CBCI, to *something* that would throw me a bone to chew on. Who was Angstrom? Someone Maddy regarded as important. When he gave an order, Daddy jumped.

'Are we going to sit like this until I leave?' he said, breaking a long silence.

'I don't have anything to say.'

'Oh, Maddy.'

The waitress passed, wiggling the coffee jug at me but I shook my head since it would mean lowering my paper and Maddy was looking everywhere but at her father.

'How's the job?' he asked.

'All right.'

'Do you like it?'

Was this where she exacts her revenge by saying it's not Lucy Clayton's but screwing men of his generation?

'It passes the time.'

'Are you all right for money?'

'Fine.'

'Are you sure?'

'God, Dad, *please*.'

'I'm sorry.'

'If you really were, you'd do something about it.'

'We'll go skiing in December, that's a promise.'

The idea didn't hit the spot. I glimpsed her profile as she gazed sullenly about the room. My arms were aching from holding up the paper. I felt like a boxer who's gone fifteen rounds.

'I have to go,' I heard her say.

'Won't you ride with me to the airport?'

'Can't, sorry.'

'Darling—'

'I have a job, remember?'

What job let her swan around the shops all afternoon?

'Tell them you're still feeling ill.'

So that's how.

'You have to go. So do I.' No more Dad or Daddy, no more hand-squeezing, giggles and hugs. She stood, appearing above the newspaper as she guided the Chanel bag over her shoulder. His chair creaked as he stood. She said, 'Stay and finish your coffee,' but he followed her out.

I left a ten on the table. At the main doors, they stopped and Burnside held his daughter by both elbows. She wouldn't meet his eyes. He bent to embrace her but all she gave was one cheek, then the other. Then she left. He stood a moment looking anxious, then returned to the breakfast room.

She was waiting beside the doorman outside while he tried to snag a taxi. If I lost sight of her now, it was all over. Then two cabs pulled in and she entered the first.

A Japanese couple were standing with a young English-man, who ushered them to the second taxi and opened the door. I darted round the other side and stepped simultaneously into the cab and out of character.

Their escort bellowed: 'Hey, fuck off, this is ours—'

I met the startled Japanese head to head inside and shouted in his face:

'Out!' He recoiled, bumping into his wife.

'Here, they were first,' the driver said. By now, the couple were clinging on to each other on the kerb. I reached across and slammed the door shut.

'See the cab in front?' I said, pointing. 'You get double if

238

you can keep it in sight.' The driver abandoned his lecture on protocol.

'Oh, I see. Like that, is it?' he grinned, ignoring the furious young chap thumping on the window.

'Like what?' I snapped.

'Nothing.'

'Right. So shut up and drive.'

I wished Wendy could have heard me. She'd have been proud. After all the years, I'd finally uttered the words I'd written for a dozen tough guys. And they had worked.

He moved west, around Hyde Park Corner, into the park, along the south road to the Knightsbridge exit, down Sloane Street to Sloane Square. It was the first time I thanked the appalling state of London's traffic system. We had no trouble staying behind Maddy all the way to the Guards' sports ground south of King's Road, where she got out on the east side, Franklin's Row. I stayed in the cab until she had reached a block of flats and let herself in, then passed a twenty to the curious driver saying, 'Don't ask.' And he didn't. I decided if I ever got out of this, there'd be no more Mister Nice Guy.

I looked across to the cricket pitch on the far side and remembered playing there with a team consisting almost entirely of young peers. Someone had burgled both dressing rooms, a bold move seeing the batting side would have been seated nearby. The assumption was it had to have been one of the players. Only the upper classes would have had the need and the gall.

Beside the main door were the six bells below a videocom screen, but no names. Jamming the trilby down as far as it would go, I started with flat 1 and rang each until I got a response. The third was answered by a child who said its parents were out, the fourth by a woman in fractured English. The fifth was Maddy.

'Hello?'

'Hello, my name is Walters. I'm a chartered surveyor working for the landlords.'

I stood in front of the postage-stamp-sized video screen.

'What do you want?'

'I'm here to check on the repairs listed by our recent survey.'

'Who did you say you were?'

'Arthur Walters. I'm with Hobbes and Sutcliffe. Please check if you like.'

There was a pause, then the buzzer went and I pushed the door open, calling out a thank you.

According to a plan in the foyer, flat 5 was on the third floor. Ignoring the lift, I climbed the stairs. An elderly woman was standing on the second floor landing in a doorway marked 4.

'Vot you vont?' she asked, with a severe look.

I doffed my hat and smiled: 'Surveyor, madam.'

'Vot?'

'To check the building.' I continued up the stairs, feeling her eyes in my back.

The third level contained two flats, 5 and 6. Both had peepholes. I rang six. When no one answered, I kept my finger on the bell.

The other door opened and Maddy put her head out: 'They're away,' she called. 'Are you the surveyor?'

I turned round. She had taken off her jacket and was holding a glass of water.

'Yes. I understand they have flaking plaster in the kitchen.'

'They're hardly ever here.' I kept on my hat and looked down to shield my face.

'May I see yours?'

'We're OK.'

'I was told you had a leaking exterior pipe.'

'News to me.'

She stood aside and I entered. In the living room I could see a tall standard lamp, some tan-coloured armchairs and a wall of bookshelves. Along the hall was a smaller room filled with computerware. Several screens were on, showing columns of numbers. She saw me pause by the door and closed it. 'Which outside pipe?'

I took off my hat. 'Hello, Emma.'

There was a moment of confusion, a frown.

'What?'

'I'm glad to see you've recovered. From the gunshot.'

Now she remembered. I expected her to dash for the door, but she showed no fear, no alarm. My imagined reactions had I lowered the paper in the hotel were nowhere close.

'Alan. How did you find me?'

'You remember my name. I'm flattered. Oh, wait, you have a brother called Alan.'

'How did you find me?'

'I followed you.' Her hand very slightly tightened on the glass.

'From where?'

'The Ritz.'

She walked into the living room. 'What do you want?'

'I think you know.'

'No, I don't.'

'Emma, or Maddy, or whatever—'

'Madeleine.'

241

'What I want is for the police to stop thinking I'm the one who killed Arnold Hall,' I said. Whatever you do, don't take your eyes off her.

'You know I can't do that, Alan.'

'Why not?'

'How would I explain what *I* was doing in his house?'

'It's not difficult,' I said. 'You and a friend were hired by Hall to spend the night with us. Forget about the men coming with the guns, forget all that. You say, in the morning Hall drove us back to London, and that was the last time you saw him or me. That's what you tell them.'

She moved to the window and seemed to be considering.

'One problem.'

'What?'

'The papers say a man rang for a taxi and when it got there, someone jumped through a window and told him to get out quick. They think he might have been you.'

'Then tell the truth. When the shooting began, I was downstairs calling a cab.'

'Then I'd have to tell them about the gunmen. The ones who made you panic. You can't just tell *half* the story.'

'OK,' I said, hesitating. 'Tell them about the shooters.'

'The what?'

'Shooters.'

'I never heard them called that before.'

'It's slang.'

'But if I told them that, I'd have to say they were using blanks on Fiona and me.'

'No, you say they were only after Hall.'

'Why haven't I gone to the police before now?'

'You were scared.'

242

'How did we get back to London? You took the only taxi.'

'You called for another.'

'No one reported another call.'

'You hitched, Christ, I don't know. All I *do* know is there's only one person in the world who can get me out of this fucking mess, and that's you. I know about your father, I know how to find him. He thinks you're doing some ordinary job. If I have to, I'll tell him how you really earn a crust.'

'Wouldn't he read about that the moment I went to the police?' she said quietly, unperturbed.

I was losing this, and she knew it.

She turned from the window. A shadow fell across her face, but I could still see the smile.

'You were so sweet that night, Alan. I never met a client as gentle as you were. I'm really sorry it has to end this way.'

'What way?'

The first sense that came alive told me my cheek was resting on something hard, gritty and cold. The second, that there was a pervasive smell of urine. The third provided a blurred light, the fourth a roar of traffic, while the last sensation arrived as a taste of blood.

When I tried to move, an explosive pain filled the back of my head, which my probing fingers worsened. They came back with congealed blood under the nails.

I was in a derelict building close to a flyover. The urine perfume mixed with that of dark concrete, awaking long-dormant memories of air raid shelters I played in when I was small. The floor was littered with the detritus of generations of dossers; broken bottles, beer cans, newspapers and the

243

remains of a sleeping bag. The ground shook from the traffic.

I tried to stand, but the legs needed a few minutes, so I concentrated on trying to recall what had happened just prior to the mystery tour. I've only once undergone a general anaesthetic, after I broke an ankle at an indoor cricket net. One moment I was lying on a trolley answering a question about how I did it, the next I was waking up after a wonderful nap with a leg in plaster. Apart from the comfort factor, this was similar.

I'd been speaking to . . . Emma – no, Maddy. About helping me, telling the truth – then what happened? There'd been a flash of light, a spine-shattering thump from behind, then the floor had tilted and slammed into my face. She had been standing at a window, telling me how nice I was. Then she said she was sorry about something. About ending this way.

My legs awoke with a rush of pins and needles as I tried to roll on to my knees, the patellae pressing hard down on to concrete shards that sent electric charges through the system. I tottered to my feet.

I was on the ground floor of a derelict warehouse. The flyover was Hammersmith; I could make out the Ark building on the other side. The area had been gradually renovated over the years and the section I was in was part of the final stages. I heard no wrecking balls or pneumatic drills, so either this was Sunday or the development had run out of cash. Certainly the *pissoir* atmosphere indicated this section had been a homeless Hilton for some time.

I tried to keep my head still as every move brought ravaging pain, like a monstrous hangover. What did they use, a crowbar? The last time I'd looked, it was around ten o'clock. What was it now?

244

Disconnected recollections gradually started to filter through. Bullying an elderly Japanese couple out of a cab, facing down the driver, talking my way into Maddy's building, into her flat. Had I really done all this? I, who once watched a plumber connect our bath taps to the waste pipes and said nothing for fear of hurting his feelings?

All you need to know about writing screenplays can be picked up during a trip around the LA studios. Don't waste your money on the stuff that clogs up bookshop film sections: *Great Unproduced Screenplays of Our Time*, *How to Write a Million Dollar Movie*. Ignore the flakes giving seminars on how to crack the code. If they were that good, how come their names aren't on every smash hit? On *any* smash hit?

All you need do is have, or take, a set of pitch meetings across town.

You have this story. It's about an ex-Marine, a former hero, who's down on his luck and forced to commit a crime to make enough money to feed his family in Flint, Michigan. It's a hit job. However, instead of killing the mark, he befriends him and together they work their way back to the man who put out the contract, the head of a drug cartel, and deliver him to a grateful DEA. It has everything, you say, a tale ripped from today's headlines, an in-depth psycho-sociological study of modern times.

The pitchtaker behind the desk at Paramount flosses his teeth until you finish. He's silent for a moment. He's clearly moved. You think you've got a deal. Then he says:

'First up, who do you root for?'

This is absolutely basic. With whom does the audience identify?

The ex-Marine, of course.

'Ex-Marine. You mean he napalmed kids in Vietnam?'

'No, he, er, he wasn't in that war. He killed Iraqis.'

'Nix the army,' he says. 'Kids today don't want to know from soldiers. *Born on the Fourth of July* did shit at the box office, even with Tom Cruise.'

'I see.'

'Is he a schwarzer?'

'The Marine? I hadn't thought of him being black, no—'

'Blue collar, though. I mean, Flint. Auto industry.'

'Yes. Working class.'

'Unless he's played by Roseanne, you don't stand a chance. Audiences hate poor. All those barnyard movies. Billionaire stars playing Depression farmers' wives. Every one went down the tubes. Video sales too.'

'No army, no poor.'

'Right. Poor is losers, and we want people to love this guy. Make him Boston old money. Harvard Law School, but he drops out because he finds out what we all know, that lawyers are schmucks. When he chucks his books at the teacher, you'll get the viewers cheering.'

'OK.'

'Second up, you give him a starving family. Where's the sex coming from? If he has a wife with ringworm, the minute he starts banging chicks, it's bye bye female audience. And they're bigger than they used to be. Time was you made all-male movies 'cause guys like to watch guys and women ditto. Not since *Thelma and Louise*, they don't. You see any buddy movies on the circuits? They're all STV nowadays.'

'STV? Scottish Television?'

'Straight to video. Give your man a crippled mom if you have to. She had an industrial accident, got carjacked,

246

mugged, whatever, but per-lease, no wife and kids, and no best buddy.'

'What about the man he helps, the one he's hired to kill. It's a big part.'

'A star doesn't share lines with anyone else. A star has to think the next move by himself, second guess the villains, outwit the cops on his own. You won't get Sly or Clint or Arnie by having them say to somebody else: "Gee willaker, Morty, where do we go from here?" At that point, their agents stop reading the material. If you must have a friend, another man, make him blind or deaf or crippled, or kicked in the head. All he's there for is to make things harder for the star, who then has to work on all cylinders plus one extra. The star comes on in the pre-credits and he stays till the last fade-out, and most of them prefer to be photographed from the left.'

'Got it.'

'Third up, you have him handing the drug baron over to the DE fucking A? You saw *Leon*? The kids love the idea these government agencies are more corrupt than Colombian mayors. No star hands the bad guy over for a fair trial these days, not since *Coogan's Bluff*. Now they toss him into a jet engine or off the Trade Center. You have to end with his viscera on the camera, and the star turning down a medal from the Prez. Anti-authority, doesn't take shit from anybody, walks his own line, tough as nails when he has to be, and tender only when he knows it won't backfire. Today's star is a cynical sonofabitch who long since gave up believing in good things happen to good people. It's what people expect and what they pay to see.'

I'm merely mentioning this to point up one aspect of my

247

ordeal that was giving me the first twinges of satisfaction.

I was beginning to act like a star.

As I stood on unsteady limbs, watching the pell-mell traffic above, I wondered how come I was still alive. It's only in fiction that criminals kill everyone but the hero, for whom they construct an elaborate execution, allowing him time to clamber free moments before the candle burns through the rope dangling him over the shark-infested swimming pool. It's a perk of the job. When men with Uzis creep up on him from behind, they always obligingly call his name before opening fire so he has time to hurl himself sideways. Well, do you want a sequel or not?

In real life, the rules are different. I was alive because, because – because they want the police to arrest me and allow the law to take its course. "Fugitive Writer Found Exhausted. Offers No Resistance."

Which was consistent with the police car that now turned the corner at the top of the road and approached the wrecked section, slowing to a crawl. Two men inside were looking up at the façade. I stumbled over to the far side. A second car was parked at an angle to cover both doorways into the building.

Screen fugitives always climb upwards, particularly villains since it allows for a satisfying scream and splat when they fall to their deaths. I assumed that was what the cops expected me to do – they watch crap as well – and so I used a flight of concrete steps leading to the basement. The only light filtered through a narrow set of windows level with the ground outside. The glass had long since been smashed and I could smell the car's exhaust as they parked with the engine running. Keeping to the walls, I worked my way round and looked through the gaps to see the two policemen get out and approach the door above me. They were armed, pistols holstered on their belts, hands resting on the stocks like Americans. The door squeaked as they pushed it open.

Think star. There were two ways forward. The Jean-Claude Van Damme School of Heroic Behaviour teaches you to wait behind the door which you slam against them as they come in, and follow up with some rapid kung fu, mostly kicks to the balls, before stepping over them with a quip like "Sorry, guys, it's nothing personal." The other, the non-violent Harrison Ford Academy, prefers something cute to make the audience laugh. Like waiting until they're inside, then crawling out and stealing their car, leaving them to fire at the wheels and miss, then throw their hats on the ground in frustration. This is helped by the fact that in the cinema, no one takes their keys out of the ignition. Woody Allen pointed this out in *The Purple Rose of Cairo*, when the screen hero steps down from the celluloid into reality and jumps into a car that won't start right away.

A star, meanwhile, registers that the driver isn't jangling keys as he approaches the hideout.

Under the basement windows lay a roll of sacking that had long since decomposed. I trod into it, my ankles sinking deep into the foul-smelling compost, but it provided the height needed to ram my elbows through the empty frames and heave my body up. As I squeezed out, I could hear their feet crunching over broken glass inside. I came up on the open driver's door and there were the dangling keys as I had, star-like, anticipated.

I crawled inside, stamped on the clutch, jammed the stick into first and switched on. A roar echoed off the buildings and the gears whined as I shot off in a squeal of tyres. Police cars are tuned to slice through traffic, catch ton-up joyriders and for the first fifty yards I felt as if I was on an out-of-control roller-coaster. I'd reached fifty in first and when the main road hoved up two hundred yards later, the speedo was tickling seventy. I stamped on the brake and snaked to a stop, the front jutting out into oncoming traffic. I didn't realize the power of authority, the effect of a police car on the public. Everyone screeched to a halt, no one honked, no road rage tantrums. They let me into the mainstream and pulled over as I shot bucking and rolling down the middle of the road. It may have occurred to them later to wonder why a police patrol driver was dressed in a shabby pinstripe, but for the moment they let me pass in a public-spirited manner that said much for British orderliness.

I took the first turning off the main road and entered a maze of Victorian back streets. Ahead was a woman pushing a baby in a pram with a five-year-old tagging alongside. She was harassed, yelling at the older child, and showed no interest in me when I stopped, removed the keys and left the police car on the kerb. As I passed, she was saying, 'Don't hold on to the pram, Darren, I won't tell you again' – although I knew and she knew that she would.

Passing a newsagent's window, I realized how awful I looked. Like a stockbroker who'd been made redundant but hadn't dared go home for a week to tell his family. Also, some time during the last few hours I had lost my wallet, credit cards and a hundred in cash. Along with my glasses.

The Indian shop owner was at the till, trying not to stare. He must have had his share of drifters like me in this area, coming in to ask the time and pinching Kit Kats.

The only advantage I gained from an honours degree in modern history was an ability to remember telephone numbers that began with a 1. Wendy's was 1358. Nineteen years before the death of Edward the Third. She lived in Battersea, so that meant a 622 prefix. The shop advertised a public phone and I went in.

'May I use the phone, please?'

'Fifty pence local calls.'

'I'm reversing the charges.'

'Still fifty pee.'

'Look, it's an emergency.'

I knew I shouldn't have said please. A star would have fixed him with a steely glare and just said, "Phone."

'Then use the one up the road.'

I thought of saying something to spoil his day. Ask why all Pakistani cricketers cheat, but he might have been Indian and agreed. Anyway, I was in no position to create an incident that might bring in the law. However, as I left, I saw Michael Douglas in *Falling Down* in a new light.

I found the phone box and rang Wendy, heard her answering machine. Enquiries gave me Pinewood's number but they wouldn't accept a collect call until I pleaded with the operator that it was a matter of life and death.

'Alan, what's up?' Her voice created a flood of relief.

'I'm seriously up shit creek.'

'You mean you weren't before?'

I ran through the pertaining facts.

'What street are you on?'

There was a pub opposite called the Duke of Newcastle. 'There can't be too many of those around,' she said. 'Stay where you are.'

I was hurting, dehydrated and dog-tired. Outside the pub, a few drinkers were huddled around wooden tables. It must be lunchtime, since a couple of men wore painter's smocks, doing what they do best, exchanging utterly meaningless

251

conversations. After a few pints, they'd wander back to their job. The wallpaper sides wouldn't line up as well as those they'd hung in the morning and the paint would dribble on the floorboards, although never on their hands. No matter how else you can fault decorators, getting paint on their skin can't be laid at their door. God knows how they do it.

The booth became stuffy as the sun beamed in. I reckoned Wendy wouldn't get here in under an hour. Soon the drinkers would start wondering why the berk in the filthy suit was staying so long on the phone. Curiosity would become suspicion, and all it took was someone whose anger rose in direct ratio to the booze he sank, and I'd be the centre of attention. "What's your game, sunshine, you spying on us or what?" So I left and walked slowly all the way up one side of the road and all the way down the other. What I really wanted was a crap, a clean-up, a seat and something to drink, but without a penny, they were all out of reach. Maybe not the crap, but to walk into this pub looking as I did would be enough to snag the landlord's attention, especially going directly into his lavs. Maybe Arnie wouldn't have thought twice, but right now I was feeling anything but heroic.

I was in the middle of London and it felt like Borneo. A voice behind me piped:

'You've got blood all over your coat.' I turned and saw a little girl. She couldn't have been more than seven. Neatly dressed, new shoes, she was holding a packet of cigarettes.

'I banged my head.'

'You want to buy these fags?'

'I don't have any money.'

'Give us a pound.'

'I'm sorry, I don't have anything.'

She went over to the drinkers and passed among the tables, but didn't make the sale.

Wendy's car eventually puttered round the corner and slowed outside the pub. Then she saw me fifty yards up the road, accelerated, showering the painters with carbon monoxide, and cruised alongside.

'God in heaven, what have you done to that suit?'

I climbed in, every limb aching, and buried my face in her neck. She saw the contusion and the blood-glued hair. 'I seem to spend my life cleaning you up,' she said, reversing to the pub. When I climbed stiffly out, a hand-holding couple at a table saw my wounds and winced. Wendy led me to the bar.

'My friend has had an accident,' she announced in RADA tones. 'Where are your washrooms?'

A barmaid pointed: 'The gents is round the trellis.'

We found a door with a wooden sign that said 'Caballeros' beneath a sombrero. Two men were having a slash and leaned modestly forward when Wendy came in. One said, 'Here, this is the gents.'

'So act like one,' she replied, turning me round to examine the damage.

'Give it to me straight,' I said.

'They got you behind the right ear. You must have bled like a pig.' She wet a handkerchief and dabbed at the cut, loosening the matted hair. 'It's not that deep. You might get away without stitches.'

The pissers zipped up and came over.

'What do you think, lads?' Wendy asked. 'Does he need the hospital?'

'How d'e do it?'

'Asking daft questions.'

253

'I fell over,' I said.

'Nah. Someone gave you a whack.'

'All right.'

'You got mugged.'

'Something like that.'

He was looking closer at the bespoke tailoring. 'I bet they were black.'

'No,' I said, hissing as Wendy probed harder with the hankie. 'As a matter of fact, they wore bowlers and Garrick Club ties.'

'You pulling my plonker?'

'Actually, it was Lloyd's. Brought a lot of good men down.'

'Who's Lloyd's?'

'Look,' Wendy told them, 'make yourselves useful and ask the landlord for some Band-Aids and disinfectant.' When they left she said, 'You reek. Did you pee yourself or what?'

I gave a brief account of the morning and she laughed at the police car episode.

'I never thought you had that kind of thing in you,' she chuckled, unbuttoning my shirt.

When the men returned with the landlord, I was bare to the waist.

'Oi,' the landlord said. 'We can't have this in here— '

He was holding a bottle of Dettol and Wendy grabbed it.

'I meant disinfectant for a wound, not the bog,' she bellowed, deflecting his objections. 'And where are the Band-Aids?'

'Look, I'm running a pub, not a bloody hospital,' he mumbled, fishing them from a shirt pocket. He had slipped into a minor key, subdued by her Hattie Jacques manner, coming as it did from six inches above his head. Wendy poured some Dettol on to a handkerchief and dabbed the abrasion. 'You talk this way, you aren't going to win the *Evening Standard* Pub of the Year Award. Not when I tell them the Duke of Newcastle turns away seriously injured customers.'

'You ain't customers.'

'All right, bring us two pints of Fuller's.'

The landlord softened: 'What did he do?'

Whenever I was with Wendy, I seemed to become invisible.

'Banged his head, what does it look like?'

'It looks nasty, that's what it looks like.'

'That's right, make the patient feel good. Does this establishment run to a sewing circle? I need a pair of scissors.'

The other men grew bored watching and left with the landlord. I asked her nervously what she wanted scissors for.

'If someone had cut your balls off,' she observed, 'you wouldn't have got into this mess.'

'Maxie said the same.'

'You require another hair trim so I can put this plaster on.'

I went to the door and looked out. 'This is usually the moment when the landlord secretly phones the police.'

'Is he?'

'I can't see.'

I stayed apprehensive until he returned with a pair of tailor's cloth-cutters not far short of gardening shears. Wendy snipped while I bit the bullet and the landlord watched, swilling the hair away in the basin as I leaned over. The Dettol stung and made me smell even more like a lavatory. She laid three Band-Aid strips star-shaped over the cut.

'That should hold it for a while.'

'Anything else I can do for you?' the landlord said with

exaggerated politeness. I had learned sarcasm was meat to Wendy's cleaver.

'Yes. A towel and a decent bar of soap. These dispensers are disgusting.'

A pint and a Ploughman's later and smelling of Imperial Leather, I felt better. By then, Wendy had heard everything.

'You say her flat was full of computers. So unless she advertises on the Internet, she does something more than Greek, French and other assorted sexual antics.' She ticked off fingers. 'Daddy owns half Liechtenstein, or appears to. She went to a Swiss finishing school, hence the German, where she learned to yank his chain about abandoning her for his work. He thinks she works in an art gallery or wherever, but she hustles to make herself independent, and one day intends to announce her real profession at a family Christmas.'

'Hustles and takes part in murder plots,' I added.

'What about her boyfriend?'

'What boyfriend?'

'The one who put your lights out. Her pimp? He must have been inside the flat. Maybe he's the technonerd. Plugged into cyberspace, one day he meets Andree the Kraut. It's love at first byte. B-Y-T-E, get it? They e-mail into each other's knickers and eventually come up with the CBCI thing. She says she knows a chap who works there called Hall. He's seriously bent, and all they need is a fool-proof plan to take along to him.'

'No. German is the link. Bruckmeyer is, Maddy's fluent.'

'Oh, *Maddy* now, is it? So your theory is that she and Andree popped Hall.'

'It doesn't have the substance to be a theory. More an embryo.'

'So? Whither now?'

'Your place. Can you put me up?'

'If I have to.'

'And get my stuff from the hotel. Paying the bill as arranged.'

'Suddenly, it's Mr Decision Maker. Anything else?'

'Yes. I want you to help me break into a flat. Number five, Keystone Mansions, Franklin's Row, SW3.'

DATE: OCTOBER 22

FAX TO: ELAINE MORGENSTERN, C/O SAVOY HOTEL,
          LONDON

FROM: BERNARD CARLUCCI, LEGAL DEPARTMENT,
          MOVIELINE INTERNATIONAL, LOS ANGELES

Dear Elaine,

Losing the Plot

I draw your attention to an article in the London
Daily Mail show business column of October 20:

> With La-La's Land's get-in-there-first energy,
> Elaine Morgenstern, producer of *Anna Karenina –
> The Prequel* at Pinewood, tells me her company,
> Movieline International, is developing a script
> based on the recent CBCI collapse. She says it will
> be a no holds barred look at high finance, but will
> also include a plot involving a hack screenwriter
> who hilariously becomes involved in a bank robbery
> story he was actually writing at the time. Confus-
> ing? It won't be if you see the film scheduled to be
> shot early next year starring Harrison Ford.

We are well aware of the irresponsibility of the
British tabloid press and assume you gave no press
interview along these lines. However, I must ask you
to proceed no further in this project. We have
received a directive from our parent company stating
that any attempt to use CBCI as the subject of a feature film might adversely affect their trading opportunities. I am Fedexing the letter sent by their
chairman, Doktor Per Angstrom.

    Best wishes,

                                    BERNIE

As her flatmate was in Ireland on a location-finding trip, Wendy suggested I take her room. It was a sweet pretence we both maintained while I was there, like talking to children about Santa Claus as if he were a regular family friend. The room hadn't been used in ages; no pictures on the wall, a rancid new-paint smell in closets that were empty except for a few cardboard boxes still packed from the last move. And the sheets needed a day in the fresh air. Wendy hadn't even bothered to hide her friend's nightie, folded on the other side of her bed.

On the way home from Hammersmith we had swung by Keystone Mansions and I pointed out the flat.

'How do we get up there? The drainpipe?'

'I got in by saying I was the landlords' surveyor.'

'A one-off, I feel.'

'Flat 4 has a woman who sounds like Marie Ouspenskaya. I could try it out on her.'

We clattered across Chelsea Bridge to a flat which hadn't seen many cats successfully swung inside, although it might have been Wendy's build that made it look tiny. Just as Arnold Hall's proportions increased the size of rooms, she did the reverse. She couldn't even drive the car without bending her head.

A day passed while she attended to *Anna Karenina* and I struggled to maintain my star status and work out a second way into Madeleine Burnside's flat. *Topkapi* and *Mission: Impossible* had men lowered on a rope to avoid a sensitized floor. *Rififi* broke through a ceiling with an upturned umbrella to catch the plaster. Michael Caine *Deadfall*ed from a higher windowsill, while Paul Newman in *Harper* simply found the door unlocked.

Wendy returned lugging what looked like a howitzer, but

turned out to be a 1500 mm camera lens complete with a monopod.

'Pete MacAuley's doing the *Anna K.* stills. He owes me a favour.'

'You *told* him?'

'I'm hurt you said that.'

'I'm sorry. I'm on edge.' I lifted the lens, buckling under the weight. 'What do we do? Slug them over the head with it?'

'He says they use them on skinny-dipping royals.'

We parked on the west side of the playing fields, about three hundred yards from the flat. She slotted the lens into a Nikon, rested the end on the monopod and aimed it through the tall iron railings.

'You look like Edward Fox in *Day of the Jackal*.' She made adjustments until she found the third floor windows and brought them into focus.

'Their curtains could do with a clean,' she said and moved aside to let me see. The lens dragged Maddy's living room all the way across the fields until I felt I could touch the windows.

'I'm impressed. And I'm really looking forward to finding out what use it's going to be.'

She pushed me away and returned her eye. 'Was Grace so negative about why Jimmy was spying on his neighbours in *Rear Window*? Did she say, "Don't tell me you're expecting to uncover a *murder*"?'

'I only asked.'

'Call me paranoid, but if someone had whacked *me* on the head, I'd be keen to find out who it was. There's only one flat with its lights on.' She glanced at her watch. 'Gone five. People'll be coming home from work soon.'

Dark clouds were drifting across the sky and I felt rain in the air.

'Your friend won't be thrilled if you get his phallus wet.'

Two teenage girls stopped to gawp. Wendy clicked the shutter: 'Got him. Naked as the day he was born.'

'Who?' one asked. Wendy pressed the button again.

'What a dong!'

'Who is it?'

'Liam.'

'Who?'

'Liam Gallagher.'

'Liam Gallagher's over there?' the second girl yelped, making a grab for the camera. 'Can I have a look?'

'Shit, he's gone. Still, his willy should be worth a bomb.'

The first girl remained sceptical. 'He's not there.'

'No? Then read the *Sunday Sport* this weekend.'

They hung around a few moments before wandering away, unconvinced.

'It'll give them something to tell their friends,' Wendy said.

The first rain hit my cheek.

'Let's go. There's no one up there.'

'Oh ye of little faith,' she murmured. 'Her lights have just gone on.' She moved to let me look. I saw the top of the standard lamp and part of the bookshelves in the main room. Then a shadow appeared at the windows.

'Someone's at the window.' I turned the focus but made it worse. She pushed me aside and readjusted.

'It's a man. Wait—' The rain was falling in earnest now. 'No, he's moved away.'

She dismantled the monopod, detached the camera from the lens and slid them on to the car's rear seats. 'Well, at least we know someone's home. Probably the one who clobbered you.'

'I wonder how they got me out of there in broad daylight without anyone noticing.'

'When you have him tied to a chair with pliers round his nuts, ask him,' she said, starting the car. 'My guess would be the fear Brits have about confronting strangers. I mean, would *you* stop and want to know what the hell was going on?'

Well, no actually. I'd assume they were ill or drunk. She drove round the square and parked on the corner nearest to Maddy's building. The rain was setting in and drivers were turning on their headlights.

'Have you got a mobile?'

She unclipped the glove compartment and handed one over. I asked Directory Enquiries if they had a listing for Burnside, giving the address. They hadn't.

'Nothing is *that* easy,' Wendy grunted.

'Either it's ex-directory or in his name.'

We sat a while in silence.

'What do cops talk about on stakeouts?' she asked. 'You must have written a few scenes.'

'Sport, sex. If they talk at all.'

'Try sex.'

'You're not a bloke.'

'Pretend.'

'You want me to act like two cops talking about sex.'

'Yeah. Make it dirty, post watershed. None of the *Bill* shit.'

It had been some time since I'd produced Polyfilla dialogue. 'Wait. Er, "Hey, you see the new WPC they got in vice?" "No, what's she like?" "Great tits." "How big?" "Bigger'n your arse, matey." "Go on!" "Hang yer hat on them. I tell yer, she can sit on my truncheon any time." '

When I stopped, she looked across. 'Is that it?'

'More or less.'

'You're having me on.'

'That's how coppers talk on stakeout.'

'What about the smarter ones, the college types?'

'I was doing the smarter ones. What would women talk about?'

'Usually boyfriend problems or where they want to go on holiday.'

The conversation dribbled away while the wipers beat a drowsy rhythm.

'Oh,' she said, making me jump. 'By the way, have you seen the *Mail* lately?' I said no. She didn't go on.

'Why, am I in it? I am. What did it say?'

She reached behind and brought up a crumpled copy.

'Do you know someone called Elaine Morgenstern?'

'I know of her. Why?'

'She's prepping *Karenina*. It was in the showbiz section—'
'*Showbiz?*'

She found the page and pointed to the squib.

'She called my agent about this,' I muttered. 'The fucking nerve.'

I checked the date. 'This is three days old. Why didn't you show me before?' She moved uneasily in the seat. 'What was it you were shielding me from, being called a hack?'

'Mind you,' she said, 'it would make a hell of a film.'

'Thanks. I'll see to it if you get first dibs on the make-up.'

We succumbed to the hypnotic metronome of the wipers. Then a Range Rover drew up. Two children jumped down and ran to the entrance, the older one fiddling with keys, while the driver moved away to find a parking place. The

263

kids let themselves in and a minute later lights showed on the second floor.

'There are kids in number three,' I said, getting out. I ran to the door and pressed their bell.

'Hello?' a girl called.

'This is the postman. Is your name Andrews?'

'No.'

'What is it?'

'Anthea Cavanaugh.'

I was keeping my eyes on the corner where the Range Rover had turned and now a woman appeared holding a newspaper over her head. I returned to the car.

'Their name's Cavanaugh.'

'Clickety click, pop, never stop thinking.'

'*Desperate Hours*, Humphrey Bogart.'

The woman went inside and Enquiries came across with the number for Cavanaugh, Keystone Mansions.

'Let me do it,' Wendy said. 'Women trust women.' She pressed and waited, then said, 'May I speak to your mother? . . . Mrs Cavanaugh?'

She tilted the phone to let me hear.

'Yes.'

'Good evening. Meredith Wharton, from the managing agents.'

'Oh, yes, hello.'

'I'm sorry to bother you at this hour, but I've only recently taken charge of the accounts of Keystone Mansions and I'd like to verify the numbering of the flats. I already have one and two. You are three, is that correct?'

'That's right.'

Wendy repeated the number slowly as if writing it down: 'Would you know who is in number four?'

'Mrs Davidovitch.'

'Thank you – ah yes, here we are, Davidovitch. I don't suppose you could tell me five and six, to save me making more calls?'

'Five is Hardwick. I'm afraid I don't know six. The Swanns left last year and I've never seen the new owners.'

'Thank you, Mrs Cavanaugh, you've been a great help.'

'Oh, while you're on, my husband reported a smell in the hallway a month ago and it's still there.'

'I'll get on to it at once.'

'Thank you.' She disconnected. 'You hear that? Hardwick.'

'Where did you learn to lie so fluently?'

'Everything is possible, sugarlumps. Barbra Streisand said so in *Yentl*.'

The motherly tones of the Enquiries electronic voiceprint provided Hardwick's number. 1882. One year after the assassination of President James Garfield.

'Now what?' she asked. 'How do we get them out of there?'

'Could try a bomb scare. How's your Irish accent?'

'What about Daddy's back in town and wants to see her *sofort*?'

'Does he know she's shacked up here?'

'Do I keep going?' Wendy asked. 'Or do you already know what to do?'

'I know what *I*'m going to do.'

'What?'

'Eat. I'm starving.'

'You're not even going to *try* to get in?'

'With him there?'

'No, wait till he leaves.'

'Who was it only the other day waxed on about the point-lessness of searching rooms? Who maligned my talent by saying there was always a moment in my work when some-body finds a matchbook with a crucial phone number? A cigarette that bears a lipstick's traces, an airline ticket to romantic places maybe, but a book of matches, never. Well, not recently.'

She wasn't listening. She was looking up at the front of the building.

'Their lights have gone out again.'

The entrance door swung inwards and a man emerged in a trenchcoat and wide-brimmed hat. He raised the collar against the rain and walked quickly away from us, stopping at a parked Saab. He aimed a locking sensor and climbed in. There was a muffled roar, then he edged out and disappeared.

I was already pressing the number. No one answered, not even a machine. 'Did you see any more of him than I did?'

'I liked the hat,' she said.

'OK, let's go.'

'But the flat's empty. Surely there's *something* worth look-ing for.'

'We've got his name. That'll do for now.'

'I get it. You tell the police the man they want is called Hardwick, and they pay you compensation for harassment?'

'There comes a time when pretending you're the surveyor or the bloody Avon lady starts to wear a tad thin. What if we do get into the building? Do you think Hardwick leaves his door on the latch? With all that hardware inside? Take it from me, he'll have hinge bolts, a double Banham and an alarm. The only way to get in somewhere like that is when people are home.'

'All right,' she shrugged. 'I was just testing.'

We chewed through a McDonald's on King's Road then walked to the Surprise, a pub where a man could get a decent draught Bass. I'd been a regular in the sixties, when it was full of beautiful folk rubbing elbows with old timers who had staked their claim to various seats before Hitler marched into Poland. Sit in one of them and they bit you. Tonight, at seven o'clock, it was almost empty. Public houses were a dying industry. In a few years, they would just be a historical question on *Mastermind*: "What is, or was, a pub?" "Pass." "A place where people gathered for social drinking." Eh? Why do that when you can have your booze delivered via the PC and sink it watching the top-rated game show, *May We Shoot Your Dog?*

We sat in a corner speaking sotto, like extras in the Rover's Return. We debated what to do with Maddy and Hardwick. We wondered how they featured in the plot. Clearly, she was not from Rent-a-Tart, scooped up by Hall for a languid poke. 'I'm really sorry it has to end this way,' she said. *What* had to end this way? Apart from the dent in my skull and a call to the police telling them where to find me, what else did she mean? Wendy suggested she and her boyfriend were part of the planning, not just foot soldiers. Hardwick had City experience, knew CBCI were fishing in murky waters.

'He found out it was bent as a fiddler's elbow. Inside information, a nod here, a whisper there.'

I grabbed the baton: 'He hears someone's planning to skin it. Hall's name keeps surfacing. He's met him on the lunch circuit—'

'Hardwick's got a rich girlfriend, father's a Zurich gnome—'

'Who could fence the loot.'

Wendy stared at me. I stared at myself.

'Alan, that's *genius*!'

Very occasionally, I've collaborated with another writer on an assignment. No one likes it because it means splitting the fee, but the upside is you speak the plot out loud, bouncing it off each other instead of gazing at blank walls before jacking it in to watch the Test Match. And very, *very* occasionally, a breakthrough occurs. As the Americans say, out of left field, out of nowhere. Imagine Shakespeare agonizing over how to establish Othello's jealousy. Weeks pass; he paddles in the Avon, kicks stones around the Stratford lanes, sleeps late. Then one morning he sees Anne Hathaway using an unfamiliar handkerchief. It has CM embroidered in the corner. He goes berserk. 'You've been a-whoring with that no-talent faggot spy Marlowe!' His hands are round her windpipe but she manages to gasp it belongs to her cousin, Catherine Makepeace.

Will has his breakthrough.

'How does this actually *work*?' Wendy asked.

I was still bending the facts to the theory, working towards the moment when Sherlock taps out his third pipe and admits to Watson that he is a blind fool for not having seen it sooner.

'Maddy's father is riddled with guilt for leaving her at crappy boarding schools,' I said slowly. 'He'll do anything to make up for it, but he's not his own boss. There's a Doktor Angstrom making his life miserable. One day, he swears, he'll tell Angstrom to shove the job and resign. Then he can spend the rest of his days with his darling daughter, making up for the lost years.'

'Maddy knows this and pillow talks to her chap—'

'Hardwick says Hall hasn't worked out how to wash the money after stripping CBCI.'

'When Maddy says Daddy will do anything for her—'

'They talk themselves into the plot.'

'Maddy hires a German friend to set up the necessary patsy,' Wendy said, then quickly added, 'I mean—'

'You mean patsy,' I said. 'She does her homework and comes up with me. Andree tells them one of the strange things about human nature is that even the most secretive, the most powerful people in the world can't resist having movies made about them. They let researchers look through all the dirty linen, plunder the files, they lend them an air force to make *Top Gun*, armies to re-create D-Day. They like cosying up to film stars. A billionaire buys a movie studio not because he wants to make money, he knows none of them do that. It's because he's sick to death of boring old Wall Street farts around his dinner table. He wants Demi Moore, his wife wants to meet Al Pacino, his kids stop thinking he's a jerk when he starts bringing home Johnny Depp and Spielberg. Here's a man who's made money hand over fist all his life, who now starts haemorrhaging zillions for the pleasure of schmoozing with people who hardly know what fork to use, let alone be witty and amusing without a script.

'So there I am, in Hall's house the night before he takes off. A schmuck from nowhere, showing the same starfucking symptoms in reverse. I am *so* flattered that this tycoon, this legend of the boardrooms, wants *me* to keep him company, to take me to his house. Am I going to say no? After his friend Andree has agreed a contract big enough to bail me out of a financial latrine? I can see them now, looking for the appropriate goat, working through a list of suggestions. Then somebody snaps their fingers and says, "Hey, boys, I got it. Let's get a *writer*!"'

269

I was pale from all this self-flagellation and swilled down the rest of the beer.

Wendy said, 'OK. All the players are in position. How do we pinch their ball?'

I flubbed my lips. 'What we need is for that door to open and the finest hacker in Europe to walk in.'

'Failing that?'

'What about a phone number on a book of matches?'

'What we need now,' she said, 'is brute force. Did you give any more thought to my ideas on how to make the bitch talk?'

'Yes.'

'And?'

'I'm getting closer.'

A bunch of youngsters, all Adam's apples and sixth form sophistication, charged in and we left as they simulated outrage at the landlord's demand to prove they were eighteen.

The rain had stopped and we walked back to Keystone Mansions.

The lights in flat 5 were back on. I checked the parked cars but couldn't find the Saab.

'You think it could just be her?' Wendy said.

'Could be.'

All the flats were now lit except for 6. On the ground floor, a young woman was sipping wine in front of the television. A fanlight window was open and we heard the phone ring. She answered and called, 'Ally, it's for you.' Another woman came through in a bathrobe with a towel round her head, took the receiver and threw herself on to a settee, grinning with delight.

'Do we go in or not?' Wendy said.

'How?'

'Wait here.'

She hurried off towards King's Road. I walked up and down until she returned carrying a bouquet of roses.

The woman was still giggling into the phone and when Wendy pressed their bell, her flatmate went out to the intercom.

'Flowers for someone called Ally,' Wendy called, holding the roses in front of the screen. When the buzzer went, she pushed inside, letting me slip behind and head for the staircase.

The woman with the drink opened a door.

'Are you Ally?'

'She's on the phone. I'll take them.'

'Her birthday?'

'No. Boyfriend most likely.'

She took the flowers inside. Wendy opened and slammed the front entrance door, then followed me up the stairs.

'She's going to thank the bloke she's talking to,' I said. 'He'll say it wasn't him, and that'll be the end of a beautiful friendship.'

'Why is a writer's world so *dark*?'

I motioned her back when we reached the second floor, half-expecting Mrs Davidovitch with a meat cleaver. I wondered if she had once had the Gestapo visit as a child and spent the rest of her life terrified of callers. Her skylight was lit and music was playing. We edged past and continued up.

By the time we reached Maddy's floor, my heart was crashing against my ribcage. I knew something violent was unavoidably about to happen. I wanted to be anywhere but where we now stood, facing her door.

'You should have bought more flowers,' I muttered. She pointed to the spyhole and a speaker beside the doorbell.

271

Pushing me to one side, she patted her hair, licked her lips and rang. A floorboard creaked, then Maddy's voice filtered through:

'Who is it?'

'Oh, *bon soir*, madame,' Wendy squeaked, putting her head close to the spyhole. 'I am, er, I come to see zuh pipple in *appartement* six, but zey are not present.'

'I'm sorry, I can't help you.'

'I am supposed to be staying wizzem, but zere is nobody 'ere.'

'What's their name?' Maddy asked, her voice sharper. Wendy glanced at me and I shrugged.

'Zey are from Lyon. Zey are called Lamartine.'

There was a pause. Did she know her neighbours? The woman in 3 said they had just moved in . . .

'I don't know what to tell you,' she said. 'Except come back later.'

Wendy started to sniffle. 'But I know *personne* in Londres, except a woman in 'ampstead. *C'est loin ça?* Is far?'

'Hampstead?'

'Is possible to walk?'

'Not really. You can take a taxi, or the tube.' Her voice was softening.

'Oh, *merde alors!*' Wendy sniffled. I saw real tears glisten. 'I 'ave no *monnaie*. If I can *rappelle*, er, telephone. Please, madame—'

For a long moment we stood staring at each other.

Then the door opened.

Wendy rammed it with both hands, knocking Maddy against a wall. She opened her mouth to scream, but Wendy seized her throat, shutting down the vocals. I closed the door.

'Make a noise, you fucking bitch, and you can say sayonara

to your teeth,' Wendy hissed into the terrified woman's face. 'Looking on the bright side, that'd mean you'd give the best blow jobs in London, but smiles and flossing'll be a thing of the past.'

She took a handful of hair and dragged her into the living room, forcing her down to the floor. I looked in the other rooms, but she was alone. When I returned, Wendy was pinning her down with a foot on her breasts.

'I shall now pass you over to my colleague, with whom I believe you have already had the pleasure.' She took her foot away.

I was on.

'I'm sorry it has to end this way,' I said. She was shivering with terror. 'It's not an original line, but it fits.'

Maddy tried to sit up, but Wendy shoved her back. 'Stay down. I hear you're used to being on your back.'

'Alan—'

'Madeleine.'

'Alan, I—'

'Maybe I ought to leave you alone,' Wendy said. 'I know you have lots to talk about.'

'You can beat me up as much as you want,' she sobbed. 'I don't know anything.'

'What's the capital of Russia?' Wendy said.

'What?'

'The capital of Russia. What is it?'

'Moscow.'

'There, you see? You do know something. I'll bet once we get going, all sorts of things'll come to you. Did you ever see a film called *Marathon Man*?' She shook her head. 'A bit before your time. Well, there's this scene where Laurence Olivier wants Dustin Hoffman to tell him something. Besides being a Nazi war criminal, Larry's also a dentist. So he straps Dustin into a chair and holds a drill in one hand and oil of cloves in the other. One for pain, one for relief. The only difference here is I forgot the cloves.'

'I told you, I don't know anything—'

I crouched on my haunches.

'You know Andree Bruckmeyer.'

'Who?'

Wendy stood on her head until she gave a muffled yelp.

'Andree.'

'Yes!'

I fondled her sleek hair that had cascaded over my face a hundred years ago, then tightened the grip. 'You hired her to get me involved.'

'No.' I tugged and she cried out. 'It was the other way around.'

'Andree hired you?'

'Yes.'

'She's the brains?'

She nodded.

'Brains for what, hon?' Wendy asked, hovering a shoe above her nose. Maddy glared at me with the sullen reproach of a scorned wife.

'I only did what I was told.'

'Only obeying orders.'

'Yeah.'

'Like at Nuremberg.'

'Where?'

'Who's giving the orders besides Bruckmeyer?'

'No one.'

'Who's Hardwick?'

The name made her start. 'Barry's got nothing to do with it.'

'He hasn't?'

'No.'

'Then who did this?' I said, turning my head to let her see the plasters.

'That wasn't him.'

Wendy took her foot away and left the room. I heard her clinking about before she came back holding a Sabatier kitchen knife. Maddy scuttled backwards but Wendy wound her hair into a fist and placed the blade between her lips.

'Open wide, precious.'

Petrified, Maddy obeyed. Wendy jammed the tip between her two front teeth.

'What was the question again, Alan?' she asked.

'I wanted to know who hit me.'

'That's right. And she said, "It wasn't Barry." Sweetie, you must listen to the question. He didn't ask who it *wasn't*. We could sit here all night hearing who *didn't* do it. It wasn't Elton John, or Che Guevara, or Gary Cooper, or my uncle Arthur—' She accompanied each name with a jab into the cleft of the teeth, creating a spasm like an electric charge. 'Or Robert De Niro or Alan Bennett or Vanessa Redgrave, or—'

'Peter!'

'Peter who? Rabbit?'

She was terrified. Had I been alone, I'd probably have eased up, even though I knew Wendy was only fulfilling my role; working on the one person able to keep me from becoming a sex slave to prisoners who hadn't cared for my movies.

'I don't know his other name – ah!'

275

The blade was now an inch through the gap; the teeth squeaked, strained to snapping point. I felt my gorge rise.

'Wrong answer.'

'Please, don't!'

'Then don't make me,' Wendy said breezily, as if playing tickle with a child.

'I'll tell you—'

She removed the knife and Maddy's hand flew to her mouth, examining the damage.

'Who was it?' I said. For God's sake *tell* us, I prayed. I didn't think I could stand by and watch her teeth flip over the carpet like tiddlywinks.

'It *was* Barry,' she whispered, barely audible.

'And where does he fit into the scheme of things?'

'He thought you were one of my old lovers. He's very jealous—'

Back went the knife until she started to gag on saliva.

'You're insulting our intelligence,' Wendy snapped.

She began to moan. It didn't sound contrived this time. Liquid gurgled deep in her throat. Wendy withdrew the blade: 'Where does Barry fit in?' There was no answer. She yanked the girl's head up and placed the tip up a nostril, but it made no difference.

While I waited, I looked over at the bookshelf. A spine caught my attention. *The Parade's Gone By*, a classic on the silent film era by Kevin Brownlow. Next to it was *Mommie Dearest*, a tract against Joan Crawford by her daughter, then *The Films of Errol Flynn* and *Damned in Paradise, the Life of John Barrymore*. Above them, Goldman's *Adventures in the Screen Trade*, *The Fifty Worst Movies of All Time*, Truffaut's book on Hitchcock, a history of the Western, a row of paperbacks on Bogart, Davis and Cagney, leading to David

Thomson's *A Biographical Dictionary of Film*, whose only error in my opinion was to omit Sissy Spacek. On the shelf above these, I could see *Force Majeure*, a Boschian novel about a writer in Hollywood, Pauline Kael's reviews, another reviewer's opinions about Pauline Kael, Julie Burchill's *Girls in Film*, until the list stretched out of focus. On the top shelf were large reference volumes: *TV Movies*, the *Great Movie Stars*, the *Films of John Ford*, *Howard Hawks*, next to a line of published scripts: *North by Northwest*, *Les Enfants du Paradis*, *Charade*.

Wendy was looking at Maddy's slack mouth and glazed eyes. She sniffed. 'I think she's peed herself. What are you looking at?'

'Barry seems to be a bigger movie buff than I am. It's like the NFT bookshop in here.'

'I need some water. In a big bowl.'

I went into the kitchen and brought back a bowlful. Wendy threw some on Maddy's face.

'Is she faking?'

'There's one way to find out.' She dunked the girl's face and held her under. She didn't struggle, made no effort to pull herself out. Wendy laid her on her back and she stared blindly up at the ceiling.

'She's gone into shock.'

I scanned more shelves. Barry apparently had few other reading interests. There were How To books on screenwriting, acting, make-up. Photograph albums of Garbo, Dietrich and Hepburn.

'I bet if you took all these books,' I said, 'all the plots on how to frame a man for murder and boiled them down, you could arrive at the perfect crime. Look at this: the script of *North by Northwest*. Cary Grant is kidnapped by James Mason and taken to a house.' I flipped through Lehmann's screen-play. 'They force liquor down his throat, put him in a car and send it down a mountain road. He survives the crash but gets arrested for drunk driving. When he tells his story and takes the police to the house, there's no trace of Mason or the gang. Just the owners who call him Roger dear, and ask if he got home safely last night. Ring a bell?'

Wendy was kneeling beside Maddy, feeling for a pulse. 'Maddy? Can you hear me? Maddy?'

'Yes.'

'Look at me.' She moved her eyes slowly across. 'Do you know where you are?'

'Barry's.'

'Do you live here?'

'No.'

'Where do you live?'

'I want to go to the lavatory.'

'Where do you live?'

'I'm tired.'

'Where does your father live?' I tried.

'Lots of places.'

Wendy went to look around the other rooms, muttering about matchbooks and phone numbers. Maddy shifted her eyes to mine and gave a weary smile, almost of regret.

'I didn't want you to get hurt, Alan.'

'Who's behind it all?' I asked.

She yawned. 'Barry said it would all be easy.'

'What would?'

'Getting the money.'

'From the bank.'

'Yes.'

'From Arnold Hall.' She nodded. 'But Hall is dead.' Another

dip of the head turned into a shrug. 'You weren't told that was part of the plan. Barry didn't let you in on that.'

'I feel so *tired*!' She closed her eyes. I shook her.

'Who killed him?'

'I don't know their names.'

'Whose names? You mean the shooters?'

'Funny names, shooters.'

'Who hired them?'

'What's the matter with me? I can't move.'

'Maddy,' I said, slapping her face. 'Don't go to sleep, listen to me, Maddy.' I forced her to sit up. 'Whose idea was it to rob CBCI? Was it Barry's?'

Her head lolled and she smiled dreamily, picking at the wet hair that clung to her cheeks.

Wendy returned with the Chanel bag, holding up a Nokia mobile phone.

'No bog standard Sloane ever leaves home without one. And guess what? It was turned on. Everybody's logged in here. Addresses, phone numbers, fax numbers, e-mails.'

She pressed a button, bringing up a list of digits in the window. 'What's 49 international?'

'Germany.'

'41?'

'Switzerland, I think.'

She pulled Maddy's head towards the Nokia. 'Which one is Daddy's?'

When there was no answer, I said, 'One way to find out. Start calling.'

'No, don't!' Maddy pleaded, scrabbling for the phone. Wendy pulled it away.

'What's up, pet? Won't he be pleased to hear you've been consorting with crims?'

'He's got nothing to do with this!' she cried.

'Who's Dr Angstrom?' I asked. This snagged her attention. 'What do you know about Angstrom?'

'What do *you*?'

All control drained from her. She pressed her hands to her cheeks and wailed, resembling Munch's famous picture. Then she started to choke and fought to breathe, air rasping in her throat. She fell back to the floor, her legs twitching so violently that a shoe flew off.

'She's hyperventilating,' Wendy shouted. She took a deep breath, pinched the girl's nose and blew into her mouth. Maddy's other shoe bounced over the carpet as her heels hammered into the carpet. Wendy lifted her head, took another deep breath and reapplied her lips.

She came back up again almost at once with a look of surprise and slowly toppled backwards. I saw blood pouring down her leg.

Then the kitchen knife impaled in her groin.

Maddy was rolling over, struggling to her feet. She lunged for the Nokia that had fallen under a chair. I flung out an arm and hit her in the temple. She staggered back. I went after her. She pulled the standard lamp on top of me. By the time I was standing, she was out of the door.

Wendy lay looking puzzled. Then she saw the knife in her crotch.

'Shit, what's this?'

I knelt, grabbed the handle and pulled it out, releasing a torrent of blood.

'It's OK. It's all right, I've got it, take it easy, don't move, lie still.'

I rambled on, not knowing what to do other than keep my hand tight against the bloody gap in her jeans. I fished

280

out a handkerchief and pressed that into it. She was losing consciousness.

'Wake up – Wendy, wake *up*, can you hear me?'

Her hand fell by her side. I looked across at the mobile and hooked it with my foot. Holding it between blood-sticky fingers, I pressed three nines.

DATE: 23 OCTOBER

FAX TO: PER ANGSTROM, MAISON VILLEFRANCHE,
           CHAMPERY, SWITZERLAND

FROM: GEORGE KAPLAN

Houston, we have a problem. Roger has reappeared and
is in possession of too much information. Transport
is in place and ready. Do we escalate or evacuate?

                                              KAPLAN

DATE: 23 OCTOBER

FAX TO: GEORGE KAPLAN

FROM: ROMAN

It is essential the information is recovered. Employ
Frantic scenario immediately.

                                               ROMAN

The paramedics arrived inside ten minutes. My wrist was
numb from pressing the swab into the wound. While we
waited, she drifted in and out of consciousness, mumbling a
few lucid words: 'Shoulda remembered the knife . . . God,
actually b'lieved she was dying . . . Don't go on at me, sweetheart, no, don't . . .'

I kept a mantra going about the ambulance is on its way,
hang on, you're doing fine, the bleeding's stopped. All the
necessary lies. The blood sank into the carpet and my clothes,
turning from pillar-box red to terracotta. I felt it congeal on
my hands. Oh, Christ, how much has she lost? If it's an
artery, she'll be dead in minutes. There was a scene in *Cracker*.
A girl knifed on a train, blood spurting like a geyser, painting

the ceiling. My hand's gone numb; *don't let go of the cloth*! Where *are* they? How will they get in? Did I tell them what floor we're on—

When Maddy ran out, she left the door open and I heard the lift doors clunk seconds before two men and a woman in green overalls came in carrying a collapsed stretcher. One knelt and gently replaced my hand.

'What happened?'

'She was stabbed in the groin.' I pointed to the knife on the floor.

The woman raised Wendy's shirt and timing her movements with the man holding the swab, pulled down her jeans and pants. I caught a quick glimpse of a cut an inch long oozing blood, slower now. The third medic had opened a bag and taken out a field dressing which he pressed hard down on to the gash. Wendy's thigh glistened with wet blood as the two men pressed down on the dressing like plumbers trying to stem a burst pipe. The woman meanwhile was reaching in the bag and bringing out a plastic bottle and a length of tube.

'Leave the drip till we're outside,' one of the men said. 'We'll have enough on our hands taking her down the stairs.'

'How is she?' I asked.

'Are you related?'

'No.'

'How did it happen?'

'The woman who lives here did it. She took off.'

'Did you touch the knife?'

'When I pulled it out.'

The woman on the radio was calling the police. She talked rapidly in efficient, economical reportage, describing the victim, the wound, the circumstances and the address. She ended

283

by saying no, they couldn't delay, they were transferring her immediately.

Meanwhile, as one kept pressure on the wound, the other had opened out the stretcher and placed it alongside Wendy. Then the three of them bent over and, to the count of three, lifted her on to it, keeping the field dressing in position.

'What's your name, sir?'

'Tate.'

'You come with us.' The woman took charge of the dressing while the men manoeuvred Wendy through the hall and round the door. Mrs Davidovitch was standing by the lift.

'Vot are you doing?' she demanded.

'Out the way, love,' the leading medic said, turning round to walk backwards down the stairs, keeping the stretcher level. Mrs Davidovitch reluctantly stood back, peered at the blood on my clothes, then into my face. Was she remembering the chartered surveyor? She transferred her attention to Wendy.

'Who is this?'

'There's been an accident,' the medic at the rear called. 'We'll look after her, don't worry. Just move aside.'

'But she is not the vooman who liffs here—'

The descent went in stops and starts. It reminded me of moving house; lugging down a settee, the removals men calling out wait, down a bit, hang on, easy now. Adding to their problem was the woman medic, squashed against the walls as she struggled to keep the field dressing in place.

I kept a hand on the Nokia in my pocket, waiting for them to negotiate the corners. More people came out to watch, alerted by the flashing lights from the ambulance in the street. The leading stretcher-bearer kept up a running patter: 'Mind out of the way, please, watch it, thank you, step aside please, there's nothing to see . . .'

Mrs Cavanaugh took one look at the blood on Wendy's thighs and shooed her girls inside.

We reached the ground floor where the two girls in the front flat were standing in their doorway. One looked at Wendy.

'That's the woman who brought the flowers,' she exclaimed as we went past and out into the chill night air.

They slid the stretcher into the ambulance. One turned to help me up. Or was it to prevent me doing a runner? One of the men returned to the driver's cabin while the other rigged up a saline drip and attached it to a vein in Wendy's wrist. Once in place, he relieved the woman on the dressing and banged on the wall. The engine purred into life and we were moving, the sirens gathering pitch. The woman turned on a heat blaster and checked Wendy's eyes. There was a silent, military precision to their actions that pointed to regular practice. I wondered if they took their domestic partners through the day's routine when they got home or, like pathologists, found their audiences tended to reach for the sick bucket whenever they tried to describe it.

The heat was suffocating and I felt faint.

'Are you all right?' she asked. I nodded unconvincingly. 'Put your head between your knees.'

'I'm all right.'

'Do it anyway.'

The ambulance was gathering speed, the alarms loud enough to scare a tank out of the way. Everything began to rock. I tried doing what I was told and clouted my head.

'How far are we going?'

285

'A few minutes.' The vehicle ducked and weaved and I grabbed whatever was close.

The woman produced a clipboard. 'Can you give me some details?'

She asked Wendy's name and address, her age, marital status and I answered what I could. No, I had no idea if she was allergic to any medication. We were friends, but hadn't seen each other for a long time until recently. The knifing was never mentioned, who did it or why. That, presumably, was cop stuff.

'Can you give me any idea how she is?' I asked.

'We'll soon see.'

'Can she hear us?'

'No, they gave her a sedative.'

'She lost a lot of blood,' I said. Something said don't ask anything more. It might be written down and used in evidence.

The sirens diminuendoed. The gates of a hospital jolted past and we stopped. The back doors opened and the men slid the stretcher out, released an undercarriage and wheeled Wendy inside. The woman climbed down and waited for me, holding my arm as I negotiated the step and keeping hold as we followed the stretcher towards Casualty.

'Can I clean myself up?' I said.

'In a minute.'

She had called the police from the flat, so they would be here any moment. I had given my name as Tate. Even if they didn't connect me right away, the fact I was found with a seriously wounded woman would be more than enough to have them ask questions. In my pocket was the Nokia, my own personal Ark of the Covenant.

'Sit there. I won't be a minute,' she said and disappeared

through a swing door. People passed and stared. The blood-stains made me into a casualty, attracting those I-can't-bear-to-look-but-can't-resist-it glances. When a young boy stopped to gawp, his mother yanked him off as if I were contagious.

It was now an hour since I had called the ambulance, twenty minutes since the message was passed to the police. Where were they? On television, they grab their hats and are out of the door in seconds.

An overpowering urge to put my feet up and drift off to sleep deadened all reflexes. The first of the Armageddon thoughts had seeped through during the ride. If Wendy dies, it will be my fault. She wouldn't be here had I not rung her, pleading for help. Wouldn't have got stabbed, wouldn't have, have—

Don't go to sleep! Where was it, *Scott of the Antarctic, Call of the Wild, Jeremiah Johnson*? One of those snowbound sagas where men fight the temptation to close their eyes, just take a nap, feel better in a minute.

I forced myself to stand. Among the signs hanging in the corridor was Toilets. Inside, I took off the jacket, rolled my sleeves above the elbows and ran water down, watching the dried blood reconstitute and whirl round the plughole.

In *Psycho*, Hitchcock used liquid chocolate in the shower scene because red didn't look convincing in monochrome. Well, it did here. I stared in the mirror. Was this really me? Lines furrowed my cheeks, below my eyes, turning me into the man who left Shangri-La and reverted to his real age. On each temple, like tribal warpaint, were streaks of blood transferred from my hands when I had held my head in the ambulance.

While I removed the gore, I couldn't stop a ring-a-roses

287

jingle in my head: If she dies, it's down to me, if she dies, then I'm to blame, if she dies, it's all my fault – *stop it*! Forget everything but your next move. Which is what? To get out of this place. Once the police arrive, it's over.

Was that such a bad thing? Where *do* you go from here? You have the mobile with all the numbers. So fucking what? What are you hoping for? That one call to Burnside or Angstrom and they'll fold? Put their hands up and say whatever the German is for it's a fair cop? Whether it was the thought of Wendy dying, or the crack on the head now pounding like grunge rock, or the weariness of having constantly to consider what next, it all began to seem so futile. Right from the start, with or without Wendy or Maxie or Tim or Richard, I had never stood a chance. Small men only beat overwhelming odds in Frank Capra movies, and people stopped believing that crap a long time ago. Leave it, take your chances with the law. Richard said very few innocent people are convicted. At least you found someone in Keystone Mansions, someone who tried to kill Wendy. The police have to take notice of that, and of the Nokia stuff. And Tim would back me up on Andree Bruckmeyer—

A phone was ringing. Distantly, but from somewhere inside the lavatory. I looked round. Was someone in a cubicle? Then I realized it was coming from my pocket. I pulled the mobile out, peered myopically at the buttons and prodded a few until the ringing stopped.

'Yes?'

No one spoke, but I could hear shuffling, muffled voices, one a woman's. 'Hello, who's there?'

'Alan?'

Expecting Maddy, I hesitated. 'Who is this?'

'Alan, it's me.'

288

'*Maxie?*'

'Some men broke into the house—'

'Hello? Maxie, hello, *hello?*'

A man came on. Cockney, calm, controlled. 'Alan, my old love, the arrangement is, your wife for the phone you're holding.'

Then the line went dead.

Had it been her? Why didn't they let her say more? Call back.

Someone came in. I shoved the phone away, washed and dried my face in slomo while he peed, glancing my way nervously. Men who hung around lavs like this were only after one thing. He zipped up fast and didn't wait to rinse his hands.

As he opened the door, I caught a glimpse of a uniform. I looked out and saw two patrol officers. One was speaking into his radio saying they were at the hospital. When they turned the corner towards Casualty, I walked in the opposite direction.

A third patrolman was standing up ahead. Each side of the corridor were consulting rooms, nurses' offices and a cloakroom, none of which offered a hiding place. Did they have my description, apart from my last name? Did I look anything like the Brittany snapshot? Don't be furtive; walk on past, don't run until someone shouts.

I walked past him and out of the front entrance where two empty patrol cars stood in the ambulance lane. Would it be pushing one's luck . . . ?

I was in Fulham Road. Crossing into the dark side streets I pulled out the Nokia and called home.

'Alan? That you, old mate?' They were there all right.

'Let me speak to my wife.'

'Why, don't you believe we got her?'

'Put her on, you piss-brained cuntface.'

'Oooh, tem*per.*' There was a pause, a burst of static.

'Honey?'

'Are you all right?'

'Yes.'

'Are they standing next to you?'

'Yes.'

'How many are there?'

She yelped as the phone was snatched and the Cockney voice came back, this time without the jokes: 'Never you fucking mind how many we are. Just get here and bring the phone.'

'Lay one finger on her, and you don't get jack shit.'

'Gotcha.' Click.

I kept walking, away from Fulham Road, away from the hospital where the alarm must have been raised by now. The third cop would have reported noticing a man in a filthy pinstripe and they'd be racing to the cars. Ten minutes and we'd have a chopper overhead with a beam.

Both sides of the road were lined with cars and I knew how the Ancient Mariner felt about water. So often, my characters flip a door lock with a wire and a wink, fiddle a moment under the steering column and vrooom! I had no idea where to start. Smashing the window to get in was only half of it. What did hot-wiring entail? Which bits did you put together? Did it even work any more with modern vehicles?

Up ahead, a car pulled up and a woman got out. I moved forward in the shadows as she headed for a house and saw two men in the car. Their combined weight would have sent the French pack reeling at Twickenham. Carjacking

290

anyway was risky. Maxie was thirty miles out of London. The owner would contact the police, and they'd have an APB giving the registration number to all patrols within minutes.

I needed one that wouldn't be missed for an hour. Someone in a restaurant. Langton Street was nearby and had several. I cut through the side streets until I was standing outside La Famiglia, popular with luvvies and anyone who cared for authentic Italian food served without pink tablecloths or breadsticks.

Two large identical cars with consecutive number plates were double-parked in front, each with a driver inside. One had the *Sun* propped on the steering wheel, the other was dozing. I looked into the restaurant and saw a large table of ten people. Judging by the shades, sweatshirts and leather blousons, they were pop stars, or wannabes. Just the type to hire limos.

I rapped on the sleeping driver's window, working on the theory that when people are suddenly awoken, they tend to be less analytical. His eyes snapped open and he sat up, instinctively reaching for the keys that hung in the ignition. Then he realized I wasn't his client.

'You widda musicians?' I said, using ice-cream Italian.

'Yeah.'

'Your bossa wants a word.'

'You what?'

'I am the manager. He aska me to a fetch you.'

The driver yawned and got out. Leaving the keys.

I'm not asking anyone to do this at home, but since I was presently living on the long odds of survival, I was grasping at straws. My guess was he wouldn't know offhand the number of the car he was driving. These were guys who

291

worked for a hire company. They turn up, are given an address and a car, and away they go.

The moment he shuffled inside, I climbed in, switched on and moved out, to paraphrase Dr Leary, while the other driver remained deep into page three nips. I eased into King's Road and headed west. In the glove compartment were the vehicle's details along with the form the customer signs at the completion of the trip. I knew about the system because I have a long enough memory to remember when there used to be a British film industry. Everybody rented chauffeur-driven cars in those days, sometimes even for the writer. The drivers told me their routine. Better than driving cabs, squire. Better hours, better motors and better class of punter. The consecutive registration numbers had given me the clue. Large hire firms lease several at a time, straight off the assembly line.

The dashboard clock read ten fifteen, a time when traffic was at its least worst. Clubs, pubs and cinemas were still going strong, leaving the streets to the carless or those who could afford none of the above. Putney was clear, and within twenty minutes I was passing the outer galaxies of Wimbledon and Merton.

This is the point in a film where the hitherto total klutz shows his mettle. Writers always contrive to hide the change from the audience. The way it goes is, for the first three-quarters of the picture he falls in rivers, gets beaten up, wrongly arrested and dumped by his long-suffering fiancée. She's tried her damnedest but he'll never change, he'll always be a loser, so here, take the ring back and get out of my life. We're talking major twat. Harry Langdon, Martin Short. Then, just as the audience are wondering how he'll screw up the rescue mission, it's revealed that during the last set

292

of pratfalls he was actually organizing a network of counterstrikes which occur on cue, wiping out the opposition in a heart-stopping series of set pieces. The villains are blown to smithereens, his nine-year-old deaf mute daughter returns safe in his arms and the townspeople, who have always despised him, hang out welcome banners. Finally, standing to acknowledge their adulation, he spreads his arms wide and knocks the mayor's wife off the podium.

As I drove the familiar route to the house, I had everything worked out up until the moment I got there. Where was the script I needed, the result of two, three, fifteen hacks smoking up a room and yelling, "Hey, why not have him —?" I had nothing pre-prepared or rehearsed. There was no storyboard overview, no split-second anything.

In *Bad Day at Black Rock*, a one-armed Spencer Tracy is pinned down by rifle fire from an evil Robert Ryan. He crawls under his jeep, unscrews the fuel cap and fills a conveniently handy bottle, stuffs his tie in and lights the end. Ryan's finger is tightening on the trigger to fire the fatal shot when Spence stands and flings the Molotov cocktail. It smashes against a rock at just the right angle for the flaming contents to splash over Ryan and put him out of action. I first saw the film when I was around twelve and loved the moment when the handicapped war veteran Tracy demolishes a bullying Ernest Borgnine with three karate chops, to the throat, neck and kidneys. All my life I've fantasized about using them on muggers. But, I had to confess, that final aim was too good to be true. And fuel tanks aren't usually entered from *under* a vehicle. If it had been the oil sump, the device wouldn't have been as inflammatory. I like to suspend my disbelief at the start of a flick, not at the end.

The garden walls loomed up. I switched off the headlights,

pulled the wheels on to the grass verge and killed the engine.

Let's run through this again. I have the Nokia, containing numbers and names they regard as incriminating. They have Maxie. What did Danny de Vito tell the Ruthless People who kidnapped his wife? Kill the bitch, I hate her. But his wife was played by Bette Midler and it was understandable. How do I bargain with them? What do I say? "I am assuming you are men of your word." "Gentlemen, this is England. A handshake is all I require." These same men whacked their employer Arnold Hall who had hired them to assist in a charade. They took Andree's, or Maddy's, shilling and reloaded with live ammo. As Sam pointed out, unwritten codes aren't worth the paper they're printed on.

They think I'll drive to the gates and ring the bell. No, that's what they *want* me to think. They really expect me to climb over and sneak up on them. Why? What possible good could that do? They had Maxie. I could come down the fucking chimney and they could still take the mobile, then kill us both.

It had been a long while since I last heaved myself over the crumbling section of the perimeter wall. A few years ago, there'd been a power failure and the gates wouldn't work. Maxie wanted to fetch the stonemasons, but I had argued that if they repaired it, the next time the electric went out, we'd have to sleep in the road. Anyway, you couldn't see the hole, hidden behind thick brambles. It was our secret. I loved Enid Blyton as a kid, and secret entrances were staple plot ingredients for the Famous Five.

The October dew made the grass underfoot cold and wet. Through the orchard, I saw lights in the lower rooms and one upstairs. Clouds scudded across the moon in a *Wuthering Heights* back-projection effect. All it needed was an owl and

I was in *Night of the Demon*. The trees, still in full leaf, gave enough cover to move closer. The living room curtains were drawn and there were no signs of anyone keeping watch. Either they didn't expect me to hide my arrival, or they knew they held enough cards to make it suicidal.

What I did see, moving round to the rear of the house, was a helicopter. Parked slap in the centre of the rose beds. Late-blooming petals had been blown everywhere like confetti.

Since *Apocalypse Now*, helicopters have represented terror on the screen. Not even cartoons, giving them smiling faces, can remove the redolent hostility of these Brobdignagian dragonflies. In *Capricorn One*, they track down and kill people, turning towards each other in mid-air when the pilots converse. Police choppers hover over cities and older folk say the sound of their engines provokes a shiver of fear, reminding them of wartime air raids.

Seeing this thing rammed down on a lovingly planted collection of Victorian roses, the kind that still smelled, that gave credibility to the Shakespeare quote, was like watching a Russian tank crack the cobbles along Wenceslas Square.

Something was triggering déjà vu. When had I last been up close to a helicopter? *Before the Dawn* had used them for aerial footage. We'd started with a decent-sized budget so the director, a South African whose career I was thrilled to see stalled after the picture's release, this retarded Polaroid dabbler, who demanded a writing credit because he'd changed around a few commas, this streak of piss had wanted eagle's eye shots and ordered four of them. That, along with other megalomaniac excesses, was why we went into the red after three weeks, and how the ending was ruined through lack of money, and why I now claim *Before the Yawn*, as the

295

gleeful trades dubbed it, was not my fault, since it had been rewritten, every scene, every word, by an illiterate.

That was the last time I'd been this close to a chopper. Somebody had suggested using one in the final sequences. There'd been complaints from the front office that the ending lacked juice. Where were the orange explosions and killing sprees to make the audience ovulate? Working on the fag end of the wasted budget, a stuntman came up with the idea that if we could just have one machine, the heavies could take off in it while the hero, a disgraced SAS operative who redeems himself after years of alcoholism, caused by the (erroneous) belief that he'd been responsible for his best friend's death in action, could blow the thing out of the sky with a single shot from a crossbow.

We were shown precisely where the fuel tanks were located, and how an arrow bolt could do the trick.

For those who were indiscriminate enough to see the picture, and don't recall a crossbow-wielding SAS man shooting down a fully armed Apache, I should explain that by the ninth week there wasn't enough money left even to pay the caterers. The last chopper had been repossessed and the denouement consisted of orange explosion out-takes scrounged from older movies. Some directors are wise virgins, but the majority aren't.

However, fifteen years after the *BTD* fiasco, I had finally gained one small shred of comfort. The experience had taught me where to find the fuel tank.

I called the house.

'You're late,' the Cockney barked.

'There's roadworks coming off the M25.'

'How long you gonna be?'

'Twenty minutes.'

In the garden shed I found a roll of hessian and wrapped it round the Nokia. Then I took a spade over to the vegetable garden and began to dig.

Ten minutes later, the chores were done. I cleaned my hands under the hosepipe and crossed the lawn towards the darkened kitchen windows. Lights shone in the hall beyond and I could see figures moving around in the living room.

Keeping close to the walls, I reached the curtained windows. One of the drapes had not been pulled completely across and looking through the gap, I saw Maxie. She was sitting with her hands folded in her lap. One of the reasons I fell for her was the way she held her hands like that. Ask a man why he loves someone and he'll fidget, change the subject, or say because she gives terrific head. They do this because they don't know, because it relates to feelings they can't explain. Like the song says, it's the way they wear their hat, the way they sip their tea. Maxie first created an irresistible rush of affection when I noticed her holding the index finger of her left hand with her right fist. Like a child who is being told off. Sentimental nonsense, but for me it worked. And now, seeing her there, looking upwards, presumably at someone who was frightening her to death, I never felt more protective of anything in my life, and I longed for the moment when I would hand her tormentor the treatment Tracy gave Borgnine at Black Rock.

I couldn't see anyone else but picked up voices I recognized. Two accents, one northern, the other Cockney. Last heard in Hall's house saying, 'I fahnd a watch by the bed.' 'Hers?' 'Nah, a bloke's.'

Headlights flashed in the darkness. A car turned into the gates and stopped. A figure emerged and pressed the bell.

The curtains parted and I dropped to the ground. Someone looked out, shielding his eyes. Then a voice called from the hall, from the intercom: 'It's Barry!' The gates parted and the Saab drove up fast and skidded to a gravelly halt, activating the security beam over the front entrance.

Maddy was the first out, followed by the driver. The doors opened and the Yorkie greeted them.

'We thought you were Tate.'

The driver turned towards the security beam, squinting.

'You mean he's not here yet?' His hair was darker, his build slimmer and the tan had gone, but I recognized the voice that had told me about the evil men he worked for.

It was Arnold Hall.

He and Maddy strode inside as the northerner repeated my phone message. The curtains remained open and I saw them enter the room where the Cockney was standing over Maxie. Hall was saying, 'We came that way, there weren't any roadworks . . .'

He looked at his watch, no longer a Rolex.

'Barry,' Maddy soothed, 'he'll be here.'

If Barry was Hall, who had been dumped on the A34?

'What you give him the phone for, you stupid cunt?' Sarf snarled to Maddy.

'Leave off,' said Hall. 'She had no choice.'

'No *choice*? Whadde do, say please?'

'I said, leave it out, Harry.'

'We coulda bin 'alfway 'cross the world by now,' Sarf grumbled.

'Where's the chopper?'

The other man jerked a thumb: 'Behind.'

'I don't like this 'angin' about,' Sarf muttered. 'It wasn't meant to be like this.'

'S'pose he don't come,' Yorkie said. 'S'pose he says fuck her. I mean, they're divorced.'

'He won't. He'll be here,' Hall replied.

Sarf grunted. 'He don't sound no 'ero type to me.'

Oh no? All right, you cocksucker, watch this.

I crabbed sideways into view and rapped on the glass. Everyone turned like a well-drilled chorus line. Maxie leaped to her feet shouting, 'Alan!'

Sarf pushed her back, then came into the aim, the barrel a yard from my face on the other side of the glass. I raised my arms. He opened a window, clambered over the sill, slammed me against the wall and finished a rapid frisk with a professional squeeze of my balls to eliminate resistance. As my knees gave way, he threw me over the sill like a Scotsman tossing a caber. I lay on the floor with a burning groin and pinpricks of light swooping across my pupils. The Yorkie pressed his gun into my neck: 'Where is it? Where's the phone?'

I stayed wincing in agony, hands over my scrotum. Maxie knelt down.

'Honey, what happened?'

'It was just their way of showing they care,' I gasped. At this point, an admiring chuckle would have run through the cinema audience.

Now Maddy was looking down, her mind back at the flat. 'Fetch a knife,' she said.

Sarf told her to keep out of the way but she stood her ground, glaring at me with all the hatred of someone who had very nearly lost her front teeth.

'Get me a knife!' she yelled. 'I can make him talk.'

'Wait,' said Hall, joining the ring above. 'Get him up.'

I mimed the Eddie Murphy routine in *Trading Places* when he pretends to be legless, but there was no uproarious punchline here when the northerner dragged me upright. Hall held out his hand.

'The phone.'

'It's not on him,' Sarf Lunnon said.

'Where is it?'

'Let Maxie go and I'll tell you.'

The neg was slowly developing. The photograph of Hall in the newspapers had, like mine, been taken some time ago. The man before me now was similar, but not so full-faced, and the glasses made his eyes look larger. However, put the two together and you'd have trouble deciding who had the Tony.

'You have two minutes, then she dies,' he said quietly, nodding towards Maxie.

'I buried it. After calling someone to tell them if Maxie doesn't ring in one hour, he's to tell the police where to find it.'

Hardwick didn't move for a second. Then he grinned.

'Once a hack, always a hack. With plotting like that, I can see why you're in *The Fifty Worst Movies of All Time*.'

'*Charade*,' I said. His grin stayed firm. 'Walter Matthau fools Audrey Hepburn in Paris into believing he works at the American Embassy. He meets her there, using the office of the real official while he's at lunch. You've got the script in your flat.'

'Your problem is you're no Cary Grant. So little Audrey here –' he jabbed a thumb at Maxie – 'doesn't get rescued in the final reel.'

'I am not in *The Fifty Worst Movies of All Time*,' I said.

'You deserve to be. You've buried the phone, let someone know where, and if your wife doesn't turn up, they're to tell the police.'

300

'Did I overlook something?'

'We *need* it in order to let you both go, you bloody idiot. If we don't get it, we'll take you somewhere else and wait till we do.'

'Shit, I hadn't thought of that.'

'I saw *Before the Dawn* on television. Now I know why it was such a crock of shit.'

'It was rewritten by a cretin.'

He held up his watch. 'Tick tock.'

I flicked my fingers. 'Oh, I forgot something. This call I made. I also read out the German and Swiss numbers in the phone's memory. I said if he didn't hear from us within the hour, the police were to call them.'

His smile faded. 'You're bluffing.'

'Now that *is* a hack's line.'

'Wossee on about?' Sarf said, his gun wilting by Maxie's head.

'Nothing of consequence.'

'Then why'd you stop grinning?'

'Let's suppose they ring Maddy's father,' I banged on, watching her reaction. 'What's he going to think? All he was told was arrange for the CBCI cash to be lodged in the bank where Doktor Angstrom keeps his parallel world account.'

'Barry!' Maddy screamed. 'How's he know about Angstrom?'

Hardwick slipped her a killer shut-your-mouth look and came so close I could smell his breath. 'Angstrom? Who's Angstrom?'

'"Knock knock, who's there? Elvis. Elvis who? How soon we forget." Angstrom, Barry, is the one who's paying your wages. And theirs,' pointing to the shooters, then at Maddy: 'And hers.'

301

Maddy looked ready to wet her pants all over again. 'How does he *know* all this?' she wailed. I gave her a Bruce Willis smirk.

'You talk in your sleep, baby.'

She lunged forward, aiming for my throat. In the microsecond it took for the defence system to stand on alert, I saw something flash in her fist. She was holding a paper knife from the desk behind the settee. Shaped like a stiletto, it had been presented to me at the end of a film. Hardwick tried to knock it away, but she got through. I dodged, grabbed her wrist and twisted. Not in the Spencer Tracy class, but she gave a shriek and the knife fell.

'All *right*!' Hardwick yelled. 'Stop this!' He shoved her backwards into an armchair, picked up the blade and read an inscription on the handle: '"For Alan. Thanks for the words." What words?'

'Guess.'

He turned it over in his hands. 'Stiletto. Sicilian Mafia. *Two Against the Mob*.'

'You should go on *Mastermind*. "The Life and Works of Alan Tate."'

'It's more likely to be the life and *death* of Alan Tate.'

'This is all fasci-fuckin'-natin',' Sarf announced. 'But when d'we get outta here?'

Hardwick raised an eyebrow.

'Your move, wordsmith.'

'Maxie leaves now. She takes her mobile and calls when she's safe. Then I fetch yours. Then you get that chopper off my roses.'

He made as if he were considering this.

'Then you hand the numbers to the police.'

'Then you send Laurel and Hardy here to come back and

302

kill us. Come on, Barry, think *Cape Fear*. Do I want to spend the rest of my life worrying about Bob Mitchum turning up to rape my daughter?'

Another thought-ridden pause followed. 'By the way,' I said, 'how did you get into CBCI? And Hall's office? And how come the boys on the trading floor knew you?'

'I work there,' he replied. 'Or did, until we were all made redundant when the assets evaporated.'

'Hall's secretary?'

'You know her,' he smiled.

'I *do*?'

'Unless you're the fuck 'em and forget 'em type.'

My head revolved towards Maddy. A blond wig, Donna Karan suit, yep.

'OK,' Hardwick nodded.

'OK what?'

'Deal.' He told the men to put their guns down.

'Now I'm the one who's nervous.' As the great Imperial Poet almost wrote: If you can keep your head while all around are losing theirs, could it be you've overlooked something? 'Wait,' I said aloud, and the guns came out again, 'someone has to take the fall for killing Hall. I don't want to end my days in Papua New Guinea.'

'Well, don't look at me,' said Hardwick.

I wasn't. I was looking at Sarf. 'Give them the gunsel,' I Bogeyed. Hardwick erupted in Sidney Greenstreet's fruity laughter.

'My word, Mr Spade, you are a character and no mistake. There's no telling what you'll come up with next.'

Sarf's jaw fell an inch. I suppose not having seen *The Maltese Falcon* a hundred times, he had reason to be confused.

'What's he fuckin' on about, Barry? What's he fuckin' sayin'?'

'Morons,' Hardwick grinned at me. 'I've got morons on my team.'

'Maxie goes.'

Hardwick politely helped her up, saying, 'Why don't you take the Saab?'

'What do I do with it?'

Hardwick gave her a boyish grin. 'Keep it. Although there might be a problem if you get a ticket.'

'You don't have the registration,' Maxie guessed. 'And the plates aren't listed, and it was probably white when you stole it.'

'Blue,' Hardwick said, opening the door. She smiled at him and for a second, I felt a twinge of jealousy. He was flirting with her. I assumed he was just getting back because I had banged his girlfriend.

We reached the car and I hugged her: 'Go to your mother's. Don't call anyone till I get there.'

'Be careful,' she whispered, then grasped the nape of my neck: 'I love you.'

'I know.'

Ordinarily, she'd have mashed my instep for that, but these were unusual times and she let it go. I watched her drive to the gates and disappear, a throaty turbo roar echoing in the still night.

I walked them round to the vegetable garden, stopping at the shed for a spade. A minute later, I was passing the hessian package to Sarf. He stepped back.

'Take it out.'

'Afraid it's a bomb?' I said. 'I bet you saw *Leon*.'

'Who the fuck's *Leon*?'

304

'What we have here,' Hardwick drawled as he took the bundle, 'is a failure to communicate.'

He removed the sacking and held the Nokia up to the moonlight, checking the identity.

We returned inside. Yorkie asked Hardwick if that was it, meaning aren't we going to off this arsehole and plant him under the cabbages?

Hardwick made a call. 'Roman, it's Kaplan. Roger's given us the information.' He listened, then said, 'Right.' He ended the call and held out a hand for Yorkie's gun. I felt a mouth-drying shock. He raised it into my face. As Michael Caine remarked in *Sleuth*, I thought my last moment on earth would be spent looking at his cufflinks, but he flipped the barrel round, placed it against the Nokia and fired, sending plastic shards across the room.

'Time to go.'

Maddy stood, holding her wrist, and sent me a look that could prompt only one response.

'I suppose another blow job is out of the question.'

'If you breathe one word to my father about this . . .' she said.

'You'll what?'

'I'll see to it your family holds up the Hammersmith flyover.'

I grinned at Hardwick, 'The cheaper the crook, the gaudier the patter.'

She spat in my face. A sheltered life had not exposed me to such white-hot hatred before and I was genuinely shocked.

'Poor little rich girl,' I said, forcing myself not to wipe the saliva. 'Neglected as a kid, wants so badly to prove to Daddy that she's really very bright. So off she goes and gets involved in the heist of the century. After all, *someone* was

going to do it, so why not you and your insider boyfriend?'
I waded on, waiting for them to correct the scenario, but
they just stood there. 'As it turned out, the bank you picked
to wash and dry the loot was run by Angstrom, who also
happened to be on the board of one your father worked for.
Where no doubt a good percentage of it would be invested.
How am I doing?' Nobody spoke. Hardwick was gathering
together a sheaf of papers and stuffing them into a case. 'The
only detail I'm fuzzy on is who approached who? Which
one of you woke up in the middle of the night and said,
"Darling, I've got it! Why don't we clean out CBCI?"'

All Hardwick said, as he clipped the case shut and
moved to the door, was: '*Whom*. Who approached whom.
It offends my ear to hear the language of Chaucer mis-
pronounced.'

'One last question. The chauffeur. How did you get him
to think you were Hall?'

'Now I know why you agonize over plots,' he replied.
'You can't see the simplest things.'

'Tell me.'

'Make a note of this for future use. Offer a man ten thousand pounds and he'll think you're Jesus Christ, if that's what
you want.'

I went with them to the chopper. Sarf climbed behind
the controls while his mate and Maddy squeezed into the
rear seats.

Hardwick turned. 'I'm sorry about what happened to your
friend.'

'Me too.'

'Arnold Hall was a monster,' he went on, by way of an
excuse. 'What I said that night in the car? I was talking about
him. I was only middle management, but I knew the sort of
306

deals he was making. He had the means to create civil war, genocide, starvation, Lassa fever, Ebola – anything he knew he could make a buck out of. He had anyone who found out what was going on killed.' He lowered his voice and glanced up into the cockpit. 'Those guys'll tell you. They worked for him. It was a privilege to order his death.' He smiled. 'The fact we could make some cash *and* have the police blame it on him, is just one of those rare moments in life when justice is served.'

'So all the money is going to famine relief.'

He raised a Roger Moore eyebrow. 'I'm also sorry the plot meant having to drag you in.'

'Why did you pick on me?'

'Maddy heard someone in the Groucho mention you were broke. And currently banging teenagers in lieu of your ex-wife. So she got a good-looking German friend of hers, Andree Bruckmeyer, to pull you in.'

'Jesus!'

He smiled. 'Someone once compared film writers to the fish they throw to the seals at the zoo.'

'Yeah.'

'Listen, I'm also sorry about calling you a hack. You're no Robert Towne, but you're streets ahead of Eszterhas.'

'I've always strived for the Goldman touch myself.'

'I'm sure you'll make it one day.'

He didn't do anything as naff as offer to shake hands. The vanes began to rotate and he grabbed the handles to haul himself inside. The doors slammed and the blades gathered speed. I retreated to the shed and watched the grass flatten until the wheels see-sawed off the soft earth.

The machine climbed to three hundred feet and swung wide over the back fields before merging into the dark landscape. After the last sounds died, I went back to the house, picked up the phone and called a number.

'Maxie, tell the cops they're in the air. Flying below radar. Heading north by northwest.'

DATE: 28 OCTOBER

FAX TO: MORT DELANNOY, MOVIELINE INTERNATIONAL,
           LOS ANGELES

FROM: ELAINE MORGENSTERN, C/O SAVOY HOTEL,
           LONDON

Mort,

I have been trying without success to reach you, or indeed anyone at Movieline, for the past four days to find out exactly what is going on.

Two days ago I was informed by the hotel that our company credit card number has been cancelled. American Express have confirmed this. Consequently, unless I use my personal card, they will impound all my stuff until payment for the past two weeks is received. Since I don't run to anything like what is owing, help me *please*! With this coming after *Anna Karenina*'s cancellation, I believe I'm entitled to some kind of explanation, but each time I call the office I'm told that you, Bernie and just about everyone else is unavailable.

So here I sit in a room the size of a broom closet with little else to do but try and figure out who lowered the boom. Call me a pre-menstrual hysteric but I can't help thinking it has something to do with a helicopter crash we had here five days ago. Three men and a woman came down, hitting an electric pylon. Only one of them survived and he's in intensive care with a bigger police guard than the fucking White House. The papers are saying the survivor worked for CBCI (remember them?) and that he was with his girlfriend and two men. They found guns in the wreckage and are testing them against the bullet that killed Arnold Hall (remember him?).

Now Mort, you may think dumb bitch, what does she know, but I read the hard copy you sent me of Doktor Angstrom's letter. At the time, I said Doktor who? No one bothers to tell me who owns us, but some papers found in the chopper include his name. He *is* the same Doktor Angstrom, chairman of some muckety muck Swiss bank, isn't he? I mean, we're not in some straight to video shit about identical twins, one a reputable film financier, the other a mob bagman.

The high concept, as I see it, goes: 'Banker orders film company to lay off movie about CBCI robbery, is found to be involved in the theft.'

Call me irresponsible, but I am forced to conclude this has to be more than an amazing coincidence.

Since I am too tired and out of practice to go on what the politically incorrect Brits call 'the game', I have no means to get out of here with my possessions, so please advise ASAP.

If I don't hear from you within the next 24 hours, you can expect to see an anonymous leak in *Variety* that the San Fernando real estate you bought in your boyfriend's name two years ago was funded by budgetary inflations created while shooting *Satan in the Desert*, proof of which resides in a security vault of an L.A. bank.

Have a nice day,

ELAINE

'This is Wendy. I may as well fess up now,' I said. 'I'm in love with her.'

Maxie squeezed the hand above the blankets. 'I hear you're the one who made my husband look smart for a brief, shining moment.'

Wendy smiled sleepily. 'I don't know what they're dripping into me,' she croaked, 'but I've been having the most wonderful dreams. The other night I was in the team showers with the Chicago Bulls. They ask me what I'm doing there and I tell them I'm working on a basketball film and I have to research what kind of skin cleanser they use. Then they lather me all over with musk oil. I could actually smell it, in my dream. They were about to advance to stage two when I woke up, dammit. Today I was in an identical situation, except this time it was the Dagenham Girl Pipers.'

The greyness had left her cheeks, and the doctors were talking about going home. The knife had cut the femoral vein but missed vital organs by a whisker. She looked me up and down.

'You look cleaner. You're not hiding in sewers any longer?'

'Have you seen the papers?'

'No. What's my horoscope been saying?'

I told her what happened after she was knifed, ending with the news that Maddy was dead, along with the two gunmen.

'What goes 'round comes 'round,' she yawned, taking little of it in. Maxie cocked her head towards the door.

'The doc says you're out of here soon.'

'Shame. You get used to all the attention.'

'Oh, by the way, *Anna Karenina* was cancelled. They want to know what to do with five tons of snow.'

'Givum this number. I'll tellum.'

We kissed her and tiptoed out as she drifted away, murmuring, 'OK, who's next up in the showers . . .'

The television news had shown Burnside arriving at Heathrow in scandal mode – dark glasses, a minder glued to his side, spurning all questions – but the tabs learned his

311

entire family history within a couple of days. Maddy went from Mystery Woman in 'Copter Tragedy to Madeleine, 23-year-old only daughter of Anglo-German banker Dieter Burnside, 55. Thence to the lover of 42-year-old Barry Hardwick, of Keystone Mansions, Chelsea, where a woman had been stabbed only hours before Ms Burnside had died.

The following day the front pages carried the news that the missing writer, Alan Tate, had surrendered to the police but, after being interviewed for several hours, was released without charge.

This caused a tidal wave of reporters to surge down to the house where police were examining the gardens. It was like 1963 all over again. Every hour brought more revelations. Bliss was it in that dawn to be alive, but to be involved was very heaven. I longed to be in America, where reporting restrictions were non-existent; where I could have been on every chat show newscast in the land, logging up enough Hollywood brownie points to merit a seven-figure auction sale for my story. Here, they didn't quite put a blanket over my head, but Richard advised keeping my trap shut.

That didn't stop the world realizing I had a Story to Tell. What Ivanov was to Profumo, I was to CBCI; the behind-the-scenes figure, implicated with all the major players.

By day five, when we heard Wendy was well enough to receive visitors, the bullet taken out of Hall was matched with a handgun found in the wreckage. At the same time, underground sources confirmed Harry Rogers and Sebastian Wentworth were ex-SAS servicemen, currently listed in the Yellow Pages under hired killers. Meanwhile, Hardwick lay in a Stephen Ward-like coma, with a crushed ribcage and a punctured lung.

A courting couple described how the helicopter flew low

over their car. The engine had suddenly cut out, followed by an enormous flash and explosion. Rescue workers found bodies and wreckage over two hundred yards of ploughed fields. Enquiries were under way into why the helicopter was flying below radar and the cause of its sudden loss of power. Fire had destroyed the fuselage, making a detailed examination difficult, but crash experts hoped that the black box would give an indication.

A few days later, Wendy left the hospital and gave her version of events, substantiating mine, from when we met in King's Cross to the moment she was stabbed. Meanwhile, Burnside left his suite at the Ritz and could not be found at any of his addresses abroad.

I spent the days watching the plods devastate the gardens in their post mortem on the chopper's last journey, while Maxie wheeled out refreshments to the boys at the gates, a tip learned from Jeffrey Archer during his libel case. For the price of a cup of tea and some Huntley and Palmers, we melted their hearts to such an extent that when Lloyd and Sophie arrived, they were described respectively as a hunky honours student and stunningly beautiful.

The police wanted to know exactly where I'd buried the Nokia and searched the shed in a forlorn attempt to find a link between the fate of the helicopter and digging tools, lawnmowers and fertilizers. One of them kicked the coil of hosepipe attached to a water supply tap and said, glancing my way: 'All it needed, of course, was someone to pour water into the fuel tank.'

'If that someone knew where the tank was, and how to get into it,' I smiled. 'Me, I'm just a dumb writer. I can't tell one end of a chopper from the other.'

In the end, they concluded that Harry Rogers had

forgotten a vital part of his military training and put it down to pilot error.

A week later, Hardwick died from pneumonia and lacerations to the heart.

DATE: 10 APRIL

FAX TO: ALAN TATE

FROM: TIM ROBERTS

Dear Alan,

Losing The Plot

Warner's have agreed a total fee of eight hundred and fifty thousand dollars (850,000) for a treatment, first draft and two sets of revisions. This will be paid as follows:

$200,000 on signature
$100,000 treatment of no more than 40 pages
$200,000 on commencement of first draft
$200,000 on delivery of first draft
$75,000 on commencement of revisions
$75,000 on delivery of revisions

Merchandising tie-ins to be negotiated when Harrison Ford is confirmed in the lead role.

If you decide to work on the script in Los Angeles, they have agreed to provide a four bedroom house and the use of a Porsche 911, with a second car for Maxie.

These figures are guaranteed irrespective of the success of the book you are currently writing.

Love to Maxie,

TIM